Masters of Terror

A Marc LaRose Mystery

R. George Clark

Best Regards

[signature]

This is a work of fiction. Names, characters, businesses, places, events and incidents are either the products of the author's imagination or used in a fictitious manner. Any resemblance to actual persons, living or dead, or actual events is purely coincidental.

Prologue – Four Months Earlier

A Georgia-based irrigation components manufacturer received an order for a chemical injection system to be connected to an existing underground irrigation layout. The order was from a new customer, Apex Irrigation located in Aiken, South Carolina. Although this was hardly an unusual order, a few special requirements gave the order some significance.

The diagram for the underground injection system, purportedly to be installed on an exclusive estate, was not unusual. According to the details supplied by Apex, the specs of the desired system included a heavy-duty underground tank with an approximate fifty-gallon holding capacity that needed to be impervious to chemical degradation. The order further stated that the tank should be designed to be readily attached to the existing one-inch irrigation pipe and refillable from above ground as needed. This, the attached letter stated, was so chemicals could be added to the existing system and the city-supplied water as required, given the varied weather conditions during the wet springs and dry summers in the Aiken area.

In addition to the above requirements, the chemical tank would need to be fitted with a wireless unit to be controlled and monitored from a remote location, due to the size of the area to be covered. This would allow the contents of the tank to be injected into the water supply at various levels at a moment's notice, a system commonly known as fertigation.

The letter, printed on the 'Apex Irrigation, Inc.' letterhead, contained an Aiken post office box number and an email address should there be any questions regarding the request. A certified check for four thousand dollars was also enclosed to cover any initial costs for design, parts and associated labor.

Although the company's accounting department thought it a bit unusual for an established business to pay with a certified check, it guaranteed the initial payment. The request was thus processed and sent on to the company's design and manufacturing team to be completed. The lawn irrigation business, even in Georgia, is slow during the winter months.

Chapter One

Marc carefully opened the outside hatch and descended the steps to the flooded basement. Except for a few shards of light that seeped past him from the burned-out sections of the floor above, the flooded cellar was mostly pitch black. He flipped the switch on the six-volt floating lantern that he kept in the trunk of his car. If it hadn't been for a passerby spotting flames coming through the roof and the quick response of the local volunteer fire department, the entire house would have caved in.

As it was, the one-story ranch-house was a total loss. The six-foot-high cinder block walled basement was flooded with over two feet of water the firemen used to douse the flames. Debris from the five rooms above had fallen through the floor and into the water-filled cellar. Marc donned his fly-fishing waders and descended the short flight of steps.

Stopping at the bottom of the stairs, he crouched down to avoid contact with the scorched beams overhead and surveyed the task ahead of him. At first glance, he could see the rabbit ears of an old tube-type TV, the scorched remains of end tables, lamps with their shades burned away, and what looked like the back of an overstuffed chair poking above the surface of the water. He pointed his flashlight toward what he suspected could have been the source of the blaze, an oil-fired furnace reported to be at the back end of the cellar. But getting to it was not going to be easy.

As he waded into the fray, he noticed the soggy remnants of fiberglass insulation, a Formica topped table turned on its side, seat cushions, a single-wide mattress, pillows, blankets, and all manner of household furnishings in various stages of submersion. Then there was the scattered flotsam, such as the armada of empty beer cans and bottles bobbing lazily on the surface of the water.

Carefully, he made his way to the far end of the cellar. As he continued to maneuver toward where he thought the furnace was located, he noticed the heavy odor of fuel oil. As his light scanned over the surface of the water, a sheen of oil formed a muted rainbow. Number 2 fuel oil floats, just like the half dozen dead rats that were on the surface, while others, their eyes reflecting in the rays of Marc's light, squealed and clung to whatever they could to keep from sharing the fate of their drowned cousins.

Marc didn't personally know the owner of the house, but he'd heard of him; a local by the name of Cecil Robare. Besides being habitually unemployed, he had a history; numerous arrests for drunken driving, assaults, mostly involving women, and living on the county dole and disability checks. Miraculously, he still appeared capable of taking odd jobs under the table to keep his beer tap flowing.

As Marc carefully continued past the bank of debris, he cast his beam toward the far end of the basement. There, he noticed the top half of a 250-gallon fuel oil tank perched against the cinder-block's exterior wall. Looking back toward the center of the foul-smelling enclosure, he saw what appeared to be the six-inch tube of a furnace's vent pipe. It hung precariously from the scorched floor joists running toward the far side of the basement before disappearing through a hole in the top of the outer wall just above ground level. His eyes followed the furnace pipe back to its origin.

Camouflaged by the debris, he spotted the upper portion of a dated, oil-fired furnace. An air duct curved up from its top, partially secured to what remained of the floor joists. The legs of the twisting, damaged ductwork branched off to the area Marc figured had been the living room, kitchen and bedroom of the building above.

Marc went to the fuel tank. He set his lamp on top of the tank, and rolled up the sleeve of his shirt to his shoulder. He bent over and felt below the surface of the oil-slicked water. Locating the copper tubing leading from the tank's nozzle, he gripped it with his thumb and forefinger. He ran his finger along the length of the piping that had been laid on the floor. The rolled-up portion of his sleeve was now underwater. Another shirt ruined. About half-way to the furnace, he felt it—an almost imperceptible notch in the bottom of the tubing. Someone had nicked the tubing, allowing fuel oil to seep out.

"There's the cause of the oil slick," he muttered.

He straightened up, relieved to be removing his exposed arm from the filth of the bilge water. He pulled his handkerchief from his back pocket with his mostly dry hand, wiped the rancid slick from his arm as best he could, retrieved his light and started back the way he had come. As he waded toward the furnace, the beam of his flashlight passed over an innocuous piece of plastic bobbing between a few chunks of charred wood. At first, he thought it was a screw-off cap for a soda bottle. However when he picked it out of the water, being careful not to re-contaminate his fingers in the filthy sludge, he shook as much of the water/oil mixture off it as he could.

With his forefinger inserted into the open end of the cap to preserve any fingerprints on the outside, he examined it. It wasn't a bottle cap after all. It had no threads. He noticed the word "Orion" embossed on the sides of the two-inch long opaque plastic cap. There was a dark rough surface at the flat end of the cap, which helped it to float with the open end up. From his days as a New York State trooper, Marc remembered seeing hundreds of caps just like this one. It was the cap for a road flare, the kind he had used to warn oncoming motorists of an accident or other road hazard. The dark rough end was the striker, put there to light the flare, much like striking a match. Marc suspected he had found the accelerant to start the fuel oil burning, thus spreading the fire to whatever else was piled on and around the break in the furnace's fuel line.

A man's gruff voice suddenly pulled him out of his deliberations. "Hey, who the hell's that poking around down there?" The voice came from the open hatch door.

"Hello," Marc called back. He suspected it was the owner, probably a little antsy about a stranger on his property.

"Come on out of there. Who gave you permission to mess around in my cellar?" the man yelled.

Marc pocketed the cap and waded toward the hatch. "You Mister Robare?"

"My place, so I'll do the asking here."

As Marc got closer to the opening, he could see Robare, bent over, peering into the flooded cellar, a sneer exposing a mouthful of stained and rotting teeth.

"My name is Marc LaRose. I work for the insurance company. You filed an accidental fire claim. The company sent me to check out the damage."

Marc climbed up and out through the hatch and extended his hand.

Robare looked down at Marc's hand, then back up at his face, ignoring the offer of a handshake. "So, what are you doing snooping around my house? You got my damage estimate. Did you bring the check?"

Marc watched as Robare's eyes shifted to the opening he had just climbed through, then back to Marc again. "No, sorry, I don't have a check to give you. They needed confirmation of your claim and a full damage report. That's why I'm here."

Robare hesitated. "Look Mr. LaRoad, I told them insurance people all they need to know. I paid 'em good money to insure my house and now look at it," he said, motioning toward the scorched remains with a wide sweep of his arm. "It's all gone. All on account the furnace repair man fucked up when he tried to fix it. Now, what're you going to do about it?"

Marc reached under the bib of his waders and pulled a piece of paper from his shirt pocket. "Yeah, I see here that you bought a policy with our company, uh, just three months ago. Even made an initial payment, fifty dollars, but nothing since. Says here you insured your place with contents for, uh, let me see." Marc made a pretense of running his finger down the paper, stopping at a spot near the bottom of the page, "Oh yeah, here it is, ninety-five thousand dollars."

"That's right, ninety-five thousand. So where's my money?"

"Let me get this straight. You said you recently had your furnace repaired. Did the furnace repairman give you a bill for the work?" Marc asked, although he suspected he already knew the answer.

"Well, uh, I had one, but as you can see, it must have burned up in the fire."

"No problem. Just give me the name of the company that fixed your furnace and I'll contact them and get a copy."

Robare stood quiet for a moment as though he was trying to think, which Marc was pretty sure he did little of. "Look, the guy who fixed it was just a friend I know'ed. He works on his own. He don't got no regular company. But that don't make no difference. I paid good money for that insurance and you people owe me ninety-five thousand dollars for the loss of my home and all of my belongings."

"I see," Marc said. "I tell you what. I've taken a few photos of the damage to the interior and the basement of your home as well as the outside. I just have to report my findings to the company. I'll even tell them you were asking about the money they owe you."

"You make sure and do that. And tell them if they want my business, they better get me my money quick. I've had to rent a room over at my, uh, sister's house. She needs me to pay her. So tell them I need my money fast, plus expenses for my sister."

Marc turned to leave. "Don't worry, Mr. Robare. I'll tell them everything. You can count on it."

Marc walked to his car, popped the trunk and pulled his waders off, then crammed them into a plastic garbage bag. He got in and made a call to his old pal, State Police Investigator, Tim Golden.

"Marc, what's up? Haven't heard from you in months. Understand you've been busy up in Lake Placid again."

"Yeah, hopefully that's been put to bed. Look, I'm in the Village of Peru at this Robare house fire."

"Yeah. We heard about that. Newspaper said the fire started in the basement; something about a faulty furnace."

"Tim, the insurance company called me, asked if I'd take a look at it. I think this might interest you."

"Why, what'd you find?" Tim asked, hesitantly.

"Someone cut a notch in the furnace's fuel line."

"That's not good," Tim said.

"It gets worse. I found a flare cap floating in the water-filled basement."

"Is Robare still on the premises?"

"Oh yeah. He's yammering on about the money he's owed by the insurance company."

"Good. Can you hang there for a few minutes? I'll contact a uniform patrol and have them guard the scene.

"My pleasure. I'll be waiting," Marc said and ended the call.

Chapter Two

Arriving back at his condo, Marc's cats, Brandy and Rye, welcomed him with their usual chorus of meows looking for affection and whatever treats Marc had in the cupboard, which he gladly provided.

Although Marc ran his own private detective business, he was often contracted by insurance companies to confirm claims and complete damage evaluations such as the one he had conducted at the "Robare Estate," as he liked to call it. He set to work filling out the insurance inspection checklist, then emailed the report along with the photos he had taken of the remnants of the house, as attachments to his investigative summary. This included the results of the interview he had with the Chief of the Peru Fire Department. There was a notation at the end of his report, "Complete summary pending police investigation."

"Don't think Mr. Robare's going to be very happy with my report, but as they say, 'if you want to fuck with a bull, you gotta watch out for those horns,'" Marc said to the computer as it swallowed his report.

The lilting tune of Dave Brubeck's 'Take Five,' brought Marc out of his reverie. He looked at his cell phone's screen. It was a call from his office mate, Norm Prendergast. Marc and Norm had worked together when they were state troopers assigned to the Plattsburgh State Police Station. When Marc retired, he opened a private detective office in downtown Plattsburgh located over a former Chinese restaurant. A few months later, Norm also retired and approached Marc with an offer to share the space with him. Norm was opening a process-serving business, delivering subpoenas and court orders for area attorneys. The two businesses did not compete and, in fact, complimented one another. Norm knew where most of the area's low-lifes lived, and Marc knew how to deal with them.

"Norm, what's up?"

"You plan on venturing to the office sometime today?"

"Why? Your Drunkin' Donut supply running low?" Marc asked, the corner of his mouth raised slightly.

"Donuts? Sounds good, but no, no more donuts."

"What? Lost your taste for powdered sugar gut bombs pumped full of yummy, heart-stopping cream and jelly?"

Norm grumbled, "No, I haven't lost my taste for them. It was stolen."

"Stolen? Who stole your taste for... Oh, you got the results of your last physical exam, didn't you?"

"Fuck you. If you want to repay me for getting you that Libyan consulate license plate data, drop by the health food store and pick up a handful of fig bars or a box of organic graham crackers. On second thought, pick up a box of each."

Marc was momentarily astonished, but couldn't say he didn't see it coming. Norm had been a regular garbage disposal when it came to his eating habits.

"Well, if a couple boxes of health food snacks will satisfy what I owe you, I guess I could make the effort. I just returned from looking at that house fire in Peru."

"Robare's place? Read about that in the papers. I trust you enjoyed yourself. Did you stay for cocktails and canapés?"

"Naw. He lost his best grape jelly glasses in the fire. Besides, it cost me a good shirt, but it looks like it will cost Robare a lot more, especially while the insurance company is holding off payments pending the results of an arson investigation."

"Arson investigation? So, Robare torched his own place?"

"It's looking that way. He didn't appreciate the yellow 'Crime Scene' tape decorating his former abode. It appears the dumb fuck figured any arson evidence would be hidden beneath the water that filled his basement, which probably explained why he was acting so antsy when the troopers called the fire department to pump out the cellar."

"What do you think they'll find?"

"I told Golden about a nick in the fuel line and a flare cap I found bobbing amongst the rest of the shit in his cellar."

"So, you think he did it?"

"Probably, it's looking that way. It'll be real interesting if the lab can lift a fingerprint off that fuel cap. In any event, it looks like he can forget about living off the insurance company for the near future."

Later that afternoon, Marc dropped Norm's care package of fig bars and graham crackers off at the office, then made the short drive to Shirley's Flower Shop. The delivery van was parked at the end of the drive which meant she was inside. The bell over the door tinkled as he entered. Both Shirley, his ex, and his daughter, Ann Marie, were busy arranging flowers. The area around the design table appeared to be full of finished arrangements.

"Hey Dad. Just in time. How'd you like to make a flower delivery?" Ann Marie asked.

"Hello to you, too," Marc answered. "And no, I don't do flower deliveries."

"I know, just kidding. These all go to the funeral parlor. There's a showing in about an hour and a half and we still have a few more to do."

Marc exhaled. "Well, I suppose, seeing as you're in a pinch."

Ann Marie looked over at her mother, "See Mom, I told you Dad would help. You just have to know how to ask."

"So, my only daughter thinks she knows me better than her mom," Marc said.

Shirley gave Marc a smile as she continued to work. "I remember that you didn't like being cooped up in a van full of flowers."

"Smells like a funeral parlor on wheels," Marc said with a grin.

As Ann Marie finished the arrangement she had been working on, she looked up at her dad. "I was going to take this load over and get them set up. Why don't you drive? I could use your help while Mom finishes the rest of the orders. Besides, I haven't seen you much lately and it will give us a chance to catch up."

Marc glanced at Shirley. "I smell a conspiracy. Your mom knows I can't resist my daughter's plea for help."

Ann Marie and her mother exchanged a look. They both giggled.

"Thanks Dad, let's get these loaded."

It was just over a five-minute drive to the funeral home.

"Dad, I never told you how much I appreciate you stepping in with that Dave Fish thing."

It had been a few months, but Ann Marie's statement brought a flash-back of the bruises on Shirley's arm, and Fish's bloodied face as it slid down the side of his house trailer following Marc's brief visit. "Your mom ever say anything about that?"

"Not in so many words. And, as far as I know, she hasn't heard from him since."

"Guess that was the idea," Marc said as he stared at the road ahead.

A minute of silence passed between them.

"So, Dad, probably none of my business, but weren't you seeing someone up in Saranac Lake a while back? Sophie something or other?"

"Maybe. Why? Is this a Dear Abby moment between father and daughter?"

"I'm just curious. I mean, you are my father and we don't see each other much and I guess I'd like to get to know you better. Who your friends are, stuff like that."

"Sophie's been a good friend. She's had some hard times. We stay in touch, but, we're just that. Good friends."

"And how about this other woman, Sylvie something? The Quebec police detective."

"Ditto. Both good friends. So, how did you hear about them?"

"From Mom," Ann Marie said as Marc turned the van into the back entrance to the funeral home.

It took the two of them ten minutes to carry the flower arrangements into the viewing parlor. A man's body occupied a mahogany coffin set up between two pedestals holding large white candles. Someone had stuffed the poor guy into a new blue suit complete with a white shirt and red tie. Marc and Ann Marie positioned the baskets of flowers off to either side of the casket.

"Dad, can you give me a hand setting up the casket spray? It's kind of large. I'll take one end and you take the other. I have a hard time reaching over the kneeler."

Marc carefully lifted one end of the spray of flowers and, with Ann Marie's help, centered it on the bottom half of the casket. He hadn't paid much attention to the body before, but as he completed his task, he glanced down at the man's face. Even with his hair parted on the wrong side and a bit too much rouge on his cheeks to make the body look more alive, there was no mistaking the face of his old friend from the local Police Department. He'd known Sergeant Dave Rabideau from his days as a state trooper. Marc stepped back and stared.

"Something wrong, Dad?"

Marc remained silent.

"Dad?"

"Nothing. It's just, I hadn't heard that Dave had passed."

"You knew him?"

"Yeah. More of a professional relationship. I remember whenever anyone said to him, 'Hey Dave, good to see you,' he'd always come back with, 'better to be seen than viewed.'"

"Sorry, Dad. I didn't know."

"It's all right. You couldn't have."

Marc took an extra moment to make sure the casket flowers were situated properly. He then patted the back of the man's cold hand. Someone had coiled a rosary around his fingers. "See you around, old friend."

They left the funeral home and headed back to the flower shop. When he turned the van into the shop's driveway Ann Marie asked, "Have you given any more thought about coming with us to the golf tournament in Georgia next month?"

"Guess I'm sort of torn. I don't want to interfere with, you know, you and your boyfriend's trip, but the thought of seeing some of the world's best golfers sure is tempting. And of course, the weather in Georgia is so nice in the spring. It's just that, I don't know."

Marc drove the van around the back of the store and cut the engine.

"You having second thoughts?" she asked.

"Don't get me wrong, I want to go. It's just I don't know anything about your friend. Other than Jake, I don't even know his full name."

"It's McKay, Jake McKay. He's about your height, twenty years old, has blond hair—"

"I don't need to know what he looks like. Where's he from? How'd you meet him? Stuff like that."

Ann Marie hesitated. "Well, if you must know, we met in a downtown bar, Brewsters, about four months ago. He's Canadian, lived in Toronto, here on a student visa. He used to play hockey in the winter and golf in the summer, but since he's won a couple of amateur golf tournaments, he's committed to golf full time. He's left-handed, his favorite color is red and—"

"Enough, I was just—"

It was Ann Marie's turn to interrupt. "He loves pizza, graduates with a bachelor's in business next week, just before the golf tournament that I had assumed we were all going to in Georgia."

"Ann Marie, I don't intend to pry into your personal affairs. You're 18, going on 30. It's a father's job to be curious about someone his daughter's apparently been living with."

"I'm not living with him, well, not all the time."

Marc hesitated as he digested this latest bit of news. "Does he plan on returning to Canada after college?"

"Dad, really?"

Marc looked at her, waiting for the answer.

"If you must know, he wants to stay on at Plattsburgh State and get his Master's in Business and Marketing. But that might change, depending on how he does at this tournament in Georgia."

Marc was aware that the local state college depended on Canadian students to fill their enrollment.

"He can't live at the college after graduating. Does Jake have an apartment?"

"Yeah. Why?"

"Where does he get his money?"

"From his mom, I guess. Same place he got the plane tickets to attend the tournament in Georgia. What difference does that make?" Ann Marie lifted the door handle. "Forget I asked you to come along. Obviously, you're more interested in who I'm seeing than going to the tournament."

Marc touched her arm, "I'm sorry. You have to understand, you're all that your mom and I have, especially now that we're divorced."

"I'm all you have? What about Sophie, your friend in Saranac Lake?"

Marc let out a slow exhale. "Like I said, she's a friend. Besides, I haven't seen much of her lately."

It was her turn to exhale. "Come on, Dad. There's still a few more flower arrangements that need to be brought to the funeral home before your friend's viewing."

Chapter Three

The following Monday, news of Cecil Robare's arson arrest and attempted insurance fraud made the bottom fold of the Plattsburgh Standard Newspaper. Naturally, there was no mention of Marc's involvement in the investigation and, for his part, it was just as well. He didn't need Robare's family pleading for him to change the story he'd given to the police. Robare had made his own bed, now he could sleep in it, along with the rest of the inmate population at the Clinton County Jail while he awaited trial.

Before heading to his office, Marc stopped back at Shirley's Flower Shop. A GMC Yukon with Ontario license plates was parked by the curb. As he entered, he saw Ann Marie talking to a woman at the counter.

"Hey Dad, you're just in time. I'd like you to meet Jake's mom. Mrs. McKay, this is my dad."

From the back, Marc could see the woman was almost as tall as he, with flowing brown hair that curled onto her shoulders.

She turned toward Marc and extended a hand. Mrs. McKay could have easily stepped off the cover of *Vogue Magazine*.

"Laura McKay. Pleased to meet you," she said.

Her grip was soft, but firm at the same time.

"Likewise, I'm sure," Marc responded.

"Ann Marie told me that you'll be joining us on our little trip to Augusta next month," she said.

Marc detected the Canadian accent in her voice but, besides her appearance, what struck him the most was that she was also going to Augusta. After a short delay, Mrs. McKay retrieved her hand.

"Uh, yeah, I guess," Marc managed.

"You're not having second thoughts, are you, Mr. LaRose?" Laura McKay asked.

"Uh, sorry. No, of course not. I just hadn't been told there'd be four of us."

Laura McKay glanced at Ann Marie. "It's probably my fault. You see, Jake did so well at the Canadian Amateur's last year, I was able to get four tickets to attend the tournament in Augusta. It's one that

I've been interested in seeing, so I thought I'd tag along. I hope that isn't a problem."

"No, no problem," Marc sputtered. He noticed Shirley was peering at him through a veil of flower stems from behind a birthday bouquet she was working on.

"So, it's settled. That just leaves the matter of getting there. I'd considered driving, but, if it's all the same with you, I'd prefer to fly. Driving would take at least two days, however, we could fly there in a few hours. We'll rent a car at the airport."

"I don't know. Augusta's not like Toronto. It's a small town with small airports. Then there's the issue of lodging. I understand that motels fill up well in advance," Marc said.

"I've already seen to that. We'll take my SUV to Burlington, Vermont where I've secured four roundtrip tickets to Columbia, South Carolina. I've also reserved a rental vehicle and taken the liberty of booking two rooms at a hotel in a small town not far from Augusta. Ever heard of Aiken, South Carolina? I understand it's a quaint little horse town about a half hour's drive from Augusta. I'm sure you'll like it."

Marc was getting the impression that Mrs. McKay was used to getting her way. "Uh yeah, that sounds alright, I guess," he said, avoiding Shirley's glances.

"I'm just in town for a couple of days, but I'll be back in time for Jake's graduation next week. If you don't mind, I'd like to leave for Burlington right after the ceremony."

Marc wasn't sure how to respond. "I guess, uh…"

Ann Marie interjected, "That sounds great. You're okay with that, Dad, right?"

"Uh, sure, why not?"

"Well, now that that's settled, I'll be on my way. Toronto's a seven-hour trip. It's been a pleasure meeting you all. Jake's told me all about Ann Marie, but she forgot to tell me she had such wonderful parents."

"So, we'll see you at the graduation next week, Mrs. McKay," Marc said.

"Please, it's Laura," she said with a light smile, then turned toward the door.

The tinkling of the bell above the door accompanied Mrs. McKay's exit from the flower shop.

"That was interesting," Marc said.

"Sorry, Dad. Guess I should have warned you. Jake said his mom was a control freak."

"Oh, I'm sure Daddy doesn't mind being controlled by someone as pretty as Mrs. McKay. Too bad she's married," Shirley said through the flower arrangement, her tone flush with envy.

"Actually, she's not, at least not any more. According to Jake, they divorced a couple years ago," Ann Marie said.

"Can't imagine why," Shirley mumbled.

Marc got the feeling that the planned trip to Aiken wasn't the only thing about to head south. "Well, I thought I'd stop in to see if there's anything I can do but, it looks like you two have it under control." He turned toward the front door. About to open it, he hesitated. "Ann Marie, did you make arrangements for a replacement while we're gone? Mom's going to need someone to help make the deliveries while we're away."

"Taken care of Dad," she replied.

Marc dropped his hand from the door handle. "Is there any possibility I could meet Jake sometime before we fly to Georgia?"

Ann Marie seemed to think about her dad's request. "I don't see why not. He's completed his finals. Let me ask him and I'll get back to you. Maybe the four of us could go out to lunch or something."

"Lunch would be nice," Shirley said, placing the finished arrangement in the display cooler.

"Whatever. Let me know what you decide." Marc said as he left the shop.

Three days passed and Marc again found himself in Shirley's flower shop. He and Ann Marie had decided to meet at Antoine's Restaurant around noon. Shirley had closed the shop for the day and was ready when Marc arrived. She was wearing a blue and white flowered dress with black pumps and a matching purse.

When she climbed into Marc's Ford Explorer, he caught the gentle scent of her perfume. "You look nice today," he said.

"Thanks for noticing." She smiled.

"Have you ever met Jake?" Marc asked, backing the SUV out of the driveway.

"All I know is what Ann Marie told me. I have to say, she seems kind of hooked on him."

Other than the weather and talk of the pock-marked city streets, the short trip uptown passed with little conversation. When they arrived at the restaurant, Marc spotted his daughter in the parking lot waving at him. She was standing between a silver sports car and a young man about a foot taller than she. Marc found an open parking spot two spaces away.

"Hope you haven't been waiting long," Marc said as he and Shirley exited the Explorer.

"No, we just arrived," Ann Marie said.

Turning his attention to the boy standing next to Ann Marie, Marc said, "You must be Jake." Marc extended his hand, "I've heard a lot about you."

"Pleasure to meet you, Mr. LaRose."

Jake was about as tall as Marc, but his voice seemed deeper. He was clean-shaven and his medium length hair was the same color as his mother's.

"Jake, this is my mom," Ann Marie said, motioning toward Shirley as she came around the car.

"Pleasure, Ms. LaRose."

The four of them stood silent for a moment as if waiting for someone else to say something. "Anyone hungry?" Marc finally asked.

"Yeah, I'm famished," Ann Marie said.

"You're always hungry," Shirley said with a short titter.

During lunch, Marc learned that Jake's mom, Laura, owned and operated a consulting business she had acquired after the divorce from Jake's dad two years earlier. Jake's dad owned a brokerage franchise business that he and his mom had started years before their marriage ended.

"Brokerage franchise firm?" Marc asked.

"Yeah, it's kind of boring stuff, buying and selling franchises. But both Mom and Dad like it and they seem to have done well, I guess. My college major is business, but my passion is golf."

"Jake is thinking about combining the two…you know like, owning a golf course, probably in the south somewhere while playing as a tour pro," Ann Marie said.

"My dream is to one day make it on the pro golf tour. However, tournament is stiff, so I figured I might need a back-up plan," Jake said.

"Years ago, my dream was to have a string of flower shops, but I still have only the one," Shirley said, "which I suppose, was my back-up plan."

The waitress reappeared and, as she started clearing the plates, asked if anyone was interested in ordering dessert.

"Yes, I believe we would," Marc replied, speaking for everyone.

After ordering, Jake asked, "Mr. LaRose, Ann Marie tells me you're a private detective."

"Yeah. That was my back-up plan after I retired from the state police."

"Sounds kinda interesting."

"It has its moments," Marc grinned.

"Just last fall Dad saved the Village of Lake Placid from a dirty bomb attack by a bunch of terrorists," Ann Marie announced proudly.

Jake looked genuinely astonished. "Really? Ann Marie, you hadn't told me your dad was a local hero!"

Marc flushed. "Well, I'm hardly a hero. Besides, I had a lot of help."

The waitress arrived with their desserts.

Saved by the soufflé, Marc thought as he scooped up a forkful of pie a la mode.

Chapter Four

The following week passed in a blur. Marc had accepted a worker's compensation surveillance assignment in the Village of Champlain, twenty miles north of Plattsburgh. Within three days, he'd collected evidence showing the target of the investigation was working off the books at a local all-terrain vehicle garage while collecting workers' compensation benefits from his former job as an orderly at a nursing home in Plattsburgh. Apparently changing over-sized ATV tires was better suited to his job skills than changing adult diapers and dirty bed sheets.

As the day of Jake's graduation approached, Marc prepared for the anticipated trip to Aiken, South Carolina.

An online search showed him that, as Laura McKay had indicated, Aiken is a mid-sized southern town, home to a sizable equestrian community with a history of raising prize thoroughbred horses. Its latest, a three-year old named Palace Malice, had captured the Belmont Stakes a few years before.

Marc's search also revealed that Aiken had played an important part in America's cold war with the establishment of the Savannah River Site, known back in the early 1950s as the "Bomb Plant." SRS, or the Site, as it was known locally, was situated a few miles southeast of the city and produced components for the country's nuclear arsenal. Over the years, many of the engineers and other professionals who retired from SRS remained in Aiken, resulting in the development of several retirement communities.

Marc stared at his computer screen as he tried to comprehend the irony of how Aiken had developed into both an equine center as well as a producer of nuclear bomb components. Upon further investigation, Marc found the answer. Senator Strom Thurmond, the once powerful politician from South Carolina had served 47 years in the U.S. Senate and was instrumental in bringing the "Bomb Plant" to Aiken at the dawn of the cold war between the USA and the former USSR.

Marc was pleasantly diverted from his research by the familiar tones of "Take Five" coming from his cell phone. A glance at the screen showed it was his daughter.

"What's up, Anny?"

"Just checking to see if you're ready for the trip to South Carolina?"

"Yeah, I think so. My sports jacket's hanging in the closet and my carry-on bag is full. The forecast for Augusta looks pretty good. Warm, with a chance of showers early in the week, so I'm thinking something casual, khakis and short-sleeved shirts mostly, although I might take an umbrella, just in case."

"Dad, please tell me you're not wearing that Hawaiian shirt to the graduation."

"Uh, which one was that?"

"You only have one, the one with the big breasted hula girls and palm trees. You've had it forever. It's gross."

"Of course not," he replied, glancing at the open closet with the offending shirt hanging front and center.

Ann Marie hesitated. "Wear something sporty, but nice. We'll be over to pick you up in Mrs. McKay's SUV at ten-thirty, tomorrow morning. Graduation is at eleven followed by a reception for the graduates and guests at the college. Then we'll leave for the Burlington Airport."

"Can I bring a camera?"

Marc heard his daughter exhale. "Daddy, of course you can bring your camera. As a matter of fact, you should. We'll need it to take photos of Jake at the graduation as well as when he plays at the golf course. I understand you can take photos during the practice rounds, just not on tournament days."

"Great. Any other restrictions I should know about?"

Marc heard the sound of another sigh. "See you tomorrow, Dad."

"I'll be ready," Marc said to the dial tone.

The following day, the weather was sunny with a few passing clouds. Perfect for a graduation, or a surveillance assignment. Marc preferred the latter. In anticipation of the sojourn south, Marc had asked a neighbor to look in on his cats, Brandy and Rye, while he was away. He took care to fill their kibble bowls as well as the gallon-sized kitty watering fountain.

As Ann-Marie had warned, Laura McKay's black SUV pulled into the driveway a minute before the scheduled departure time. After saying good-bye to his feline friends, he grabbed his carry-on and headed out the door. Laura was behind the wheel and Jake was in the back seat next to Ann Marie.

The rear hatch door opened and he placed his bag on top of the pile already there, then climbed into the front passenger seat. Laura McKay looked ever the business professional, smartly dressed in a red blazer over a white blouse and black slacks. "Good Morning, Mr. LaRose," she said with a practiced smile.

"Morning, Ms. McKay,"

"Please, I'll do Marc, if you'll do Laura," she said.

"Fair enough."

Jake wore his graduation gown and held the cap on his lap. After a few pleasantries, the short drive to the college campus passed with a few comments about the weather and other useless conversation that strangers often rely on to help them get better acquainted.

Laura seemed aloof as Jake, accompanied by other members of the graduating class, filed into the commencement hall. Ann Marie, sitting between Marc and Laura, was obviously excited as she waved and shouted. Marc noticed Jake wore several colored cords around his neck. He assumed they were academic honors of some sort. Obviously, the kid was smart.

The commencement speaker was a woman that Marc had never heard of. He vaguely remembered that she was introduced by the college's president as the director of some collegiate association that he'd also never heard of, and really didn't care to hear of again. Just as he felt himself nodding off, he was brought back to consciousness by the sound of polite applause. The speaker had apparently ended her presentation.

Then it was time for the college president to hand out the diplomas. Despite the 400 graduates, the presentation went relatively quickly. Ann Marie was visibly excited as Jake's name was announced. Marc had brought a camera with a zoom lens attached and snapped a few photos as Jake accepted his diploma.

After a serve-yourself luncheon, the group piled back into Laura's SUV for the ferry ride across Lake Champlain to the Burlington Airport. Without mentioning it, Marc had secreted his H&K handgun in his suitcase that was checked through to their final destination.

After a short stopover in Philadelphia, they caught the connecting flight bound for Columbia, South Carolina. Upon boarding, however, they discovered that the seating arrangements had been changed. Marc's seat in the first-class section had been re-assigned.

As Laura McKay was about to protest, Marc intervened. "It's no problem. Business class will do just fine." Marc felt he needed a little down time to be by himself. He grabbed his carry-on and followed the flight attendant back a few rows to his new seat with a window view. The seat next to his was empty. A few moments later a gentleman shoved his carry-on into the overhead bin and plopped down next to Marc. Up ahead, Marc could see Ann Marie sitting with another female passenger in the first class section.

As the plane taxied away from the terminal in preparation for takeoff, Marc's seatmate introduced himself as Hank from Rock Hill, South Carolina, and soon the pair engaged in friendly conversation.

"Is this your first trip to the south?" Hank asked.

"Yes, it is."

Marc explained the purpose of the trip and that his daughter and her boyfriend were accompanying him. He motioned toward the first-class section.

"That's nice of you. Pony up first-class seats for them while you suffer back here in business," Hank said with a toothy grin.

Marc didn't feel he needed to explain, and responded, "Sometimes you do what you gotta do."

As they chatted through take-off, Marc let it slip that he and his daughter were ultimately headed for the golf tournament in Augusta.

"Oh, lucky you. If you don't mind my asking, did you get your tickets through the lottery system?"

"No, actually, my daughter's boyfriend won an amateur event last year and was awarded tickets for us to attend."

Hank seemed genuinely impressed. "You don't know how fortunate you are. There is so much demand for tournament tickets that the golf club has developed a complicated system of allotting tickets through some sort of computer algorithm."

"How's that?" Marc asked.

"The way I understand it, if you, as a regular fan received tickets last year, chances are you probably would not get them again, at least for a while. Maybe never."

"Wonder why that is? I mean, it's a golf tournament, not an audience with the Pope," Marc said.

"Demand," Hank replied. "The Savannah River Golf Links is the place to see the world's best golfers, and to be seen. The regular cost of a weekend day pass is around a hundred bucks, but a scalper could sell the same ticket for over a thousand. Scalping tickets for the tournament is big business and the tournament committee has become very selective about who receives them."

"I didn't know that," Marc said.

As Hank was about to say something, the plane's captain announced they had reached their cruising altitude and that it was safe for passengers to move about the cabin.

"Oh, yeah," Hank continued. "I've even heard there are categories of eligibility that must be satisfied just to be considered to receive a pass to get through the gates at the tournament."

"Really?" Marc prodded.

"They've designed it so that practically everyone attending the tournament is from outside the Augusta area. Think about it. These people need a place to stay and eat while they're not actually attending the tournament. They have money to spend and these people are not going to stay at just any dump. They're willing and able to spend money on nice hotels and good restaurants. What's good for Savannah River Golf Links is good for Augusta."

"Interesting," Marc said.

"And that's just the tip of the proverbial iceberg. You have the mega-corporate types, you know, the really big businesses. They bring in prospective clients and guests to schmooze, rewarding them with the prize perk of a golf pass, keeping the client happy. Plus, the business can write it off as an expense."

"That makes sense, I guess," Marc said.

"And then there are the great unwashed," Hank said making air quotes. "You know, the stars of stage and screen, politicians, past presidents or secretaries of state, whoever. They provide snippets of excitement for the cameras to pan-in on as they scan the throngs watching from the sidelines. Of course, to fill the galleries, they allocate a good block of tickets to regular folk. But as I pointed out, these are mostly out-of-towners, like yourselves, to help prop up the local economy."

Marc thought about what Hank had said. "So, it sounds like there is a symbiotic relationship between the golf tournament and the city."

"It's worked well for all these years, and believe me, neither the city nor the golf course wants anything to change, except maybe to increase the income the tournament provides."

"Sounds like we should be very grateful that our boy made the cut, allowing us to attend."

"Enjoy the tournament, and if something comes up, or you decide not to go, give me a call." Sam reached into his shirt pocket and handed him a business card. "Sammy's Used Cars" was printed across the top of the card. He then reclined his seat back as far as it would go. "I could probably get a thousand dollars for a day ticket. I'd even split it with you," he said with an oily smile.

When Marc looked over again, Hank had closed his eyes.

A small bag of pretzels and a half hour later, Marc felt the plane begin its descent to the Columbia Airport. After deplaning, a one-hour drive brought the foursome to the city of Aiken.

As they unloaded their suitcases from the SUV Laura had rented, she announced, "I could only get two rooms for our stay here, so I thought that if Ann Marie and I stayed in one room, Mr. LaRose and Jake could stay in the other." Her comment appeared to be directed at Jake and Ann Marie.

They traded glances.

"I guess that would be appropriate," Marc said. "But I wish you'd at least allow me to pay our half of the room rental. After all, you've provided the tournament tickets plus the airfare."

"Nonsense. It was Jake's and my idea to come to the tournament in the first place. No, the rooms are pre-paid. If you'd like to pick up the tab for dinner tonight, that would be fine," Laura said.

Marc knew there was no use in arguing with Laura McKay.

Chapter Five

The following morning was the tournament's first practice day. That's when amateurs, like Jake, as well as all who qualified went to sharpen their skills on the rolling hills and undulating greens of the Savannah River Golf Links. Marc had watched the tournament for years on television, but having never attended, was excited to see first-hand what all the excitement was about.

While the great majority who came to the tournament had to park outside the gates, the passes that Jake had acquired for being the low amateur allowed his small entourage to pass through the heavily guarded entrance. Once inside, they were directed to the player's parking lot, secreted well away from the clubhouse and out of sight of the gallery and TV cameras.

When Laura parked their SUV, two golf carts appeared and the four of them, along with Jake's golf clubs were transported to the main clubhouse. Jake was informed by one of the club's marshals that his clubs would be taken to the visitor's bag room where his caddy could retrieve them. Marc noticed the confused look on Jake's face.

"What's the problem?" Marc asked.

"I hadn't thought much about a caddy. I've usually carried my own clubs, except when I played in the amateur championship at Pinehurst. Then, I used one of the club's caddies."

The grey-haired marshal raised his bushy eyebrows and his mouth turned up in a grin. "We hear that a lot from the amateurs. You could use one of our club's caddies. Of course, should you win the tournament, you'd have to share your winnings with your caddy. Oops, I forgot, amateurs aren't allowed to accept prize money. No matter, an amateur has never won the Monarch Golf Tournament."

Jake's expression was one of uncertainty.

"I'll caddy for you," Marc said.

The marshal looked over at Marc as if seeing him for the first time. "You sure you can handle this? Looping three practice and four tournament rounds, providing your boy here makes the cut, can be pretty strenuous," he said, nodding toward Jake. "Plus you'll need an intimate knowledge of the rules of golf to advise your player on what and what not to do."

Marc knew the term looping was golf caddy speak for carrying a golfer's bag of clubs around the course. "Not a problem. I haven't carried for a while, but I'm sure I can handle it," Marc said with more assuredness than he felt.

"Mr.LaRose, er, Marc. I think we should discuss this," Laura said.

Marc saw the concern on her face. "I've played golf for well over twenty years and even caddied as a kid. Although I've never been involved at this level, I'm quite sure I can handle it. Besides, it would be a good opportunity for me and my future son-in-law to get to know each other."

This comment not only brought a wide smile to Ann Marie's face, it also seemed to mollify some of Laura's doubts, although he knew she was still not thoroughly convinced.

"Alright. Let me see how things go with the practice rounds, then we'll take it from there," she said.

The marshal glanced at his watch, then up at Jake. "Son, your tee time is set for a little over an hour from now. If you, and your, uh, caddy, will follow me, I'll show you to the locker room where you can change and get ready. That should give you about forty-five minutes on the practice range before you'll be called to the first tee."

Ann Marie gave Jake a hug. "Better run along, Jake. We'll look for you on the range."

Marc grabbed Jake's clubs and the two of them left, following the marshal to the player's locker room. Jake was shown his locker, while Marc was directed to a separate caddy's locker room where he was furnished with a tournament bib and a copy of the course yardage book.

Fifteen minutes later, Marc and Jake headed out onto the practice range, Marc carrying Jake's clubs along with a mesh bag full of range balls. There were just two other players on the range.

Marc admired the lush practice range. "The conditions here are certainly a long way from the driving range at Day's Marina up in Plattsburgh, plus we practically have the whole place to ourselves."

"Yeah, that's probably because many of the pros played in a tournament last week and haven't arrived yet," Jake said.

While Jake went through a stretching routine, Marc opened the mesh bag allowing several balls to roll out onto the thick carpet of grass.

Armed with a short wedge, Jake chipped a few balls. Then he grabbed a nine iron out of the bag and proceeded to launch a dozen balls toward a flag positioned about 170 yards away with consistent precision.

"You keep that up and that marshal will have to eat his words about an amateur never winning this thing."

"My problem is, hitting balls on the practice range, then hitting them on the course where they count, are two different things. It's the pressure. Gets to me every time. Especially being an amateur," Jake said.

"Just think of how you got here. Take this one shot at a time."

As Marc was saying this, he noticed a golf course tractor pulling what appeared to be a large tank of liquid slowly making its way from the direction of the maintenance barn along the first fairway. It eventually disappeared over the rise as it continued in the direction of the eighteenth green, not far from the clubhouse.

Probably a tank full of liquid fertilizer, Marc figured.

A sudden metallic 'thwack' brought Marc's attention back to the moment as Jake had switched from hitting irons to his driver. Marc caught sight of Jake's ball as it bounced then settled in the middle of the range, well beyond the 300-yard marker.

There was the low murmur of approval from the small crowd of golf patrons sitting on the bleachers along with Laura and Ann Marie.

"Yeah, you keep hitting them like that and you'll have a good chance of making some history."

"Thanks for the encouragement, Mr. LaRose. I'm going to need it.'

At their appointed time, Marc and Jake were on the first tee box. It was a 430-yard par four that doglegged uphill and turned off to their left. Except for Jake's mom and Ann Marie plus a few passing spectators, they were alone. As this was a practice round, the club had allowed ample time for the players to hit multiple shots on each hole. Jake hit two balls, both landing near the middle of the fairway.

A smattering of applause from the small gallery caused Jake to smile.

"Nice start," Marc said, as they trudged off to where Jake's shots had landed. Using a wedge, Jake hit approach shots, both balls finding the middle of the green. Despite the super-fast putting conditions, Jake managed most of the following holes with little trouble. Marc made notes of the approximate pin placements planned for the first two days of the tournament, and Jake took several practice putts from different locations on each green. He knew that if Jake made it past the second day below par he would have a good chance of making the cut, allowing him to finish the final two days of the tournament.

Three hours later, the pair, followed by their small, but supportive gallery arrived at the eighteenth fairway. Jake had again driven two balls onto the narrow uphill fairway, both barely missing a large sand bunker that was set off to their left. Up ahead, Marc noticed there was a thick stand of pine trees behind the bunker that extended to within twenty yards of the green. Three sets of long metal bleachers had been constructed at the back of the green for patrons to sit and observe as the players finished their rounds. A large scoreboard was positioned between the thick section of trees and the green, allowing the contestants as well as the gallery to observe each player's position as the round progressed.

Marc estimated the distance from Jake's second shot to the center of the green was about 185 yards. "What do you think, eight iron?"

Jake nodded as Marc handed him the club.

"Thwack," Marc watched as Jake's ball drew slightly to the left and with a single bounce, stopped at the front portion of the green.

"Provided there's no wind, I think that would be the club of choice, keeping the ball below the hole," Jake said and handed the club to Marc.

"You wanna try another?"

"Sure, give me the seven," Jake replied.

When Marc handed him the club, he noticed a movement in the trees up ahead, which he suspected was probably a few golf patrons taking in some of the action.

"Thwack. " Jake's ball again curved slightly to the left and this time landed at the back of the green. "Leaves me a downhill putt, unless, like you say, there's wind in our face."

Both Laura and Ann Marie approved with another cheer.

When the pair approached the green, they noticed that it indeed sloped slightly upwards from front to back. Marc again referred to the course yardage book to locate the possible flag, or pin placements for the first two days of the tournament. Jake took his time lining up his putts before sinking them with the standard two strokes for pars.

Having finished their first eighteen practice holes Marc noticed there was another twosome standing in the fairway with their caddies patiently waiting for them to leave the green. Marc and Jake joined Laura and Ann Marie who were standing just outside the ropes. As they left in the direction of the clubhouse, Marc glanced to where he'd noticed movement in the trees just minutes before, but now, all he saw were the tops of the pine trees, swaying in the gentle breeze. Apparently no one was interested in following a little known amateur.

After returning to the driving range and depositing Jake's clubs in the member's bag storage, they left the grounds of the Savannah River Golf Links then headed back to Aiken and their hotel. Although the day was just a practice round, Marc was impressed with Jake's play and felt certain he was capable of completing the course below par and told him so. Ann Marie was excited to hear how well Jake had done.

Laura didn't seem so sure, however. "Unlike some, I've had the advantage of following my son's career in competitive golf for the past two years. I've seen what he is capable of, especially during tournament. Doing well in a practice round is one thing. It's success under pressure that counts."

Were he and Ann Marie the "some" Laura was referring to, Marc thought? Laura's statement confirmed what he had suspected. The woman was more than a perfectionist, she seemed driven to the point of compulsion. Apparently, failure was not an option for Laura McKay, and Marc was beginning to fear that Ann Marie might be putting herself into a situation she could regret down the road.

Chapter Six

When they arrived back at the hotel, Ann Marie asked if anyone wanted to join her and Jake for a walk through the center of town to do some window shopping.

Marc suspected the couple really wanted a few moments alone and Ann Marie was asking out of courtesy.

"When do you expect to return?" Laura asked, glancing at her watch.

"Depends. If it's all the same, we thought we'd look for a diner, somewhere for a light supper."

"Sounds good. Mind if I tag along?" Marc asked.

"Sure thing, Mr. La… I mean, Marc," Jake replied, then glanced at his mom with a questioning look.

Laura sighed, "Why don't you all go ahead. I still have some unpacking to do. Just don't be all evening. You have another long day of practice tomorrow."

Marc watched as she exited the vehicle and walked through the hotel's main entrance.

"Jake, when you get back, let's plan on going over the notes I made today in preparation for tomorrow's round."

"Where are you going, Dad? I thought you were coming with us?" Ann Marie asked.

"I think you two would rather be alone, besides, there's something I want to check out. I'll see you later."

"Okay, Dad. See you after supper then," Ann Marie said with a light giggle as she and Jake drifted off in the direction of the city center.

Marc turned and headed toward Whiskey Road, the main drag leading from the older section of town past a row of stately homes surrounded by brick fences and crepe myrtle trees. Fifteen minutes later he found what he was looking for, The Palm Tree Golf Club. A sign in front of the building said, "Private." Marc had read about The Palm Tree Golf Club and knew that it had its beginnings a few years before the Savannah River Golf Links in Augusta was founded.

Passing the sign, he entered the club house through its front entrance. Marc wasn't there to make a tee time and, rather than stopping at the check-in counter, he made his way to the interior of the clubhouse. He was immediately impressed by the collection of club memorabilia that adorned the walls of its history room. He found a plethora of photos of past members of the club, plus those of Presidents Eisenhower and Taft, actors Fred Astaire and Bing Crosby as well as notable golfers, Ben Hogan, Byron Nelson and Sam Snead.

As Marc was perusing the array of artifacts, he heard the old wooden floor creak behind him. He turned and saw an elderly gentleman sauntering into the room. Marc looked over at the man and nodded. "You work here?" he asked.

"Well, you could say that, 'cept I don't get paid. Guess that makes me a volunteer of sorts," the old man answered with just a hint of a southern drawl.

The old fellow looked like he'd just stepped out of a Norman Rockwell painting. His wire-rimmed spectacles covered a pair of intense blue eyes, and were perched precariously on the end of his nose. He wore a paisley bow tie that was obviously hand tied and was slightly askew at a 10-4 angle.

Those are the eyes of someone who pays attention to things that matter, Marc thought.

"I've heard about your collection. Thought I'd like to see it for myself," Marc said.

"Yeah, as you can imagine, it's taken a few years to compile. Go ahead and look around. I'll be out behind the check-in desk if you have any questions," he said and started to turn away.

"Tell me, I've heard that this course and the Savannah River Golf Links in Augusta share a bit of history," Marc said.

The old fellow stopped and turned, "In fact, it does. Of course, The Palm Tree Golf Club has been around a little longer. Why do you ask?"

"I'm caddying for an amateur at the Monarch Tournament this week and I'm kinda new at caddying. Actually I'm just doing the kid a favor and I was hoping I could pick up a few pointers on how to advise my young friend on what to expect while playing the Savannah River course."

The old guy scratched his head and gave Marc a light smile. "Well, you've come to the right place. You got a few minutes?"

"Sure do." Marc said, extending his hand as he introduced himself. "My name's Marc LaRose."

The old man took Marc's hand. "Ned, Ned Bunker. Most people just call me Ned. The Club's put up with me hanging around here, for the past forty years."

Marc heard the front door open. When he looked over, he saw a middle-aged man and a teen-aged boy enter and head for the check-in counter. The boy was carrying a small golf bag containing a few clubs.

"If you'll excuse me a moment, Mr. LaRose, I just have to get these fellas taken care of," Ned said, and ambled off toward the newcomers.

"Like I said, I'm in no hurry," Marc said, then continued to peruse the walls of memorabilia.

"Hey Ned, we were hoping we could get in a few holes today," Marc heard the man say.

"Sure thing. It's kinda slow right now, Mr. Osbon. This your grandson?"

"My nephew, actually. Visiting from Charleston. He's in town to watch the Monarch Golf Tournament. Tim, say hello to Ned. Ned's the club's main man here."

"Hello, Mr. Ned," the boy said.

"Glad to meet you, Tim," Ned replied. "Should be no problem, Mr. Osbon. I'll have Bill retrieve your clubs from the bag room and set them on a cart for you."

"Thanks, Ned."

Marc heard the screen door slam shut as Osbon and his nephew left through a side door that led to the first tee.

"Jim Osbon's a life-long member. I remember when he first joined the club thirty years ago," Ned said.

"You still golf much?" Marc asked.

"Me? Oh, I chip and putt around a little, mostly on the practice green. Occasionally, I'll go for a ride in one of the golf carts, but my back won't let me to take a full swing."

Both men remained quiet for a moment.

"So, how about the Savannah River Golf Links? Are there any secrets you can share about the course?" Marc asked.

Ned hesitated as he seemed to consider Marc's query. "Well, you gotta be good, damn good to win there, and that's just for starters. Then you gotta be patient. It's a tough track. Even the best are gonna make mistakes, especially the rookies like your young friend. What'd you say his name was?"

"Jake McKay. He was runner-up at the U.S. Amateur in Pinehurst which qualified him to get into the field for the Monarch Tournament," Marc replied.

"Well, that should make him good enough, all right. But how come you're his caddy? Usually kids who get as far as this Jake has gotten have their own."

"Apparently, he doesn't have a big desire in turning professional, at least not yet. His main interest is business. Guess I just happened to be in the right place at the right time, plus, he and my daughter are an item."

"An 'Item'?" Ned said with a confused look.

"Yeah, uh, they're dating, you know, going together."

"I see," Ned said, again scratching his head as he seemed to think about Marc's question. "Well, if there is any one thing I can say that might help, would be that if you and Jake are unsure which way a putt will break, nine out of ten times, it will break toward the river."

"Toward the Savannah River?" Marc asked.

"It's the only one around. For some unknown reason, that river, running southeast towards the Atlantic the way it does, seems to pull the ball toward it, even on a flat lie. Of course, you have to remember you didn't hear that from me."

"Mum's the word," Marc said, as he thought about what Ned had told him. Just then, the front door opened and another man entered.

"Hey, Ned. I was hoping to get in nine holes today. Any chance?"

"Sure thing, Mr. Simmons," Ned replied, obviously acquainted with this new arrival. "Jim Osbon and his nephew left a few minutes ago. I think they just teed off."

"Maybe I could catch up and join them. I doubt that Jim would mind."

"Where's Mr. Saylor? He's your regular Tuesday partner. Not feeling well?" Ned asked.

"Zach? Yeah, well, his wife called the house and left a message. Said he had some kind of accident at work. Doubt it's anything serious. What could happen at a place where they make PVC irrigation pipes?"

"Yeah, see what you mean. Good luck catching up with Mr. Osbon. At any rate, have a good round," Ned said as this new arrival left the clubhouse.

When Ned returned to where Marc was standing, he said, "Look, Mr. LaRose, as you know, this is a private club, but with your situation, caddying for someone playing in the Monarch Golf Tournament, I'm sure the members wouldn't mind if you wanted to play a round here sometime.

"Thanks, Ned. That's very generous. I'll keep that in mind." Marc glanced at his watch. "Guess I should be heading back to the hotel. I'm sure my daughter will be wondering where her old man has wandered off to."

"Alright, but if you have any more questions, don't hesitate to stop by. I'm usually around during the day and always have time to share what I know, especially if it will help an amateur."

"Thanks, Ned. I appreciate that." With a wave, Marc left the clubhouse and headed back toward Whiskey Road. Taking his time, Marc retraced his steps down Aiken's main thoroughfare with a heavy stream of traffic passing by the otherwise idyllic residential setting. He thought about the information he had gleaned from Ned and how it could help him as Jake's caddy. But as he walked along there was something niggling at him. Something he had heard while in the clubhouse. He hadn't been there very long, but it was like an itch you get, then it leaves you before you have a chance to scratch it.

Wonder what the kids are up to? He thought. The itch was gone.

Chapter Seven

The following morning Laura again drove the foursome to Augusta for Jake's second practice round. Unlike the day before, the check-in routine was expected to go much smoother. Jake's scheduled tee time wasn't until eleven o'clock.

As they were crossing the Savannah River on I-20 into Georgia, Ann Marie asked, "So Dad, yesterday afternoon while we were downtown, you headed off. Said you wanted to check out something. Did you find what you were looking for?"

"If you must know, I went over to The Palm Tree Golf Club."

"Like you didn't have enough golf, caddying for Jake for over four hours, you needed to look at another golf course?" Ann Marie asked.

"The Palm Tree Golf Club was designed by the same guy who set up Savannah River Golf Links. I thought by checking out The Palm Tree course, I might learn what the two had in common."

"And what did you learn?" she asked.

"Other than the fact that both courses had the same designer, probably not much. But, I don't think the visit was totally for naught, however."

"Oh?" she questioned.

"The old guy behind the counter invited me and Jake to play a round. I don't think we'll have the time to do that, but I thought it was nice of him to make the offer."

As Marc turned to look at his daughter, he caught Laura rolling her eyes.

"I'm sorry, Laura. You disapprove?"

She remained quiet for a long moment as the SUV's tires thumped rhythmically over the breaks in the pavement. "My son needs a caddy, someone who will give him advice on how to win a golf tournament, not arranging for free play at a secondary golf course."

"Sorry you feel that way. My intention in going there was not to find a place to play. We already have that. I went there thinking I might learn something, and I believe I did. Just like any business, it doesn't hurt to check out the area and introduce yourself to the locals."

"Whatever," she said, dismissively.

"Mom, I have to agree with Marc," Jake said. "Yesterday, we worked well together. He only gave me advice when I asked for it. Then after a full day of practice, he went out on his own to conduct some research. I've never had anyone do that for me."

Marc could see Laura was not happy with her son's comment, but at least she didn't repeat the eye roll.

"We'll see," she said.

Laura exited the interstate at the Washington Street turnoff. Though the tournament traffic was heavy, the obvious police presence provided an orderly flow. For the second day in a row, the weather was sunny with a light breeze. After checking in, Jake went through his forty-minute warm-up regime that included some stretching as well as hitting every club in his bag. Afterwards, Marc and Jake walked to the practice putting green. Marc noticed Jake's putting seemed to improve with every stroke. When they approached the first tee, they passed a throng of fans who'd gathered along the way, many holding hole-flags, caps and brochures. Several in the crowd pleaded with the more famous pros for an autograph. Jake, a virtual unknown, was only asked for his by a few as they looked curiously at this young unknown. Marc handed Jake a Sharpie pen he'd kept for marking Jake's golf balls. Jake gladly signed a few autographs and chatted with his young admirers.

As they continued to the first tee, Marc noticed the gallery lining the fairway had doubled in size from the day before. For today's practice round, Jake had been paired with another golfer, a professional who had won a major tournament a few years in the past. Although that win qualified him to play, Marc suspected that the golf gods had not been kind to him since. Marc noticed the pro and his caddy spoke English, but with an accent that Marc couldn't place. When he looked at the player's bag, he recognized the flag of South Africa affixed to it along with the name, Luther Van Zyle.

Although introductions went smoothly, rapport between the two players seemed stilted. The old pro apparently didn't appreciate being paired with an amateur, even if it was for a practice round.

Finally, Willum, the caddy, asked, "Would you like us to go first?"

Although his accent was thick, Marc had no trouble understanding what he had said.

Jake smiled. "Sure, go right ahead."

The South African teed his ball, then with practiced precision, hit a fine shot down the center of the fairway.

Jake nodded his approval.

The South African displayed a pleasant smile.

Then Jake hit his drive. They watched his ball sail past the South African's by at least thirty yards.

Laura and Ann Marie clapped politely.

Willum looked at Marc and smiled. "The kid is pretty good, no?"

"He's got potential," Marc replied.

The second and third holes went just as smoothly. However, Marc noticed there seemed to be more than the usual number of security officers present, especially for a practice round.

When they arrived at the fifth tee box, a female security guard with a K9 stood close by. Curious, Marc asked, "There seems to be a lot of extra security today. Expecting problems?"

The guard hesitated before answering, "Nothing in particular, just a precaution." She then pulled on the dog's leash and moved away, apparently reluctant to discuss the subject any further.

Marc recognized the dog's breed as a Belgian Malinois, known for its keen sense of smell and commonly used by the police for locating contraband drugs and even hidden explosives.

"I heard what you asked the guard," Willum said. "I must say, it feels like we're playing on a course back home. Intense security is the norm in South Africa."

"Up to today, I've only seen the tournament on television and I understand that thorough gallery screening is standard practice at the Monarch Golf Tournament. But somehow, I get the feeling this is a bit unusual."

"In our years on the tour, we've seen some crazy stuff. However, with your foreign secretary attending the Sunday round, I suppose the organizers would rather plan for the worst and hope for the best," Willum said.

"You're probably right," Marc replied. It was news to him that the U.S. Secretary of State would be attending the tournament. And although it would certainly be an honor to meet him, Marc knew that, at this moment, it was more important to concentrate on Jake's progress.

As they continued with the round, Marc could see that Jake's self-confidence was building as he succeeded in reaching all par fives in just two shots, even making an eagle on the last. The few times that his shots were errant, rather than criticize, Marc simply encouraged Jake to put the wayward shot out of his mind. It was more important to recover and move on to the next swing. Also, Marc felt that as Jake's confidence increased, his own ability to help Jake improved as well.

When they completed the round, Jake and the South African player shook hands as did Marc and Willum. They wished each other good luck in the tournament, now less than twenty-four hours away.

By the time Marc, Ann Marie, Jake and Laura returned to Aiken, it was late afternoon.

"I've taken the liberty of making a reservation for the four of us at a nice Italian restaurant downtown. A place called Casa Della's," Laura said.

"Sounds nice, but only if you allow me to take care of the check," Marc said.

Laura hesitated then retrieved her cell phone from her purse. "I suppose. I made the reservation for seven thirty, so let's plan on meeting in the hotel lobby in about an hour. It's about a ten-minute walk to the restaurant."

Jake was standing nearby. "Mom, would you mind if Ann Marie and I leave a little earlier? We'll meet up with you at the restaurant."

"Oh, I don't know. How do you feel about that, Mr. LaRose?" Laura asked.

"Sure, why not. Sounds like the kids want some time by themselves."

At seven fifteen, Marc was sitting in one of the lounge chairs in the hotel's lobby. A young man about Jake's age was playing the piano. It took Marc a moment to recognize the tune. It was "Hotel California." Although he'd heard the recording many times before, he'd never heard it played on the piano. Immersed in the song, he caught a movement off to his right from the landing that led to the elevators. It was Laura. She was wearing a dark green knee length skirt, a white blouse and a pair of black low-heel pumps. She was carrying a matching purse in her right hand. She seemed to focus on the guy playing the piano. Without her usual scowl, she was actually attractive.

Remember Marc, he told himself, this is Rose Hill, not Hotel California.

He stood as she descended the landing. His movement caught her attention.

"Ah, Marc, there you are. I wasn't sure if you'd be ready quite yet."

"I like to be prompt. Besides, I was enjoying the ambiance of the hotel's lobby."

"Good choice, by the way."

The fact that she'd addressed him by his first name was not lost in the din of "Mission Bells" flowing from the piano.

Laura glanced at her watch. "Yes, well, I'd love to stay and listen to the music, but I suppose we'd best be on our way."

As the two walked out of the hotel's entrance, Marc couldn't shake the feeling, is this really heaven, or could this be hell?

Chapter Eight

The following day the weather turned nasty, especially if you were playing golf. Winds averaged around 20 mph, gusting to 25. Although the rain was light, it was steady, just south of a heavy mist. No lightning was in the immediate forecast, which insured the tournament would go off as planned. Because all patron tickets were presold long before the start of tournament, other than the hot dog vendors, the biggest losers would be the fans who had coughed up big bucks to see the best golfers in the world play while holding an umbrella and/or wrapped in one of the cheap see-through ponchos that were sold in the gallery golf shop. Although the weather conditions had a perceivable effect on fan enthusiasm, the turnout, as well as the abundance of security, appeared about the same as the day before.

Jake declined the umbrella and was happy with his rain suit; however, Marc kept the umbrella handy to keep the golf clubs and score card dry. It was the first day of regulation play, and although Jake had made it this far, to make the cut and play the final two days would require above average rounds. The cut line depended on how well the leaders played. Jake and Marc knew that making it into the final two days would be an achievement in itself, let alone even thinking about winning. After all, the field of 120 players included some of the best in the world.

Jake was paired with a previous Monarch champion, Teddy Doubles. Doubles had won the Monarch twice before and Marc knew he had his sights set on a third win. It was common knowledge that Doubles was a fan favorite and although Jake was a virtual unknown, being teamed with this prior champion would bring more attention to Jake, thus increasing the pressure on him to succeed.

"Just play your own game. Remember whatever Doubles does, we have to keep our cool and take it one shot at a time," Marc counseled.

Marc hoped the "we" would give Jake some comfort, that he was not in this alone, and that they were a team.

Jake's face broke out in a wide grin, "Marc, I not only appreciate your advice, but at this stage of the game I would be completely lost without it."

"You've got game, Jake. Just trust your ability and we'll do fine."

Marc knew that playing in the same group with Teddy Doubles, a previous champion, would bring a large fan following, plus extra media coverage. Of course this had the effect of increased scrutiny of not only Doubles, but of Jake's play as well.

Doubles' first drive was not just long, but also very accurate, leaving him with no more than a pitching wedge to the first green.

Jake's drive was almost as long, but his ball leaked off to the right side of the fairway into the first cut of rough. When they arrived at Jake's ball, Marc saw that although it was not far off the fairway, the grass was thick. The one bright spot was that Jake had caught a break. The ball was held up by the thick mat of grass, making his attempt to get it on the green doable.

Doubles' pitch was accompanied by cheers as it landed in the middle of the green, but the cheers quickly turned to moans as his ball checked up, then spun back off the front of the green.

Jake's pitch landed at the front of the green, then rolled to about three feet left of the flag. This was followed by light applause, except for Ann Marie who squealed with delight. Laura was much more subdued, offering applause and a smile.

Doubles went on to make his par and Jake's birdie putt found the middle of the hole.

"Nice recovery and a good start to the round. Sure you haven't played here before?" Doubles said with his natural grin.

"No, not before this week," Jake answered.

At the second tee box, Marc spotted the same security guard with her K9 that he had spoken to the day before. As the men approached, the guard again pulled on her dog's leash.

"Good Morning, officer," Marc said in an attempt to get a response. She gave Marc a quick smile and a nod, then slipped away toward the ropes that separated the fairway from the gallery.

Oh well, worth a try, Marc thought.

The two men continued to play well for the remainder of the day, with the lead between them trading hands. When they finished the round, Doubles was one stroke ahead of Jake and just four strokes behind the leader.

The mini tournament between Jake and Doubles had been good, especially for Jake. Marc believed it was because both men had something to prove. Doubles, the accomplished champion didn't want to be outshone by this newcomer, and Jake intended to show that although he was an amateur, he had something to prove. Marc also suspected that Jake needed to show his mother he was good enough to play on the pro tour.

After returning to the hotel, Ann Marie announced that she and Jake had made plans to go to a restaurant later that afternoon, and made no secret that they wanted to be alone. Laura, although not outwardly pleased with this announcement, seemed resigned to her son's intentions and simply indicated that she'd probably find something to eat at the hotel before turning in for the evening. It was still relatively early, so despite the lingering mist that had plagued their day at the Savannah River Golf Links, Marc drove the rented SUV to The Palm Tree Golf Club to see if his new-found friend, Ned Bunker, was still minding the store.

As he pulled into the clubhouse parking lot, he noticed only three cars there and figured that one, an older model Buick parked between a late model Lexus SUV and a Land Rover, was probably Ned's.

Inside the clubhouse, Marc found Ned was still busy with the memorabilia he had been working on the day before, dusting and cleaning before returning them to their traditional places of honor. Marc could see there would be no problem determining which pictures went where because of the outline shapes that each portrait had left on the faded wallpaper. Ned again was wearing a bow tie; however today it was slightly turned to an 8-2 position.

"Hello, Mr. LaRose. Didn't think we'd be seeing you around here so soon now that your amateur is faring so well at the Monarch. Looks like congratulations are in order."

"Jake had a good day, but there's still tomorrow. And with the rain and softening course conditions, anything can happen."

"I'll say. So, what brings you here on such a dreary afternoon?"

"I just stopped by to thank you for that little tip you gave me."

"Tip? What tip was that?"

"The one about how some putts tend to turn toward the Savannah River, even when they're on a flat lie."

Ned hesitated as he continued to straighten one of the pictures he had just re-hung to its traditional position on the wall, "I don't know what you're talking about," he replied, then looked over at Marc and gave him a quick wink.

Marc remembered. Ned's "tip" was to be kept between the two of them. "Don't worry, that's our little secret."

Ned didn't reply and continued working, apparently not wanting to broach the subject any further.

Marc decided to ease out of the conversation with some idle chit-chat before returning to the hotel. "Looks like the weather's put a damper on your business today."

"Yeah, well, the weather's had some effect on play, but that's not the only reason for the day's low turnout."

"Oh? I understand The Palm Tree drains pretty well, even in the wettest of conditions."

"You're right. We do have a fine course, and, like you just mentioned, it drains really well, even after a good soaking. But that's not the main reason for the lack of play. One of our members passed this week."

Marc hesitated before answering, "Sorry to hear that. Hope it wasn't too unexpected." Marc had heard that a few of the club's members were octogenarians and older.

"As a matter of fact, Mr. Saylor was one of our younger members, forty-five or so. Seemed healthy as a horse. Plus, he was a scratch golfer."

Marc thought a moment, "Oh yeah, I recall overhearing his name mentioned last time I was here. Something about an accident at work?"

"That was him. Don't know exactly what happened. Just that it was deemed an industrial accident of some sort."

Marc hesitated. "Yeah, didn't he work at a plant that produced PVC piping or something?"

"You have a good memory, Mr. LaRose. Apex Irrigation is the name of the place. Zach, er, Mr. Saylor, had worked there for years. Not certain, but I understand that Apex was bought out last year. 'Twas a small, family-owned enterprise specializing in custom irrigation work. It was rumored, however, the business was circling the drain, so when an out-of-town buyer approached them, the owners apparently jumped at the offer."

"Did Mr. Saylor leave a family?"

"Just a wife. His second. Zach remarried when his first wife ran off and left him. That was just after their third wedding anniversary. Story goes that despite working at an irrigation supply plant, old Zach was sorely lacking in the plumbing department, if you catch my drift," Ned said with a wink of his eye.

"Poor guy, unlucky at love, and unluckier at work, I guess," Marc said.

"Unlucky may be a little understated. I believe the funeral is tomorrow. Won't be much to see though. I heard they've cremated what was left of him."

"What was left? You mean there was a fire?"

"I guess. Not much's being said about that. Understand they had things pretty much cleaned up by the time the fire department arrived.

"They? You mean the company, Apex Irrigation?"

Ned was quiet a moment. "You'd have to ask them, but don't expect much. They're pretty hush-hush about the whole thing. There wasn't much in the paper about it either. Just a column about an apparent spill, followed by a fire. As you can imagine, that covers a lot of territory."

As Marc was thinking about Ned's recollection, a flash of bright light from one of the side windows filled the room. This was immediately followed by an explosion of thunder causing the old building to shudder.

"That was a close one," Ned said. "I only have a couple twosomes out on the course. I suppose I should get them in before we lose another member."

With that Ned laid his dusting cloth on the counter. "If you'll excuse me, Mr. LaRose, I should activate the inclement weather warning alarm."

"Need any help, Ned?"

"No, thanks. We use a public address system. I don't even have to go outside.

"Okay," Marc said as he glanced at his watch. "I probably should be heading back to the hotel."

"Stop in again when the weather gets better," Ned said as he turned toward the check-in counter.

"Will do, and good luck getting your members out of the storm."

As Marc left the clubhouse, he heard the blast of a horn over the club's PA system. This was immediately followed by another rumble of thunder coming from somewhere in the distance.

You wouldn't have to warn me to come in out of the rain when there's lightening in the area, especially if I was standing in the middle of an open fairway holding a four iron above my head, Marc thought as he climbed into the safe confines of the SUV.

When Marc arrived back at Rose Hill, he noticed Laura was seated in an overstuffed chair in the hotel's lounge. She was nursing a glass of white wine and appeared quite content. The evening's entertainment was provided by a young lady strumming softly on an acoustic guitar. Marc recognized the tune. It was "Lara's Theme," Lara, Laura, close enough. Wonder how much she tipped the girl to play a song she probably thinks was written just for her? he mused.

Marc lowered his head and continued toward the landing and the hotel's elevators just beyond.

"Mr. LaRose. You're not trying to avoid me, are you?"

Was I that obvious? Marc stopped in mid-step, one foot still on the landing, "Oh, hello, Laura. Sorry, I was just thinking about the tournament tomorrow."

"I'm sure you were," she said with little conviction. "But look, the evening is just getting started. Let me buy you a drink."

Although Marc felt uneasy about Laura's offer, he let his foot slide back off the step, then glanced at his watch. "I suppose I have time for one. There's a few things I need to do to get ready for tomorrow." *Hope that didn't come across as lame as it sounded.*

"Oh, come now. Jake and Ann Marie haven't returned from dinner yet. Come, sit by me," she said, patting the seat of a chair next to her.

Cautiously, Marc took the proffered chair. "Alright, but only on one condition."

As Laura drained her glass, Marc suspected that was not her first for the evening.

"And, what condition would that be?" She asked, setting the empty glass on the table between them.

Marc felt the radiation of her provocative stare that bore into his eyes. "Two conditions actually."

When Laura looked like she was about to protest, he held up a hand.

"First, no wine. Bourbon, Woodford Reserve."

"My, I'm already beginning to like your conditions. And the second?"

"Drinks are on me. You've already done enough."

Laura seemed to give Marc's suggestions some thought.

"Sure, why not," she said with a light smile.

Marc got the waiter's attention and ordered the drinks. As the attendant turned to head back to the bar, the guitarist finished the set and announced she was taking a five-minute break.

"Potty time," Laura said.

Marc started to get up from the chair.

Laura put a hand on his knee, "Not me, I meant the girl playing the guitar. Sounds like she's in need of a bathroom break."

"Sorry," Marc said, slightly embarrassed.

"So tell me, Marc, you don't mind if I call you Marc, do you?" Without waiting for his response, Laura continued, "Jake says you're some kind of private investigator. What kind of things do you investigate?"

Where's this going? "It depends."

"Depends? That's not much of an answer. Would you mind elaborating?"

Marc hesitated. "Pretty simple really. Depends on what people want me to do for them."

"I see. So you're not a specialist, like in computer fraud, forensics, or risk assessment. You're more like a small town doctor, an investigative general practitioner."

"Yes, I suppose so. Sounds like you've had some investigative experience yourself," Marc said.

"No. Let's just say I've had a challenging business career."

Marc didn't know exactly what she meant by that, and, at this point, didn't really want to.

Their drinks arrived. The waiter set two glasses of bourbon and a container of ice cubes on the table between them. "Shall I start a check, sir?"

"That won't be necessary," Marc said and handed him a fifty-dollar bill. "That should cover it."

"Thank you, sir," the waiter said appreciatively, then turned and left.

Marc touched his glass to Laura's, "To Jake. May the golf gods shine down on him tomorrow."

Laura lifted her glass, "And the day after."

They clinked their glasses, then each took a sip.

When Marc looked over his glass, she was staring back at him.

"Umm, nice," she said.

"Glad you like it."

"Yeah, the bourbon is good too." Without waiting for a response, she set her glass on the table, "As you may have suspected, Marc, I appreciate fine things."

"Yes, I've noticed."

"I don't think I've told you how much your help means to Jake, and to me as well."

"Don't mention it," Marc said as he took another slow sip.

Laura started to say something, then hesitated as the guitarist returned and began her next number. As she strummed a few notes, Marc recognized the tune. It took him back to his childhood when his mom played it on the family's record player. It was an old Bobby Darin favorite, "*Mack the Knife.*"

"When that shark bites, with those teeth dear," Marc was momentarily lost in the young performer's rendition of the song, then glanced over at Laura. She was smiling - at him - again.

She said something, but Marc, distracted by the song could only think, yes, your teeth are indeed, pearly white. "Sorry Laura, I didn't catch that, what'd you say?"

She took another sip and set her glass on the table. She then reached over and covered the back of Marc's hand with hers, "Just that, I'm truly gratefull for what you're doing and I'd like to pay you back sometime."

Marc hesitated as he suspected he knew where this conversation was headed. "I think you already have. I mean, just by bringing us here to this splendid hotel and to the tournament."

"No, Marc. I'm thinking something more personal." She raised her glass with her free hand and took another slow sip of the sweet, smoky libation.

Marc, not usually at a loss for words, could only return Laura's glassy-eyed stare. In the background, the soloist continued, "Just a jackknife, has old Macheath babe, and she keeps it, out of sight…"

"Well, don't you two look cozy?"

Shaken from his reverie, Marc looked up. It was Ann Marie. She and Jake had returned from their outing and Marc, busy fending off Laura's advances, hadn't seen them enter the hotel. He casually withdrew his hand from beneath Laura's and picked up his glass. "We were just talking about you," Marc said calmly, swirling the remains of his drink.

Laura glanced at her watch. "Oh dear, look at the time. It's already after nine o'clock and we have a big day ahead of us tomorrow." She looked up at her son, "I suppose we should turn in. Jake will need his rest if he wants to make the cut tomorrow."

"Yes, I agree," Marc said. He finished his drink and rose from his chair.

As Marc and Ann Marie made their way to the elevator, Marc heard the soloist continue, "Someone's sneaking 'round the corner, could that someone be Mack the Knife?" Marc shuddered as the elevator door closed.

Back in his room, Marc had given the larger of the two beds to Jake, while he had taken a twin that was separated by a corner close to the single bathroom.

"So, what did you guys do for supper," Marc called out around the separation.

"Just went out for a burger. Some place down the street, Betsy's, or something like that. Looks like you and mom were hitting it off nicely in the lounge."

"No, it was nothing like that," Marc said defensively. "We were just talking about how well the day went for you at the course today."

"Uh huh," he said, his tone leaving little doubt Jake was unconvinced.

"Hope you don't mind if I shower first tonight. Like your mom said, we have a big day tomorrow."

"Sure thing, Marc. Take all the time you need."

Chapter Nine

Overnight, the damp weather that soaked the area the day before had moved on, allowing the sun to rise over Aiken and the Savannah River Golf Links. Laura drove the SUV out of the hotel's parking lot and headed west toward Augusta. Although Jake had drawn a ten-thirty tee time they had all agreed to arrive early enough to grab a breakfast at one of the course concessions.

On the first tee, both Jake and his playing partner for the day, a good player who had won for the first time in his career the previous year, greeted one another. Adam Sink was an affable fellow and although Adam was a few years older than Jake, the two men seemed to hit it off right away.

The small crowd gathered around the first tee greeted both players with light applause as their names were announced. Jake was first to tee off and, unlike the previous day, hit his drive well over 300 yards straight up the center of the fairway. Adam's drive followed Jake's at practically the same length. Both men and their caddies knew this day was important because making the cut depended on how well everyone, especially the leaders, played today. If their play fell short of the cut line, it was adios amigo, better luck next year. Although Jake had played well the previous day, setting him up for a good chance to make the cut, Marc knew that good play today was imperative to getting into the weekend for the final two days of tournament.

When they reached the fifth hole tee box, Marc again saw the same female security guard with her dog that he had seen before. "Good morning, officer. Another fine day, don't you think?" Marc asked, in an attempt to start some conversation.

The officer smiled. "So far, so good," she said, then, not unlike before, she made a kissy noise and tugged lightly on the dog's leash. "Come on, boy," she said. The dog responded and the two moved away.

She's either following instructions not to talk to anyone, or she's introverted.

As the day progressed, both Jake and Adam played consistently through the first nine holes. Jake arrived at the tenth hole three strokes under par, while Adam was two strokes behind. On the fourteenth, par three, Adam faltered when his tee shot found the pond guarding the raised green. Unfortunately for Adam, he never regcovered from that one bad shot and went on to finish at five over par, missing the cut by two strokes. Jake's play was exemplary. He finished with two birdies, leaving him four under par for the round.

Laura and Ann Marie joined Marc and Jake and after congratulatory hugs, waited around the eighteenth hole for the final players to finish. Although Marc was confident Jake would be playing the weekend, he wanted to see just where he would be standing for the next day of play and also who Jake would be competing against.

"I don't know about you guys, but I'm starving," Jake announced.

"Me too," Ann Marie chimed in, "walking eighteen holes has given me an appetite."

Marc knew there were at least ten pairings left to complete their rounds, so after securing Jake's golf bag in the player's bag storage, he led the group to one of the outdoor cafes reserved for players and their guests not far from the eighteenth hole. As they were being seated under an umbrella, Marc noticed a man walk by wearing a set of drab green work coveralls, which made him stand out from the passing crowd of golf patrons. Marc's attention was momentarily interrupted as another group was seated at a table nearby. Then, as his gaze shifted, he again caught sight of the back of the coveralls. "Apex Irrigation." Then, just as quickly, the coveralls melted into the river of colorful golf shirts. He thought back to The Palm Tree Golf Club and Ned. Apex was the company Ned had mentioned where one of its club members was employed when he was killed in some kind of work-related accident.

"Welcome, folks. How about a cold pitcher of Arnold Palmer Iced Tea to start with?" a waiter said, bringing Marc back to the moment.

As Laura ordered a glass of sweet tea, Marc continued to look for any sign of the workman, but the slow-moving train of golf attire had completely swallowed him up.

"And for you sir?"

"Oh, uh, the same, please," Marc managed, unsure of what he'd just ordered.

Ann Marie gave Marc a *"Something bothering you?"* look. "Are you okay, Dad? You seem a little pre-occupied."

"I'm fine. I was just thinking about Jake's round today," he said, not wanting to share his musings with his daughter, especially with Jake and Laura within earshot.

"Okay, while you're enjoying your drinks, I'll leave you with today's lunch specials," the waiter said as he dealt the paper menus around the table.

Later, that afternoon, on the trip back to Aiken, Marc was quiet, thinking about Jake's play, and the man with the coveralls with Apex Irrigation stenciled on the back.

Laura said, "Marc, why don't we go out someplace different for dinner tonight?"

"I suppose. Want me to make a reservation for the four of us, say around seven o'clock or so?"

"Actually, Mark, I was thinking it would be for the two of us. I'm sure the kids wouldn't mind, would you, Jake?"

"Sure. You two do your thing and we'll do ours," Jake said.

Marc could see Ann Marie in his rear-view mirror, poking Jake playfully while giving him a smile.

"Yeah, Dad. I think that's a great idea. You guys can talk adult talk. We'll be fine on our own."

Marc knew there was no use in arguing. "Any place in particular, Laura?"

Laura paused. "I thought it was the gentleman who made dinner arrangements."

"Alright, but I can't make any promises. After all, we've only been in town for a few days and other than Casa Della's and Rose Hill, I haven't had time to check out another place."

"You're a big boy. I know you'll think of something," she said.

I'm thinking of a few things right now, but I don't think they're what you have in mind.

When they arrived at the hotel, Marc went to his room and immediately took a long hot shower. He soaped up and let the water ease the tension from his muscles that had built up from the day on the course.

After showering, he donned a pair of khakis and a short-sleeved button-down collared shirt that he felt would be appropriate for the evening's dinner. Jake had left earlier and Marc guessed he and Ann Marie were out looking for someplace to have dinner alone, without parental supervision. He pulled the nightstand drawer open and, next to the Gideon Bible, found a local telephone book. *Surprised they even print these things anymore.*

Finding what he needed, he left the room and headed for the elevator. The hotel's dining room was already quite busy and practically every table was full. From their dress and demeanor, Marc could tell most of the diners were golf fans just returning from the day's tournament in Augusta.

He stopped at the bar and ordered a diet Coke, figuring it was too early for alcohol; besides, he suspected this could be a late evening. Marc found a stool with a view of the hallway that led to the elevators. A three-piece band was beginning to set up near one of the fireplaces in the hotel's lobby.

"My, you clean up well, Mr. LaRose," Marc heard the familiar voice behind him as he was scanning the crowd assembled in the lobby. When he turned, he saw Laura walking toward him. She had apparently taken the stairway on the opposite end of the hallway, from where the elevator was located. Marc stood to meet her. She was dressed in dark leggings and a flowing white top. Her spiked heels brought her eyes almost even with his and she carried a small leopard skin clutch purse. *Graaauu!*

"You look nice as well. The crowd at McDonald's is gonna love that purse."

"McDonald's?" she said a little too loud, which caused a few nearby heads to turn. Then, as a grin crept across her face, she said, "Oh, I should have known." She glanced around with an embarrassed look on her face. "Jake told me that you're quite the kidder. Come on, let's get out of here."

Once outside, Laura handed Marc the keys to the SUV which was parked a half block away on a side street. The car's locking mechanism chirped as Marc pressed the button to unlock the doors. He held the passenger door open and she climbed inside.

"Well, thank you, Mr. LaRose. Good to know you have a few domesticated qualities."

Ignoring Laura's quip, Marc got behind the wheel and started the engine. He retrieved his cell phone and tapped in an address.

"Looks we're going somewhere mysterious. Must be quite a restaurant," she said.

"Actually, before we have dinner, I need to check out something. Should only take a few minutes."

"Let's make it quick. My stomach's beginning to protest."

Marc made a left turn and drove to the center of town. After a few more turns, he found the street he was looking for. The address he had found in the phone book took them toward the edge of town. The few streetlights that were working were just coming to life. Marc noticed they were in an area of mixed light industry and a scattering of private residences, mostly of the double-wide variety. The place he was looking for turned out to be a cinder block structure surrounded by a ten-foot-high, chain-link fence topped with three strands of barbed wire angled away from the building. A lighted sign hanging off the front of the structure read, "Apex Irrigation Supply Co." Darkness was less than a half-hour away and the security lighting mounted at close intervals around the building was already lit. A gate connected to the fence at the front had been left open. A sign hanging in the glass doorway that appeared to be the building's main entrance indicated the business was closed for the day. A few fluorescents had been left on inside, and light seeped through the glass. Marc stopped on the street in front of the building.

"If that is the place you've made reservations for, it looks like we got here a little too late," Laura said.

Ignoring the comment, Marc turned the SUV through the open gate. The crushed stones that formed the parking lot crunched under the tires. Parked just inside the fence were a couple of sedans that appeared to have out-of-state license plates, along with a dark colored SUV. In the diminishing remains of daylight, Marc could see a line of vans parked along the side of the building with the company's name adorning their sides. He brought the vehicle to a stop in front of the entrance door.

"Looks like there's someone inside. Stay in the car," Marc said.

As Marc exited the SUV he heard the passenger door open. Against Marc's instructions, Laura had decided to join him. He knew there was no use arguing with this woman, although he did enjoy watching her maneuver around the front of the SUV, her spiked heels sinking deep into the crushed stone. He shook his head and continued toward the building's entrance.

He peered through the glass portion of the door with a "Closed" sign dangling from a small chain. A long counter ran past the door he was looking through. The counter formed an open hallway ending at a partition at the far end of the room. Marc could see several desks with computer screens sitting on them. A solid door at the far end of the hallway had a sign attached to it: "Employees Only."

Using the back of his hand, Marc tapped on the door's window. His State Police retirement ring made a piercing, metal-on-glass sound.

"I believe it's after business hours, Mr. LaRose. Besides, why are you in the market for irrigation supplies? You thinking of doing some landscaping?"

Marc ignored Laura's comment and tapped on the window again, this time a little harder. After waiting a long minute, there was still no answer.

As he was about to try one more time, he looked upwards and noticed what appeared to be a security camera mounted under the building's overhang. Thinking there was possibly someone inside looking back at him, he retrieved his New York State Police retirement credentials that included a gold shield and held it upwards toward the camera for a few seconds. He took the chance that someone inside was paying attention, but not looking too close.

Laura asked, "That your go to jail free card?"

Marc heard the distant thump of a door closing and when he looked back through the entrance door's glass again, he saw a man approaching from the "Employees Only" door, wearing a respirator with a face shield. Marc snapped his credential holder shut and replaced it in his shirt pocket.

When the man got to the door, he removed his respirator. It was then that Marc recognized him from his visit to The Palm Tree Golf Club two days before. His name was Jim Simmons. He heard the locking mechanism disengage, and the door opened.

"Sorry for the delay, officer. We mistook you for someone from the press. You know how nosey those bastards can be."

"No problem. Tried to call, but when no one answered, we thought we'd see if there was still someone on the premises."

Simmons hesitated. "Look, if this is about the incident that occurred the day before yesterday, you should've heard that it's been taken care of. Someone from the police along with the fire department came out and since then we've hired a chemical spill service to clean things up."

Marc glanced at Laura. "I'm aware of that. It's just that the officer who was originally assigned to investigate the incident had to leave town. Family emergency. We've been tasked with following up. Hope this isn't a bad time."

Simmons hesitated, apparently unprepared for this sudden appearance of the police. He glanced over his shoulder back toward the door with the "Employees Only" sign on it.

"Oh, excuse my manners," Marc said and extended his hand. I'm Detective Ryan, and this is my partner, Detective Burns," Marc said, motioning toward Laura, attempting to urge Simmons along.

Simmons reluctantly shook Marc's hand, but only gave Laura a quick glance. "I'm Jim Simmons, one of the managers, sort of. But, as you can see, we're still closed due to the accident and the cleanup. Wish you'd have called ahead. Could have saved you a trip. Besides, you must be aware that I gave the responding officers a complete statement. I'm sure you have a record of that somewhere."

"Uh, yes we do. We just have a few more questions. Only take a moment."

Simmons glanced at his watch. "I'm sorry, detective. But can't we do this another time? As you can see, we're still busy trying to get things back in order." He glanced over his shoulder again.

Marc noticed a few beads of sweat forming on the man's brow. He suspected Simmons was under some kind of pressure to end this conversation and get back inside. "We understand. Like I said, this should only take a moment," Marc said.

Simmons started to protest again, but Marc cut him off. "According to the information I received, Mr. Saylor died from a chemical spill, correct?

"Yes, but--"

"What kind of chemical?" Marc asked.

Simmons glanced back through the door a third time. "Surely the other detectives must have told you, it was simple chlorine. We use it to sanitize our equipment before sending it out to the field.

Unfortunately, for Zach, uh, Mr. Saylor, he must have accidently inhaled some of the pure chlorine before it was diluted. I've known Zach for years. Heavy smoker. I suspect years of inhaling cigarette smoke didn't help. Plus, according to the autopsy, he also had a heart condition that even he didn't know about. But like I just told you, the responding investigators have all this information."

"Chlorine? Are we talking about bleach?" Marc asked.

"Sort of, but chlorine in its purest form is much stronger. We really don't know how he ingested enough to kill him. There are strict safety regulations we follow when handling these chemicals, and to the best of my knowledge, everyone present at the time was properly protected. It was just some kind of freak accident. But now, if you'll excuse me, I really must return to my work. If you need to get in touch with me, please call during regular business hours."

With that, Simmons produced a card from his shirt pocket and handed it to Marc. "My cell is the first number. I'm usually available after lunch," he said and grabbed the door handle.

Marc held up his hand, "When do you think the cleanup will be completed?"

Simmons gave his head a quick shake, "Not certain. Actually, we're not sure that we will even reopen the business. This whole thing has been very tragic, for all of us."

"Sorry to hear that. Did Mr. Saylor have any family?" Marc asked.

"Yeah, a wife and two children. His kids are married and they don't live around here. Now, if you'll excuse me, I really have to return to work. Still have lots to do."

"All right then, Mr. Simmons. Appreciate you taking the time to talk. We'll be in touch."

"Yeah, thanks," Simmons said and shut the door. Marc watched as he walked the corridor formed by the counter and the wall. He stopped a moment to secure his face mask, then he disappeared behind the door.

Marc turned and headed back toward the SUV and slid in behind the wheel. Laura got in beside him.

"What the fuck was that all about?" Laura asked as she buckled her shoulder harness.

He started the engine and swung the nose of the SUV back onto the street. He turned in the direction they had come. "Probably nothing," he said.

They rode in silence for a few hundred yards. Marc could feel the intense stare he was getting from the passenger seat.

"'Probably nothing? You take me to a business that has just experienced a chemical spill. You have us, you and me, falsely impersonating police officers sent to investigate the spill, and on top of all that, the chemical spill has apparently resulted in at least one fatality. You have a weird conception of what 'probably nothing' means,'" Laura said, her annoyance as intense as the polish reflecting off her cherry-red fingernail extensions.

"Take a breath, Laura. I can explain everything over a very dry martini and a nice relaxing dinner. Why don't you pull your cell phone out of that cute little clutch purse you're carrying and get us the directions for the General P.T. Beauregard Restaurant. It's somewhere on the outskirts of town. I just don't have the exact location."

"Look, Mr. LaRose. The only directions I'll be giving you are the ones that take us back to our hotel. That's where I want to go. I've had enough fun for one night."

"Why? You afraid of a little excitement in your otherwise uninspiring existence? Or is it because, for once, you are not calling all the shots and feel like you're not in control?"

Laura looked away, toward a collection of double-wide mobile homes passing by her side window.

Marc heard her exhale, then saw her dig into her purse.

"What did you say the name of that restaurant was? Beauregard something?"

"It's called the General P.T. Beauregard. It shouldn't be far. I just can't remember the name of the street it's on."

After a few moments of fiddling with her phone she said, "Take the next right hand turn. It should be on our left, about a half mile after the turn."

A few minutes later Marc pulled the SUV into the restaurant's parking area and maneuvered into what appeared to be the only available space that was left.

By the time Marc had come around the SUV to open Laura's door, she had already made her way out and was walking toward the restaurant's front entrance. Marc followed her up the entrance steps. A small man with a gray pencil-line mustache met them as they entered. He wore a nametag, "Maitre d' Oliver."

"Good evening. What name is your reservation under?" Oliver asked.

Laura started to say something, but Marc interrupted, "Sorry, we don't have a reservation. We just stopped in on the off chance that you might still have something available."

The man glanced at the clipboard he was carrying, "You're in luck. We've just had a cancellation. Right this way, please," Oliver said and led them to a small table situated next to a curtained window that looked out toward the street. Except for this table, the restaurant appeared to be full.

After they were seated, Oliver asked. "May I get you something from the bar?"

"Yes," Laura said, "A double martini, Bombay Sapphire, if you have it. Rocks on the side."

"Certainly, and for you, sir?"

"Goose Island IPA, please."

As the Maitre d' drifted back towards the bar, Laura asked, "Beer?"

"I don't drink hard stuff when I have to drive. Besides, I like beer, and I've recently developed a taste for IPA's."

The two sat in silence with the typical hum of background restaurant noises filling the space around them.

A few moments later, their drinks were delivered.

"Would you like to hear this evening's specials?" Oliver asked.

"I'd like a steak. A big one. Very rare, with whatever comes with it. No salad," Laura said.

"Same for me, but not as rare as hers, and I'd like a salad as well," Marc said.

"House dressing?" The man asked.

"House dressing would be fine," Marc replied.

Laura took a long swallow of her drink then, set her glass on the table. "So, are you going to tell me what the fuck we were doing back at that irrigation supply building?"

"Just checking something out, it's probably nothing." Marc answered.

"Why do I get the feeling you're feeding me a line of shit?"

Marc used his napkin to wipe the beer foam from his upper lip. "During one of my trips to The Palm Tree Golf Club this week, I learned that Mr. Saylor, the deceased, was supposed to play golf with a friend of his that day. His friend was Jim Simmons. However, due to an accident where he worked, he couldn't make it. Later, I learned that Saylor died from the injuries he had suffered from in the accident."

"Okay, but why are you so interested in an accident that occurred at some irrigation supply company. Has someone hired you to look into it."

Marc glanced out of the window as he thought how to answer Laura's inquiry. "When we were at the golf course today, did you happen to notice a man wearing a set of work coveralls with Apex Irrigation imprinted on the back of them?"

Laura seemed to give Marc's question some thought. "No, not really. There must have been twenty thousand people milling around. Should I have?"

"Not necessarily. But I did."

Just then, Marc's salad was delivered, along with a basket of rolls and a small dish of butter pats.

While Marc broke one of the rolls in half, Laura took another long drink of her martini.

"So, you think there's a connection between the man you saw at the golf course and the accident that occurred at the irrigation supply plant," Laura said.

"Don't know. Just thought of the coincidence," Marc said as he buttered his roll. "I mean, we really don't know anything yet, other than there was some kind of accident at Apex. A man is dead and Apex apparently does some kind of work at the Savannah River Golf Links."

Laura grabbed the other half of Marc's roll and took a small bite. "You know what I think, Mr. LaRose?"

"I'm afraid to ask," he said, taking a swallow of his IPA.

"I think you've been in the PI business a little too long. You're letting your suspicions divert your attention from the real reason we're here in Aiken, South Carolina."

"Believe me, I know where I am and where I'll be tomorrow morning. Being aware of what's going on around me has kept me alive for as long as I can remember. I guess it's some kind of innate ability I was born with."

Laura drained her glass, then held it up to her lips as the lone olive slipped from the glass and into her mouth. She slowly chewed the olive. "Speaking of innate abilities, Mr. LaRose, I have a few of my own," she said as a light grin creased her face.

I bet you do, Marc thought.

A waitress appeared carrying two plates. Their steaks had arrived. Marc instinctively leaned back, allowing her to set them on the table. "Will there be anything else?" The waitress asked.

"Yes, I believe the lady would like another double martini," Marc said.

Laura did not protest and as she cut into her steak, blood oozed onto her plate. "Um, fresh meat, my favorite."

Chapter Ten

When Marc awoke the following morning, the events of the previous evening were still fresh in his memory—the visit to Apex Irrigation, the discussion with the plant's owner and dinner afterwards with Laura McKay. He took a long shower, then dressed for another day at the Monarch Golf Tournament. Jake had arisen earlier and left the room, probably to meet up with Ann Marie somewhere. A copy of the day's local newspaper had been pushed under the room's door.

When he glanced at the lead story, he was momentarily stunned. "Canadian amateur makes the cut at the Monarch." A photo of Jake walking off one of the tee boxes followed by Marc carrying Jake's bag was under the headline. Marc's face was partially hidden from the camera's view by the bill of the golf cap he was wearing.

Good thing I had my head down. That Simmons guy over at the Apex plant doesn't need to know my connection with the golf tournament. At least not yet.

Emerging from the front door of the hotel, Marc found that Saturday morning's weather looked promising; a cloudless sky accompanied by a gentle breeze. An hour later, with Marc at the wheel of their rented SUV, Jake's entourage arrived at the golf course just in time to take advantage of the breakfast offerings before a morning warm-up at the practice range. The cut line had been established and only the top fifty-five players, plus ties remained, reducing the number of golfers competing over the weekend to nearly half of the original field. Although Jake was deemed an amateur, he had played well enough the previous two days to place him somewhere near the middle of the remaining competitors. The downside was that he was ineligible to receive any prize money because of his amateur status, no matter how well he did. He was playing for status and recognition, should he decide to turn professional.

On the way to the breakfast concession, Marc stopped by a kiosk and picked up a couple of the day's pairing sheets, one for him and Jake and another for Laura and Ann Marie. The sheets displayed the names of the players and their tee times. Although Marc knew Jake's approximate tee time, he hadn't heard who they'd be paired with. The amateurs were usually the last to know. As they sat down for breakfast, Marc scanned the sheet and saw he was paired with the South African Jake had played with on Wednesday's practice round. Marc hadn't noticed the man's name on the tee sheet the day before and figured he'd missed the cut, but of course he wasn't looking for him either.

After a full breakfast, Marc gave Jake the news of his pairing.

"Luther Van Zyle? I remember his caddy, Willum. He seemed a friendly sort, but Van Zyle, not so much."

"Might have had something to do with the language. I've heard that Afrikaners aren't as outgoing as some. I'm sure we can warm him up though," Marc said.

"That might depend on how well he plays," Jake answered.

Marc and Jake headed for the bag room to retrieve Jake's clubs while the girls left to find a good vantage point to watch the golfers warm up.

Marc gave Jake's name to the storage clerk who went to retrieve his golf clubs. Jake asked, "So Marc, have you given any thought to a strategy for today?"

Marc could see by Jake's expression that the pressure of actually making the cut was just beginning to settle in. Jake busied himself by juggling golf balls, a habit some golfers use to relieve the tension. "Yes, I have. The strategy for today is the same as we had the first day we arrived here."

"Uh, what strategy was that?" Jake asked. He'd stopped his juggling and looked at Marc, waiting for an answer.

"It's the most basic rule in golf. You hit one shot at a time."

There was a long pause.

"That's it? Hit one shot at a time? Marc, you know I appreciate your help, but…"

Marc interrupted. "'Look, you were perfect the first day because you didn't know what to expect. You played as you always have and, three days later, here you are, only the second amateur in this year's field to have made the cut. That alone could be worth an invitation to play at a few other professional tournaments. Just relax and don't get ahead of yourself. If you make a mistake, take a deep breath, readjust, and hit it again. Don't try to make up for a bad shot;

that will only lead to another miss-hit. Remember, as Bob May, one of golf's greatest players once said, 'you play the game of golf one shot at a time.' You have loads of talent. Just relax and have fun. You'll be fine.'"

"Okay, I guess," Jake said.

"Remember, Jake. I'll be right there beside you all the way from start to finish. You're not in this alone."

Jake paused as he seemed to give Marc's advice some thought. He exhaled deeply. "Thanks, Marc. That means a lot."

"Alright then, let's show this crowd what you're made of."

With Marc shouldering Jake's clubs, the pair made the short walk to the practice range. Unlike the earlier practice days when the bleachers were only partially occupied, today there were few, if any, empty seats. A huge throng had gathered to watch some of the best golfers in the world go through their warm-up routines. Despite the crowd, Marc had no trouble locating Ann Marie and Laura, sitting in the front row. Ann Marie's face beamed with pride as the crowd erupted with applause.

As was usual for Jake, he first went through a short stretching routine. Then he went to his wedges and slowly proceeded through each of his longer irons before reaching for his driver. His first practice drive sent the ball to the far reaches of the range, practically to the television broadcast booth that sat at the far end. This brought a reaction of 'ooohs' from the bleachers.

"Are you showing off for your girlfriend or your fans?" Marc said with a smile.

"I'm not showing off," Jake said. "I really believe I can do this."

"Good attitude. Now let's hit the practice putting green before you take out one of the announcers."

When they got to the putting green, Marc noticed that Jake's playing partner, Luther Van Zyle and his caddy, Willum, were already there. There were also a few other players practicing while waiting for their respective tee times.

Marc dropped three balls on the green about ten feet from a hole. Jake easily putted the first two in, but the third one missed, just going over its left edge. Jake looked a bit confused as he stood back and eyed the miss.

"You probably pulled it a little," Marc said. "Just take a deep breath and try to relax."

Jake then tapped three more in from the same distance with no trouble. "I guess you're right. Must be the pressure," he said.

Soon after, Willum came over to where Marc was watching Jake.

"Congratulations on your boy here making the cut," he said, nodding his head toward Jake. "For an amateur, that's a pretty big deal."

"Yeah, thanks, and same to you and your man. We've been so focused on making the cut, we sort of lost track on how Luther was doing."

"We didn't do well on Thursday, but Friday we turned things around and here we are."

The two men stood for an awkward moment as they both watched Jake sink a few more putts.

"Well then, I guess we'll see you on the first tee in," Willum said, then glanced at the clock the players used to keep track of their tee times, "about fifteen minutes."

"Good. See you then," Marc replied.

Marc watched as Willum trundled off to confer with his pro, then motioned toward the clock. Returning his gaze to Jake, Marc said, "Let's try a few long putts to get the speed of the greens. They'll be calling your name in a few minutes."

As Jake finished up on the practice green, Marc noticed a substantial crowd had gathered down both sides of the first fairway. A narrow clearing had been roped off allowing Marc and Jake to get to the tee box. While they waited their turn, Marc could see the pairing in front of them had hit their second shots and were making their way to the first green, some four hundred and sixty-five yards away.

Marc and Willum reported to the starter and advised him that their players were present and ready to play. A few moments later, the starter announced that it was time for the ten o'clock pairing. He first introduced the former winner of the tournament, Luther Van Zyle of South Africa to the Monarch Golf Tournament and instructed him to tee off. There was polite applause in respect for the former champion. After a couple of practice swings, Van Zyle hit his drive down the middle of the fairway. This was followed by another round of applause from the crowd. After Van Zyle's ball stopped rolling, the starter announced it was Jake's turn to tee off.

"Ladies and Gentlemen, it is my pleasure to welcome the second amateur to make the cut in this year's Monarch Golf Tournament. From Toronto, Canada, Mr. Jake McKay." A roar from the gathered assembly erupted as the throng welcomed Jake to the tournament. Marc looked at Jake. He could tell by Jake's expression he had not expected such an overwhelming introduction.

Marc pulled the driver out of the golf bag and handed it to Jake. "Remember, one swing, one hit, one shot at a time."

Jake nodded, then pushed his tee into the ground. After a single practice swing, Jake hit his first drive of the day and, like the practice round he had played with Van Zyle before, Jake's drive flew past Van Zyle's by about forty yards. A truly impressive golf shot. The crowd again erupted in applause, cheering with shouts of encouragement.

As Marc and Jake made their way down the center of the fairway, toward Jake's ball, Marc noticed that a sizable crowd had broken from the first tee area to follow Jake's progress. Marc also noticed that among Jake's new fans was a group of young girls, who, to the displeasure of Ann Marie, giggled and clapped at every swing Jake made. It didn't seem to matter if Jake liked the shot or not, they were apparently delighted just to watch him swing the club.

By the time Marc and Jake arrived at the fifth hole, Jake was up three shots over Van Zyle. Although the gallery following the pair of golfers had thinned somewhat, there seemed to be a buzz in the air that this amateur actually had a chance to win the tournament, which would be an historic first. Marc also noted the security, which appeared to have steadily increased since the first day of the tournament.

Jake made another birdie, putting him four up over Van Zyle. As the players walked off the green toward the sixth tee box, Van Zyle looked at Marc. "You have coached your young player quite well."

Marc was surprised as this was the first time Van Zyle had spoken directly to him. He spoke clearly with just a hint of his homeland Afrikaans language. "Yes, he is quite gifted and shows promise. My job is simply to keep his mind focused on the game."

"That must be a challenge, especially with his mother and that group of young girls tagging along, and now, with all the extra security people. I understand your foreign minister is supposed to attend the tournament either today or tomorrow, but even with that, the number of officers appears a bit overwhelming."

Although Marc had been concentrating on Jake's play he had noticed an excess of uniformed security officers, as well as local sheriff's deputies, patrolling the course.

Wonder how many undercover officers are mixed in with the crowd?

Marc chided himself for letting his mind wander from the tournament at hand.

The remainder of the round went well for Jake, but not so much for Van Zyle. Jake finished the day at six under par, putting him in a tie for seventh place overall, well ahead of the other amateur. Marc and Jake bade Van Zyle and his caddy, Willum, good luck with the remainder of the tournament, although with only one day of play left, Marc knew Van Zyle had lost too much ground to make any serious money.

While Ann Marie, Laura and Jake headed back to the car, Marc went into the bag storage building to drop off Jake's clubs.

"I see your boy did pretty well for himself today," the storage attendant said. Marc saw that the man's nametag read, "Sammy." Like many of the club's caddies and attendants, Sammy was African American. His short white hair was tightly curled, close to his scalp. When he smiled, his white teeth were brilliant against his smooth ebony skin.

"Yes, he did," Marc said. "But, as you know, the tournament isn't over until tomorrow afternoon. We still have 18 holes of golf left. I'm sure you've been around long enough to know anything can happen."

"Oh yeah. Been working here for over twenty-five years, and I've seen quite a lot. It's not over till the last golf ball falls in the hole."

Marc found Sammy's accent and friendly demeanor homey. He smiled, and with a nod, turned to leave. Then, a thought struck him. He turned back.

"Forget something, sir?" the attendant asked.

"Sammy, just curious. Why do you think there's so much security about?"

Sammy stopped wiping the leftover soil from Jake's clubs, looked at Marc and shrugged. "As you probably can guess, tournament rules regarding patrons viewing the tournament are pretty strict. They have to be so's their actions don't affect the quality and pace of play." He then returned his focus to cleaning Jake's clubs.

"I understand," Marc said. "It just seems peculiar that, while the field of players has been reduced to about half since the cut, the number of officers patrolling the course appears to have almost doubled, and that's just those you can see. I suspect there's quite a few more mingling with the gallery not wearing uniforms."

"Don't know nothin bout that, sir. S'pose you'd have to ask one of them that wear the uniform."

"Tried that. They're pretty tight-lipped about their purpose."

Sammy finished wiping Jake's clubs and laid his cleaning cloth off to one side. He gave the entrance door a furtive glance and leaned in close to Marc. They were still alone in the storage room. "Understand, this didn't come from me, but I heard tell that the United States Secretary of State will be on the premises tomorrow to watch the last day of the tournament. That's probably one reason."

"I've heard that, too. What'd you think could be another reason?"

Sammy seemed to think how to answer, "Ya'll don't live round here, do ya, sir."

"No. I live in upstate New York, but right now, we're staying in Aiken."

"You ever hear of a place called The Savannah River Site? Around these parts, it's known as SRS. Some even still calls it the Bomb Plant."

"Yeah, I've heard a little about it. Guess it's not far from Aiken, or Augusta for that matter," Marc said.

Sammy's eyes danced toward the entrance again. "Yes sir, they make bombs, and a whole lot more. They make parts for nuclear bombs. Something they call, Pits."

"Pits? What's a Pit?" Marc asked.

"Don't really know much about them sir, just that they make a nuclear bomb explode, kinda like a triggering device, I guess."

Marc thought a moment. "What does any of this have to do with the security at the golf tournament?"

Marc noticed Sammy's furrowed brow begin to glisten.

"I've probably said too much already, sir," Sammy said as he recovered the cleaning cloth from the side of the counter.

"Sammy, we're just talking here. Most of what you've told me, I've either read in the newspapers or heard from others," Marc said, in an attempt to assuage Sammy's fear of revealing something he thought may be confidential.

Sammy carefully placed the golf bag in a storage bin with Jake's name stenciled at the top. He retrieved a handkerchief from a back pocket and wiped his brow while his eyes moved between the entrance and Marc still standing at the counter. "Rumor has it there's a big meeting happening day after tomorrow, right after the tournament."

"What kind of meeting?" Marc asked.

"The United States Secretary of State, the head of the Energy Department, the CEO at SRS and even somebody from Israel. I overheard a couple of those security guards talk'n about it."

Marc hesitated as he thought about what he'd just heard, "You'd think the location of important government officials would be kept low-key. Surprised the guards wouldn't have been more careful," Marc said.

'Mister, look at me. I'm just an old black man. I clean golf clubs and shine shoes. It's all I do. Guess they just didn't think – or care – that I was listening. Besides, they didn't actually use their names. They used code names."

"Code names?" Marc asked.

"Sure. You know. Secret Service code names. Fadeaway is for the United States Secretary of State and Sparky is for the Secretary of Energy. You can find them online."

Marc grinned. Sammy was obviously wiser than he let on and admired him for his cleverness. "So, you think the reason that security is so high is because these government officials have included a few days of watching the tournament before heading over to the meeting at SRS on Monday?" Marc said, mostly to himself as he tried to make sense of it all.

Sammy had pulled a pair of golf shoes from under the counter and started brushing them with a well-worn shoe brush.

"Sir, I don't think about nothing. I just do's my job. Cleans golf clubs, polish golf shoes and stows 'em for the next day," Sammy said with a thick, melodious drawl.

Marc was again about to turn and leave when another thought crossed his mind. "Sammy, what do you know about a company called Apex Irrigation?"

Sammy again stopped what he was doing and gave Marc a look. "Apex? What about 'em?"

"Just curious. I thought I saw one of their trucks on the course a couple days ago."

"The only thing I knows 'bout Apex is they work on the irrigation. Takes a lot of water and fertilizer to keep this grass as green as it is, especially for the tournament. Why do you ask?"

"No reason. Have they always provided irrigation services to the course?"

Sammy hesitated and looked up. "No sir. They just started working here a couple months past. I guess they got a contract with the course, or something. Why? You think they got something to do with the security?"

"Like I said, just curious," Marc thought about the previous evening's trip to the Apex plant in Aiken. He pulled a fifty-dollar bill from his wallet and dropped it on the counter.

Sammy looked at the bill, "what's that for, sir?"

"For cleaning my boy's clubs, of course. See you around, Sammy."

"Thank you sir, and tell your boy Sammy says, 'Good luck.'"

"Thanks, Sammy, I'll be sure to tell him."

Marc was thinking about his conversation with Sammy as he walked past the tables where he had eaten breakfast just a few hours before. In the parking lot, Jake and Ann Marie were standing outside the SUV. Through the tinted windows, he could see Laura sitting in the passenger seat.

"Hey Daddy, thought you got lost," Ann Marie said.

"No, just dropped Jake's clubs off at the storage barn." Marc did not mention his discussion with Sammy.

Chapter Eleven

The traffic was thick, but orderly, as Marc maneuvered the SUV through the lines of vehicles exiting the golf course. Laura sat stoically while Jake and Ann Marie, sitting close to each other in the back seat, chatted about things youngsters talk about. Their unintelligible banter was occasionally marked with giggling. Marc could see in his rear-view mirror that Jake had his arm around Ann Marie.

As they arrived at the outskirts of Aiken, Laura turned in her seat and said, "Jake, you do realize you are in seventh place in one of the most prestigious golf tournaments on the PGA tour." Her tone was direct.

"Mom, thanks for telling me what I - and everyone else - already knows."

"Well, you don't seem to be taking this very seriously. Seems to me, you should be thinking more about your strategy for tomorrow rather than playing footsy with your girlfriend. After all, when will you ever get another chance to win the Monarch Golf Tournament?"

Jake removed his arm from around Ann Marie. "Mom, I appreciate everything you've done, and are doing for me, but Marc and I have a strategy and so far, it appears to be working pretty well. Whether or not there will be other girls is my business. I'm very happy with Ann Marie."

Laura turned in her seat and resumed starring out at the road ahead. "People change their minds all the time, but assuming a place in history is forever."

"Whatever," Jake said.

As Marc was about to make a turn on a street leading back towards their hotel, the mother/son banter was suddenly interrupted as a dark colored sedan cut in front of the SUV, compelling Marc to slam on the brakes and veer to the right. Marc missed the car, but only because of his defensive driving skills. Out of frustration, he laid on the horn, but the offending vehicle quickly drove out of sight.

"'Sorry about the horn, but I must say, people in the south seem to employ a unique driving technique. "Out of my way, y'all, I'm coming through."'

"Could've had something to do with the cell phone that guy was holding to his ear," Jake said.

"Southern hospitality. A hackneyed phrase that seems to have outlived modern reality," Marc muttered.

"Not sure, but it looked like that car was carrying an out-of-state license plate," Laura said. "I'm not familiar with license plates in the states, but I don't think it was a South Carolina or a Georgia license plate."

"Couldn't tell, I was too busy just trying to avoid a crash without running off the road to notice," Marc said.

By the time Marc found a parking space on a side street near the hotel, the incident with the reckless driver had taken a place on the back burner of his mind. "I know it's still early, but anybody thought about dinner tonight?" he asked.

As the four climbed out of the SUV, Laura replied as if she'd been thinking about Marc's question in advance. "You know, I think it's time for a girl's night out. It would give Ann Marie and me a chance to get to know each other a little better. This way the boys can discuss how they might want to handle their final day at the tournament."

Marc was pleasantly surprised by Laura's suggestion. The thought of not having to spend another evening sparring with her was a relief. He noticed, however, the look on Ann Marie's face which told him she had other plans.

"I'm game," Marc said. "How about it, Ann Marie?"

"Um, I don't know. Why don't we…"

But before Ann Marie could finish her thought, Jake jumped in, "Sounds fine, Mom. There's a few things I'd like to discuss with Marc and no sense in boring you and Ann Marie talking about golf strategy. We can all meet up in the hotel lobby after dinner."

"Great, it's settled then. Jake and I will find something close by and the girls can take the car if they want to," Marc said.

Ann Marie was noticeably silent.

"Without the men hanging around, this would be a swell time for us girls to get better acquainted, right, Ann Marie?" Laura said with a practiced smile.

Ann Marie managed a nod. It was apparent she hadn't quite recovered from Laura's "footsy" quip. With a forced smile, she turned toward the hotel.

Marc handed Laura the car keys. "Call my cell when you think you'll return to the hotel and we'll meet you for a nightcap."

"Fine, but remember, no alcohol for Jake. He needs to be at the top of his game tomorrow."

"Yes, Mother," Jake's response was accompanied with an eye-roll.

Marc glanced at his watch, then at Jake. "Let's meet in the lobby around five thirty. That should give us plenty of time to shower and change."

"Sounds good, let's do it," Jake said.

Ann Marie and Marc stood outside and watched Jake and Laura disappear through the hotel's front door.

"Thanks, Dad," Ann Marie said. Her tone had a disapproving quality. Marc knew she was unhappy with the arrangements he had made for the evening.

"I'm sorry, but Laura is right. Jake and I need to talk about tomorrow. If you're as serious about this boy as I think you are, then this would be a good time to bond with his mother."

"Bond? Really?"

Marc sighed, "I know, she can be difficult, but she is Jake's mother. At this point in her life, besides her business interests, he's about all she has. I think beneath that crusty exterior, she deeply cares about her son, and I think she likes you as well."

Ann Marie appeared to give her father's comment some thought. "Guess you're more optimistic than I am."

Hope springs eternal, Marc mused and headed toward his room.

After showering, Marc changed into a casual set of evening clothes. Jake was watching a replay of the tournament highlights on the room's TV.

"So, did you make the news tonight?" Marc asked.

"Naw, they've been concentrating on the top pairings."

"Big names at the top of the leaderboard always make for a good story. Why don't you go ahead and take your shower, Jake? I'll watch and see if they mention your name."

Later, as Marc and Jake walked through the hotel's lobby, Marc saw the same young man that was there a couple evenings before, singing his version of "Hotel California," again. *Must be a crowd favorite,* he figured. Marc loitered for a few moments, listening to the song.

Although the incident he and Laura had at the Apex Irrigation Company the night before was still fresh in Marc's memory, preparing Jake for the last day of the tournament had pushed that incident to the side, for now.

When Marc stepped outside, Jake was waiting for him in one of the rocking chairs that were arranged on the patio in front of the hotel. He was surrounded by a half dozen people. By their dress, Marc surmised they were golf fans who had apparently heard of Jake's success at the tournament. He stood off to the side for a few moments, listening to what Jake's new-found admirers were saying.

"Did you ever think you would be this successful at a major tournament?" One asked.

"I try to stay positive," Jake replied. "But to tell you the truth, just being here, in the position I now find myself, is more than I could have hoped for."

"Depending on what happens tomorrow, where will you go from here?" another man asked.

"For now, probably back to Canada."

A few of the men chuckled.

"If you mean where this puts me in my career, there's no doubt I'll be thinking about turning pro."

As another was about to ask a question, Marc interrupted. "Excuse us folks, but Jake and I should be going or we'll be late for an appointment." Marc hooked Jake by the arm in an effort to lead him away.

Jake gave Marc a puzzled look, then, realizing he was looking to get on with their evening's plans, he said, "Sorry folks. My manager says it's time for me to go. Hope to see you all at the eighteenth hole tomorrow when we finish. Meanwhile, wish me luck."

After hearing a few "Aw's," from the gathered circle, Marc ushered Jake around the corner of the hotel toward downtown Aiken's business district.

"I apologize for taking you away from your newfound admirers, but we have a few things to discuss. Besides, what you need right now is a relaxing evening and a good night's sleep. You need to be fresh in the morning."

"Guess this sudden interest in my golf game is something I'm not used to. Glad you're here to help me navigate the way," Jake said.

Just then a car slowly passed and a passenger leaned out the window and yelled, "Way to go, kid. Kick ass tomorrow!"

Jake returned the comment with a fist-pump.

"Looks like you've become an overnight sensation. How does that feel?" Marc asked.

"Quite frankly, it's a little overwhelming."

Marc pulled out a wide-brimmed hat that he'd previously stuffed into his back pocket, and along with a pair of dark sunglasses, handed them to Jake. "Put these on. Hopefully, they will help make our evening a little more private."

Jake hesitated, then pulled the hat down to his ears. The pair crossed the road and headed for Laurens Street located in the heart of downtown.

"I've read about a nice place for supper. Understand the food's good and it's not far from here. Hopefully, it will be reasonably quiet where we can eat and talk about our strategy for tomorrow."

"Have you talked to Ann Marie? Where do you think they will be going?" Jake asked.

"No idea. But I'm sure your mom has the evening all planned out. Besides, I think it would be best to compartmentalize your feelings."

"What do you mean?"

"I know my daughter, and I think I know how you feel about Ann Marie, but for the next twenty-four hours, it's important that you concentrate on your golf game."

"I'm not sure what you mean, Marc," Jake said, putting on the dark sunglasses.

"I'm saying that starting now, at this moment, your total focus should be on tomorrow's tournament. Ann Marie wants only the best for you. But for you to be at your best, you may have to put your feelings aside until the tournament is over. What you do tomorrow will help determine what kind of life you and Ann Marie could have together."

The pair walked in silence for a while. "I know what you want me to do," Jake said. "But you have to understand, I've never felt about any girl the way I feel about Ann Marie. I knew the first time we met that she was the one, and I think she feels the same about me."

Marc stopped at the corner. There was a crosswalk with a public mail drop box bolted into the concrete. The "Don't Walk" sign was staring back at them. He turned towards Jake, "Obviously, your feelings for my daughter are pretty strong, and, believe me, I'm happy about that. But now, it's crunch time. Time to focus on tomorrow's match."

As Marc was concentrating on their conversation, he heard an electronic clicking sound. He glanced up to see the walk sign had started counting down the seconds to safely cross, and the two men started off. When Marc's foot left the curb however, he heard the sound of a car approaching at a high rate of speed. A quick glance showed that a dark-colored sedan was heading directly toward him and Jake. Marc grabbed Jake and pulled him back towards the sidewalk. Jake's foot caught on the curb, sending him to the sidewalk on all fours. In the background, Marc heard the car's screaming engine as it seemed to be bearing down on them. Grabbing onto Jake, Marc lunged for the cover of the mailbox. His foot cleared just as he heard the car's tires scrub against the side of the curb, missing the men by mere inches. He looked up and watched the vehicle as it accelerated away from the intersection.

Marc pushed himself upright. Seeing that Jake appeared uninjured, he looked up and tried to get a description of the vehicle as it sped away. A few quick seconds later, the car disappeared around a pickup truck heading in the same direction. "You okay?" Marc asked, helping Jake to his feet.

"I'm fine, but what the hell was with that jerk?" Jake asked, brushing the dirt off his trousers.

"Whoever it was is obviously in a hurry." Marc said. What he didn't say was that the car looked suspiciously like the one that had cut them off less than an hour before, out-of-state license plate and all.

"Seems that your point regarding the myth of Southern hospitality may be well taken," Jake said.

"Jake, were you able to see the license plate?"

"No. I was too busy thinking about Ann Marie and what we were talking about when I heard the car approaching and was pushed back onto the sidewalk. Thanks for that, by the way."

The crosswalk sign had reverted to "Don't Walk," and Marc pushed the "Walk" button again. "Maybe this wasn't such a good idea," he said.

"No big deal. I'm sure the town is full of strangers here for the tournament. No doubt, many of them are as unsure where to go as we are," Jake said.

"Maybe," Marc said, skeptically.

A few minutes later Marc spotted what he was looking for. The restaurant's weathered sign, "The Billiard Palace," was visible a hundred feet away. Inside the diner, Marc found the place was already crowded with what appeared to be a cross section of the local population. There were several blue-collar types as well as a few out-of-towners wearing Monarch Golf Tournament hats and golf shirts. Marc spotted a table along the wall at the rear of the large room, adjacent to a couple of pool tables presently manned by who he suspected were a few local hustlers.

"This place is noted for its chicken livers and sautéed mushrooms, but I think I'll stick with a burger. How about you?" Marc asked.

"Chicken livers?" Jake said curling his upper lip. "You got to be kidding. That makes a burger and fries sound real good."

A moment later, a waitress approached, "Hey fellas, what can I getcha?"

Her question was punctuated by the sharp collision of a cue ball with a fresh rack, then the announcement by one of the players at the pool table, "I've got stripes."

Marc looked back at Jake, "Care for a beer?"

"No, diet something. Coke, I guess."

"Good choice. We'll each have a burger and fries, one diet coke for my partner here and I'll have an IPA, whatever you have," Marc said.

The waitress scribbled on her pad, "Two dead-ass burgers with fries, a diet and an All Day IPA. Anything else?"

"That should do us for now," Marc replied.

"Coming right up," she said and turned toward the kitchen. Her departure was marked by the sharp clacking sound of another billiard ball, followed by a cry of "Yeah, baby," from one of the players.

"Ever played?" Marc gestured towards the pool match.

"A few times, when I first started school in Plattsburgh. A place out on Route 9, Eight Ball Billiards. Never really got the hang of it though, putting English on a ball is what a golfer tries to avoid when he can. Besides, I really needed the time to study for my classes."

"What got you started playing golf?" Marc asked.

"My dad. He was good. Took me out to the range after school and weekends back when I was about ten or so. Not long after, he brought me to a course and taught me some of the basic rules."

"Did you play golf in high school?"

"I made the Junior Varsity team in the seventh grade and played right through my senior year. Except for a couple of years playing ice hockey, golf was my only sport."

The waitress returned with their drinks. "Burgers should be out shortly, fellas." She then moved off to answer a call from another table.

"Do you see your dad much?" Marc asked.

Jake took a sip of his soda. "Once in a while. He lives in Lawrence Park, a suburb of Toronto. He has a live-in girlfriend and she has a daughter. He calls about once a week and we talk. Unfortunately, I don't see him often enough. He's always busy with work, and besides, his house is full of strange women."

Marc smiled at the thought. "I know the feeling. You think you're outnumbered, even though you aren't."

Jake smiled. "Yeah, something like that."

The two sat quietly for a moment, enjoying their drinks and watching the men playing pool.

"Heard anything about the weather tomorrow?" Jake asked.

"I understand it should be pretty much the same as today. Possibility of showers late in the afternoon. I'll have the foul weather gear handy, just in case," Marc replied.

"So, I guess it will be another day of 'One shot at a time,' right?" Jake asked.

"Yes, possibly with a few adjustments."

"What do you mean?"

"Depends on where we stand as the tournament proceeds. If we get near the top of the leaderboard, we might want to play more conservatively. You know, take fewer chances. However, in the unlikely situation that we find ourselves falling down the leaderboard, then, I might advise we gamble and try to climb back up. I'm not expecting the latter, but we have to be prepared."

As Jake was about to say something, the waitress arrived with their meals. "Here you are, fellas," she said, placing the food on their table. "Anything else I can getcha?"

Marc glanced at Jake.

"Uh, do you have any malt vinegar?" Jake asked.

"Malt vinegar? Sure, I guess," she said raising her eyebrows. "Be right back," she said and left in the direction of the bar.

"I forgot how Canadians like vinegar with their fries," Marc said. "Reminds me of a case I worked on, not long ago up in Montreal."

A minute later, the waitress passed by and dropped a cruet of vinegar in front of Jake. "Here you are, enjoy!" she said, giving Jake an uncertain look before moving on to another table.

Jake sprinkled the vinegar over his fries, held one up and shoved it in his mouth, "Um, not bad, maybe just a touch more salt."

Marc smiled, enjoying Jake's momentary diversion from Ann Marie and the intensity of the discussion about the golf tournament. As he was about to comment on the quality of his food, there was another clacking sound coming from the area of the pool table.

"That's from the boys at H Canyon," the young player yelled, apparently proud of his prowess with a pool cue.

A group of people, obviously friends of the two men stalking around the table, were egging the players on with taunts and cheers, "Give'em hell, Brad," one of them called out.

Marc looked over at the group. They were a mix of men and women, some middle aged, most were younger. He thought one of the women glanced in his direction, then just as quickly, she seemed to have returned her attention to the pool game.

"No way, all the way with K," the opponent shouted good-naturedly.

"We'll all find out soon enough when the Czar gets in town!"

Jake swallowed and looked over at Marc, "H canyon, K, Czar? Wonder what that's all about?" he asked.

Marc shrugged his shoulders, "Beats me. Sounds like they probably work together, I suppose."

One of the men in the group looked in the direction where Marc and Jake were sitting. He had apparently caught Marc glancing over at them. "Hey guys, I think we better cool it." The pool players glanced at each other, then continued the match, but without the bravado.

As the waitress passed by, Marc asked, "Miss, can you tell me what these guys are talking about when they mention H and K or whatever?"

She hesitated. "You're not from around here, are you?"

"No, we're just in town for the golf tournament," Marc responded.

"Don't pay those guys any mind. They just got off a twelve-hour shift out at the Site. They come here about once a week to play a little pool, eat burgers and let off some pent-up steam."

"The Site?" Marc asked.

"Yeah, SRS, the Savannah River Site. They're referring to H canyon and K area. The K area stores plutonium produced at the H Canyon which is a radiologically-shielded chemical separations facility. There's a constant feud between departments as to who is the more efficient."

"So who's this Czar they're mentioning?"

"Probably the U.S. Secretary of Energy. Word is, he's supposed to visit the Site this week. Something about a big announcement. Could be another new mission, who knows?"

"Hey, Linda. Can we get a couple more beers when you're done socializing?" Someone yelled from the other side of the pool table.

The waitress glanced back at Marc. "Sorry, guys, got to go." She turned back toward the pool players. "Hold your horses, be right there!"

"Plutonium?" Jake said as he pushed another vinegar-soaked French fry in his mouth.

Marc took a sip of beer. "Yeah, according to the local newspaper, there's apparently been renewed interest in the Savannah River Site because of this new project coming there. Apparently the Site's been tasked with producing something called 'Pits.' According to a guy I was talking with at the golf club, 'Pits' act as a trigger for a nuclear bomb."

"Seems kind of scary to think that those guys drinking beer and playing pool could be making nuclear bombs," Jake said, glancing toward the crowd gathered around the pool table.

"'I'm sure they're qualified. It's just when you see people relaxing outside of their realm of expertise, they often say and do things that don't seem professional. I think it's called, 'blowing off steam.' It's not unusual."

"I suppose," Jake said.

Marc detected a hint of doubt in Jake's voice.

"One thing I'm am sure of, this is one helluva burger," Marc said.

Jake swallowed. "It's okay, I guess."

"What? You don't like it?"

"The burger? Yeah, it's okay, I mean, it's good, really good. It's just, I dunno..."

"You're thinking about Ann Marie, aren't you?"

Jake sipped his drink, "That obvious, huh?"

"Let's just say that in the short time we've known each other, I have learned a little of what bothers you and what doesn't. Not being with Ann Marie bothers you."

"Yeah, guess you're right." Jake replied, his eyes lowered toward his plate.

"Look, what you're feeling is perfectly natural. The problem is, there are times when you're going to have to live without her if you're going to succeed at golf, or practically anything else."

"What do you mean, learn to live without her?" Jake asked.

"Like when you're playing a golf tournament, or sitting behind a desk making decisions, Ann Marie can't always be right there by your side. I'm sure she will be with you in spirit, just not physically."

"Yeah, I know that. It's just that, well, you know."

"I know you love my daughter, and that's a good thing. And I'm really happy that she's found someone that I can like as well. It's just that there are times you and Ann Marie will function well, if not better, when you're not physically tied to each other."

"Like on the golf course," Jake said.

"Like tomorrow, on the golf course, yes. I'm not saying that you have to forget about her. I know you can't do that, neither can I. But, for you to perform at your best, you'll have to put your feelings aside for about five hours and concentrate on what's in front of you. Namely, playing the best golf of your life."

Except for the occasional clacking of pool balls and the drone of conversation throughout the establishment, the two ate in silence. Jake appeared solemn. Marc had the feeling Jake was digesting what they had discussed, along with the burger and French fries.

The return of the waitress broke their reverie. "What do you say, fellas, want to hear about our desserts?"

The two exchanged glances. Jake shook his head.

"Just the check, please," Marc said.

"Suit yourself, but they tell me the banana cream pie is to die for."

"Sounds tempting, but we've got another big day ahead of us tomorrow. Need to get some rest."

The waitress tore the check from her pad and dropped it on the table. "Good luck with that. Y'all come back and see us again soon, y'hear?"

"Will do," Marc said as he scooped up the bill. Sliding out of the booth, he looked over at the group of pool players. The girl he had seen before was no longer there.

Chapter Twelve

When they left the restaurant, Jake again pulled on the hat and sunglasses that Marc had given him. "Thanks, Marc."
"For what, the burger, or the disguise?"
"I was referring to your lecture about keeping my priorities straight. Guess I haven't given that much thought."
"That's what a coach and a caddy are for. Just trying to help you keep your head in the game."
But Marc was the one who was distracted, not by his daughter, but by the near accidents - those occurrences having taken place in the short time since they had returned from the Savannah River Golf Links. Were they just coincidences? Marc was skeptical.
As the two headed back toward Rose Hill, streetlights buzzed to life as the sun slowly slipped behind the live oaks that lined the city streets.
"You think Mom and Ann Marie have finished their dinner?" Jake asked.
"Probably not. I'm sure you know how women love to talk, especially when food is involved. More food means more conversation."
"I won't tell Mom you said that."
Marc grinned. "Nice to know you're a quick study, not only in golf, but also in some of the basics of manhood."
They approached Laurens Street, the city's main drag. Music could be heard in the distance. Continuing in the direction of their hotel, the music's volume increased. A signpost reading 'The Alley,' led off to their left, which appeared to be the source of the tunes. A crowd was gathered along one side of the street.
"Want to check it out?" Marc asked.
"Sure," Jake said. "They sound pretty good, whoever they are."
Marc didn't care for modern music, but he understood why Jake could be attracted to it. As they continued, Marc noticed that The Alley showed signs of having undergone recent restoration, probably a remake of the City's center to accommodate an influx of upscale

restaurants and boutique shops, he figured. About midway down the street, a mostly younger crowd had gathered in front of a bandstand. Some were dancing, but most were just standing and swaying with the music. A combo was assembled and the female lead singer, wearing distressed jeans, a few tattoo's and a black tee shirt, was belting out a pop tune.

Jake seemed slightly more enthralled than Marc, as his body moved in time with the others in the crowd.

"Wonder what they're playing?" Marc shouted over the noise.

Jake looked at Marc with a puzzled look, "Come on Marc, you must have heard of Selena Gomez. She rocks."

Marc had never heard of Selena Gomez, but he could see that Jake was getting into the music as he bobbed up and down. "Want something to drink?" Marc shouted.

Jake glanced at his watch, "Yeah, maybe a soda, Coke or something?"

"Wise choice. I'll be right back," Marc shouted and headed for an outdoor bar set up next to the bandstand. After waiting in line for a few minutes he paid for the drinks and returned to find Jake talking to a girl about his age, maybe a little older. She appeared to be asking Jake if he wanted to dance.

Marc handed Jake a foam cup of Coke. "Who's your friend?"

Before Jake could answer, the girl asked Jake, "This your Dad, or something?"

"He's my ca…"

"Father-in-law," Marc interjected, fearing that Jake was about to reveal he was Jake's caddy.

"Oh, so, you're like, married?" The girl directed her query toward Jake.

"I'm afraid so," Marc said. "Who are you?"

"Never mind," the girl replied. Then, with one last glance toward Jake, she turned and left.

Marc lost sight of her as she passed through the crowd of spectators.

"Sorry, Marc. She just walked up to me about the same time you were returning with the sodas and asked me if I wanted to dance."

"Well, did you?"

Jake hesitated. "I guess the thought crossed my mind, but you know I wouldn't have. I'd rather dance with Ann Marie."

"I know, forget about it. If you want, let's listen to this next set. Then I think we should head back to the hotel. The girls will probably be returning from dinner soon."

Fifteen minutes later, Marc and Jake turned the corner. The sign for the Rose Hill Hotel and Restaurant was visible a block away. Marc could hear kids playing in the pool. He looked, but didn't see their SUV in the parking lot.

"Either the girls haven't returned yet, or they've parked somewhere else," Marc said.

The sudden cry of "Daddy, Daddy," caused Marc to shift his focus to the front of the hotel. Ann Marie was running toward him. He could see she was crying.

"What's the matter?" Marc asked as his daughter fell into his arms.

Ann Marie continued sobbing, trying to catch her breath. "It's Laura," she gasped between sobs.

Marc held his daughter at arm's length, trying to assess the problem. He could see the front of Ann Marie's blouse had been torn.

"What happened? Where's Mom?" Jake asked.

"I don't know, they took her," she managed between sobs.

"You're not making sense. Tell me what's going on." Marc said, handing her his handkerchief. Ann Marie's sobs slowed, but she was still out of breath. Marc led her to the pool area where they sat around a table. After a few seconds, Marc could see his daughter was beginning to collect herself.

"So what happened?" Marc repeated.

Ann Marie exhaled, "It was all so fast. We'd just left the restaurant. We were walking to the car when some men stepped out of the shadows, like they were waiting for us."

Ann Marie stopped to blow her nose and wipe more tears that streaked down her cheeks.

"Go on," Marc urged.

"One of them said, 'Good evening, Detective Burns.' He directed his remark towards Laura. I don't know why he called her that. Naturally, Laura said she wasn't a detective and that he must have her confused with someone else. Then the other man said something like, 'Don't you know it's a serious crime to impersonate a police officer?' Laura told the man he was mistaken, and that they should leave us alone or she would call a real police officer."

At this point, Marc could see that Ann Marie was tearing up again. He laid his hand on top of hers, "That's okay. You're doing good, baby."

Marc thought of the incident at the Apex Irrigation Company the previous evening. A pang of guilt coursed through him. "What happened then?"

"I heard something, a hissing, like the sound of an aerosol spray. I think one of the men sprayed something in Laura's face. I heard her starting to scream. I couldn't see much in the darkness, but the other man grabbed her arms and pinned them behind her back. I screamed at the man and tried to help Laura get free, but he pushed me back and I fell. When I looked up, the men were dragging her into a waiting van that was parked on the street. I could hear Laura resisting, but I think they had put something over her mouth because her screams were muffled."

"Okay, anything else you can remember?"

"I tried to get up to help Laura, but this other man grabbed me and held me down. He said, 'Shut up, or we'll spray you too.' Then, he threw something toward the front of the restaurant. 'There's your car keys, little girl.' He said if I wanted to see my future mother-in-law again, I should be quiet and just leave. That's when they put Laura in the van and left. It took me a few minutes to find the keys in the grass. I came back here and parked in the first spot I could find."

Marc looked at Jake. He appeared upset and probably torn between how Ann Marie had been treated and the apparent kidnapping of his mother.

"Can you remember anything else?" Marc said, thinking about what he and Laura had encountered the evening before.

"Just that the man holding me had a message for you."

"A message for me?"

"Yeah, he said to tell you, he called you by name: Mr. LaRose. He said not to call the police, the real police, to mind your own business, and that you should pay more attention to Jake's golf game. He also said that you shouldn't bother yourself with affairs that don't concern you and that there would be no further warnings."

Jake went to Ann Marie and hugged her, inducing a fresh batch of tears.

"Daddy?" She asked.

"What, dear?"

"Why would these men call Laura a detective and for you not to call the real police?"

Marc sighed, "It's a long story. I'll tell you about it later, I promise. But for now, I think we should get you cleaned up and ready for bed."

"But don't you think we should report this to the police or somebody?" Ann Marie asked.

"Let me handle that," Marc turned to Jake. "Would you mind taking her to our room? Stay with her. There are a few things I need to do."

"Okay, but are you sure you don't want me to go with you?"

"No, I need you to stay with Ann Marie. Besides, you need your rest."

"Marc, my mother is being held hostage somewhere! I can't even think of playing golf tomorrow."

"Let me take care of your mom. You take care of Ann Marie."

After Ann Marie and Jake left, Marc found their rented SUV. He opened the rear hatch and retrieved the H&K semi-automatic pistol he had hidden in the spare tire's wheel well. Marc didn't have a South Carolina pistol permit, so he was careful that it wasn't seen. At this point, however, he felt the risk of being caught with an unlicensed handgun was a small price to pay.

The SUV's dash clock indicated it was almost nine. Darkness covered downtown Aiken and the streetlights were on. He would start with a check of the Apex Irrigation building where he and Laura had visited the previous evening. It was a risky move; the kidnappers were probably expecting him. He drove to an area a couple blocks from the Apex plant. There were a few residences scattered among the commercial buildings. He parked and locked the SUV, then headed out on foot. It was quiet except for a few barking dogs, apparently stirred to life by this stranger walking by just as darkness was falling.

When he was a half block from the Apex building, he spotted an abandoned gas station set back off the street. There was a poster wired to an old Texaco signpost planted at one end of the lot. The old gas station's windows were boarded up. Marc suspected the building was probably used for storage. Using the dim lighting provided by a single streetlight a half block away, he cut through the rear of the lot and found a break in the chain link fence that surrounded the station on three sides. He cautiously stepped through the deep grass and turned in the direction of the Apex building.

Another few minutes of slow going brought him to the perimeter fence that surrounded the Apex building and its offices. Aware that the uppermost strands of the fence might include sensors, Marc scanned the fence line for another option.

Suddenly, a loud grunting came from somewhere along the fence line ahead. Marc stopped, his H&K at the ready. Cautiously, he proceeded along the fence looking for a way through or over it. Once again he heard grunting, this time just a few feet away. Then, a dark flash and a squealing gave Marc a start as whatever it was ran past him toward the wooded area to his right.

"Wild boar," Marc whispered. He had heard there were feral hogs about, but didn't expect to find one so close to the Aiken City limits. He knew that boars rarely attacked humans unless they were cornered, or protecting their young, but he also knew that a boar's razor-sharp tusks were nothing to be taken lightly. Creeping along the fence, Marc found where someone or something had dug a channel under the fence.

Probably the boar, he figured. Could be that the boar was living inside the fence line, safe from any wild dogs roaming about. Marc crept to the channel and with his hand, felt around beneath the bottom of the fence.

With what light that trickled in from the streetlamps and the sliver of moon coming over the horizon, Marc couldn't tell if there were any sensors. If there were, whoever was monitoring the system should be aware that boars lived in the area. Would his attempt to crawl under the fence through the channel made by the boar seem any different? There was only one way to find out. Lying down, with his back on the cool earth and pushing with his heels, he inched his body under the fence. A minute later, he was on the other side. No sirens or alarms sounded, but he knew if the system was wired with a silent alarm, not hearing one didn't mean he was out of danger. Marc lay in the cool grass, listening.

After hearing or seeing nothing unusual, he continued in the direction of the street and the Apex building. He could see there were a few lights on inside, some at the front of the building where he and Laura had confronted Jim Simmons the evening before. Most of the light, though, was coming through the windows, located at the rear of the building.

The fenced-in lot was mostly empty, save for patches of overgrown grass, weeds and the rusted-out hulks of a few discarded vans that were lined up and left to deteriorate. Even with the dim lighting and faded paint, "Apex Irrigation" was still visible on their sides. Using the vans as cover, he quietly stalked from one to another, slowly making his way toward the back of the Apex plant.

As he closed in, he could see that the building formed one side of the fenced-in lot. Light from inside seeped through the two industrial window casements set into the cinder block wall at the back of the structure.

Marc figured if he could get to the windows, he might determine if Laura was being held inside. However, when he made it to the back wall, he discovered the windows had been frosted over making it impossible to see what was happening inside. In the still darkness, he listened intently for any sounds, but all he heard was the passing of an occasional vehicle on the street that ran by the front of the building, or the buzzing of a cicada that had recently emerged from its seven-year nap. The wild pig that had startled Marc earlier had apparently wandered off in search of more tender grasses or berries, or maybe an elusive canebrake rattlesnake.

Marc studied the window. Its glass was six panes across and six panes high. Each pane was held in place by a rusty metal frame. He pushed in on one of the inner panes and felt it give way. He examined the window again. The middle panes, about six feet off the ground, were separate from the outside panes and were tied to an interior hinge that allowed the center portion of the window to tilt in, apparently for ventilation. Someone had forgotten to relock the section, probably after the chemical spill that resulted in the death of Zach Saylor.

As Marc was about to push on the section again, he heard the sound of muffled voices coming from somewhere inside. Marc stood motionless, but with the thick glass he could barely make out what was being said. "Why did you bring...here?" After a pause, a different voice replied, "Where ...we take her?" Then, "Take...plant."

Marc strained to listen, but the voices seemed to retreat to another part of the building. As he pushed in again, the rusty hinge emitted a high-pitched squeak. Marc froze. He strained to listen. Silence. Either no one inside had heard the noise or they had and were waiting to see what happened next. He rose up on his toes, trying to look inside, but the inch of clearing between the glass and the frame was not enough to allow him to see anything. Then, he heard the sound of a car engine starting up at the front of the building. Whoever he had heard talking before was apparently leaving.

Marc went to the corner of the building and through the cyclone fence saw two people walking toward a sedan parked where he had seen the vehicles the evening before. When the car door opened, someone was being shoved into the car's rear seat. The person appeared to be a female and was handcuffed with her hands behind her. *That's got to be Laura, but where are they taking her?*

Marc ran back to the opening in the fence he had crawled under minutes before. In the distance, he heard the muffled sound of car doors slamming shut. Racing toward his SUV, there was the sound of tires on the crushed stone parking lot. As he rounded the corner of the Texaco station, the sedan passed by on the street out front. With the car key in hand, he jumped in the SUV and took off after the sedan. But when he got to the roadway, there were no taillights, just darkness illuminated by a scattering of streetlamps. He floored the engine in an attempt to catch sight of the vehicle. As he passed several streets that ran perpendicular, he slowed and glanced down each one, hoping to locate the sedan. At the third intersection, he caught a glimpse of a car's taillights a few hundred yards off to his left. The car was turning.

Marc slammed on the brakes, backed up and made for the intersection. However, when he arrived at the turn, there was nothing but another string of streetlights. He pushed down hard on the gas pedal and as the last streetlamp whizzed by, he saw another sign, "Aiken City Limits."

"Where the hell does this road go?" he whispered. Undeterred, he forced the SUV forward at top speed, hoping to again catch sight of the now familiar taillight configuration. Through the darkness he could see he was coming up on an intersection. It appeared to be a main thoroughfare. There was a steady stream of car lights traveling in both directions. The traffic light facing him was turning red. As Marc slowed, he saw a road sign, "Whiskey Road." The intersection was illuminated with lights from the gas station on the corner. As Marc's vehicle came to a stop, he spotted movement to his right. Someone was walking toward the gas station. Marc knew the walk. It was Laura.

Relieved that he'd found her, but pissed that he had not been there for her, Marc tapped the SUV's horn and pulled into the station's lot. Laura turned, came around to the passenger side and got in. Her face was wet with tears and contorted in apparent anger. Was she mad at her captors or someone else? He would soon find out.

"You alright?" Marc asked.

"No thanks to you!" Her response was quick and terse.

Guess we know who she's pissed at, but why? "What happened?" he asked.

"Those assholes handcuffed me and forced me into their car."

"What did they say?"

"Basically, they said for us to fuck off, mind our own business and that the next time it will be your daughter they take and that you'd never see her alive again."

There was the sudden sound of an angry car horn. Marc had inadvertently blocked a gas-pump lane. He waved his apology and pulled around the pump to a parking spot in front of the station.

"So, why did they take you?"

"How the hell do I know? To deliver the warning, I guess."

"How many were there?"

"Two. Both fairly good-sized, white, and like I said, assholes."

"Did they hurt you?"

She hesitated, rubbing her wrists, "No. Handcuffs were too tight, but nothing other than that."

"Was the guy we talked to at Apex Irrigation one of them?"

She snuffed back more tears. Marc handed her his handkerchief. She took it, blew her nose and wiped her face, then let out a long exhale. "No. I don't believe so."

"Look, Laura, I apologize for getting you involved in this. It was a bad call on my part. I was curious about the alleged accident that occurred there earlier in the week, and, at the time, it felt like portraying us as police officers would work. Obviously, I underestimated them. The good news is no one got hurt."

"Easy for you to say," Laura replied, clearing her nose again.

Marc sensed that although Laura was still upset, she had relaxed to the point where she might become reasonable. He put the car into drive and turned toward Rose Hill.

"So, you said there were two of them. Can you remember anything about them?"

"Yeah, they were both assholes."

Marc's lips turned up into a small grin. He turned toward his side window in an attempt to hide his amusement.

"It is not funny," she said.

"Didn't say it was," Marc said, attempting to plead his innocence.

They rode in silence for about a mile. "One of them was big, strong as a fucking ox. His hands were like a vise grip. He's the one that grabbed me, put me in handcuffs and threw me in the car."

"Did he say anything?"

"No, the other guy did all the talking, what there was of it. They were both big, but the other guy, the driver, warned me that the trick we had played, impersonating police officers, was pretty dumb and that we should be paying attention to Jake's golf game and stop nosing around."

"Wonder how they knew who we were, and about Jake?" he said.

"I have no clue. But I assure you, as soon as Jake finishes the tournament tomorrow, we're getting the fuck out of South Carolina and back to Ontario."

When they arrived at their hotel, they found Ann Marie asleep. Jake had covered her with a blanket and was sitting on the edge of her bed. When he saw his mother, he went to her and wrapped his arms around her.

"Mom, you okay?"

"I'm fine, but it's been a long day for all of us, and obviously, tomorrow's going to be another long one for you." She glanced at the clock on the bedside table. "It's already after ten and you need to get some rest."

"But…" Jake started to protest.

"No buts, Jake. You need to be at your best tomorrow. The only way we can do that is to put today's events behind us and get you ready for the tournament in the morning."

"Come on, Jake," Marc said. "Your mom's right, you need to conserve your energy and get some rest."

Jake knelt down next to Ann Marie and gave her a peck on her cheek. "Suppose you're right," he said as he straightened up. "See you in the morning."

Jake left the room, leaving Marc and Laura alone with Ann Marie sleeping soundly. "Guess I should be getting along as well, but before I do, I just want to say that…"

"Save it, Marc. You've already apologized and I accept it. I'm too tired to get into why you did what you did. I'm sure you had your reasons, but I think it's best to save this argument for another time."

The two held each other's gaze for a moment, then Marc nodded his assent and left.

When Marc opened the door to his room, Jake was already in bed.

"Marc, is everything alright with you and my mother?"

"Everything's fine. Why?"

"It's just, I know how Mom can be, and if we are going to be a family some day, I think it's important that we get along, that's all."

"I appreciate your concern, Jake, and I agree. We just have to get past tomorrow."

Jake was quiet for a moment, "You have to understand. She can be kind of funny, but her intentions are good. She just has an odd way of expressing them."

Marc grinned. "So I've learned."

Then they were both quiet. "Look Jake, I'm going to turn the light off and let you get to sleep."

"Where are you going?" Jake asked, stifling a yawn.

"Downstairs to the bar. I can use a nightcap.

"All right. See you in the morning," Jake said as he pulled the covers up to his chin.

"Goodnight, Jake," Marc hit the light switch next to the door.

Chapter Thirteen

Marc quietly shut the door and made his way down the hallway toward the stairs and the hotel's bar, where he saw that business appeared to be slow. The sound of piped-in jazz filled the room. He slid onto a stool and ordered a bourbon, Woodford Reserve, on the rocks. When it was delivered, he took a slow sip, savoring its smooth oak finish. Reflecting on the events of the past evening he felt the presence of someone sitting next to him. He set the glass down on the bar and looked over. It was Laura.

"You always drink alone, Mr. LaRose?"

"Only when there's no one with me."

Marc was puzzled by Laura's sudden appearance. "Is this a social visit, or do you want to continue to complain about our episode at the irrigation plant?"

Ignoring Marc's question, she said, "I like my martini dry, with olives."

"Yeah, I know." Marc motioned to the bartender and ordered Laura a double martini, dry, with olives, rocks on the side.

"You remembered," she said.

He glanced at her. "Some things are hard to forget."

Her drink was delivered. She spooned a few of the ice cubes into her glass. "I'm sorry," she said, then sipped her drink.

"Not sure exactly what you're sorry for, but I'm not going to look a gift horse in the mouth." Marc took a sip of his bourbon, "I accept."

"I apologize for overreacting. I shouldn't have said some of those things. I was pissed about the way those men treated me and I took it out on you."

Marc set his glass on the bar, "I appreciate that, but just so you know, I think you had every right to be upset. I miscalculated and didn't think they would come back at you and Ann Marie the way they did. That's on me, and I like I said before, I'm sorry."

"So, now that we got that out of the way, where do we go from here?" Laura asked.

Marc glanced at his watch, "I suppose we should be going to bed, er, maybe that didn't sound right, I mean…"

She placed her hand on his arm, "I know exactly what you meant, Marc. You want to do the right thing, the thing that brought us to Aiken. You want to get ready for my son's tournament tomorrow. Trouble is, those bastards who roughed up your daughter, then threw me in the back of a car and dropped me off in the middle of fucking nowhere are up to something and we both know it. They know who we are and that my son's competing in the tournament. They fucked with us. I think we need to fuck with them."

Marc swirled his drink as he thought about what Laura had said. "You know they're not just a bunch of smalltown goons. What are you proposing?"

"You suspect they may have something going on at the golf course, the Savannah River Golf Links, don't you?"

"That's a distinct possibility. But like you said, it's just a suspicion. I don't know for certain, otherwise, I'd alert the authorities."

"And what is it that's so suspicious?"

Marc took another swallow as he thought how to answer, "It's not just a thing, it's more of a feeling. You have the Apex employee that died, Zach Saylor. He supposedly died from chlorine inhalation. Apex happens to do a lot of work for the Savannah River Golf Links and this is their big week, with the tournament and all the out-of-town patrons attending, not to mention government officials."

"Government officials? What are you talking about?"

Marc swirled the remains of his drink. "I learned from a source at the club that the U.S. Secretaries of State and Energy as well as a few other government officials will be attending tomorrow's tournament."

"First time I've heard. Is that supposed to mean something?" Laura asked.

"Not sure, but it's been my experience that cabinet level officials don't usually attend a public event unless they intend on making some kind of policy announcement."

"You were at the golf club caddying for my son. A place that, until recently, you'd never been, and while there you had time to get this information from 'a source' at the club?" Laura asked, making air quotes with her fingers.

"Let's just say that I get around, and I like to ask questions."

Laura took another swallow while she seemed to digest this new revelation. "So, why do you think the Secretary of State is attending the tournament? I can understand the Energy guy coming, with the Savannah River Site just down the road, but the Secretary of State?"

Marc glanced over at Laura with a surprised look, "Didn't realize you knew about the Site?"

"You think that because I'm Canadian I don't read the newspapers? You forget, when the U.S. sneezes, Canada catches a virus."

"As long as it's not of the novel corona variety," Marc quipped. "Look, I don't know about Canada, but to have these government officials at the tournament tomorrow gives me the creeps," Marc said.

Laura threw back the remains of her drink. "So, getting back to those two jerks who manhandled your daughter and me, what are we going to do about that?"

Marc hesitated. "I don't think we should do anything. In the first place, we don't know who we're dealing with. They could be just a couple of goons hired to protect the irrigation plant. Like the old saying goes, where there's smoke, there's fire. But I didn't come here to fight a fire, I came here to be with my daughter and watch your son play golf."

"So you don't care that Ann Marie may have been scarred by the way those assholes manhandled her?"

"Of course I care. But you have to remember, we're on their turf. I have an idea what they're capable of, and if my suspicions are right, they will stop at nothing to carry out what they've been hired to do. They've warned us and I think it's prudent to back off, at least for now."

"So you're afraid?" She said, almost tauntingly.

"Maybe I am, but not for me, for Ann Marie, and..." Marc let his thought drift off.

"And, who else?" Laura asked.

Marc exhaled. "For your son and you."

The two remained silent for a full minute.

Marc glanced at the time on his cell. "It's just nine-thirty. I wonder if Zach Saylor's widow is still up?"

"Who's Zach Saylor?" Laura asked.

"He's the guy that died at the Apex Irrigation Plant. I hate to bother her. It's only been a couple days since her husband died, but I wonder if she has any thoughts about his death and what's been going on at the plant."

"Let me see your phone," Laura said.

"Why?"

"Maybe I could find a phone number."

Marc slid his cell across the bar.

Laura fiddled with it for about a minute, "Here it is, Zachary Saylor, Colleton Avenue, Aiken." Laura pushed a button and held the phone up to her ear.

As Marc was about to protest, Laura held up her hand, "Hello, Mrs. Saylor?" She paused before continuing. "Yes, Mrs. Saylor, my name is Laura McKay. You don't know me, but my associate and I are familiar with the unfortunate passing of your husband. Please forgive me for calling at such a late hour, but we were wondering if it would be possible to talk to you tonight?"

Laura looked at Marc and gave him a wink.

"No, we're not selling anything. We're just in town for a few days and it appears that we've come across a few things that seem to be connected to your husband's previous employer that we'd like to speak to you about. No, unfortunately, it really can't wait until tomorrow."

There was another short pause.

"Yes, we understand the inconvenience, but...alright, that would be great. Hold on a second." Laura made a writing motion with her hand toward the bartender, who gave her his pen.

"Okay, Ms. Saylor, go ahead with that address."

Laura scribbled the address on a napkin.

"Great. We're staying at Rose Hill."

"Five minutes? Okay, see you then," Laura ended the call.

"Good luck. Seems Mrs. Saylor has got about as much use for the Apex Irrigation Company as we do. Said 'she'd love to speak with us.' Here's her address," Laura said, sliding the napkin with the address on it toward Mark.

"According to Mrs. Saylor, it's about a five-minute drive from here."

Marc stood, finished his drink and glanced at his watch, "Guess we shouldn't keep the lady waiting."

Using Laura's cell phone, they quickly located the Saylor residence. A light was on above the expansive porch that curled around the side of the house leading to a three-car garage. After parking the SUV, the pair climbed the three wooden steps to the front door and as Marc was about to knock, it was opened by an attractive woman about the same age as Marc.

"Hello, Ms. Saylor? He asked.

"Yes, yes, come in, quickly, please," she said, holding the door open. Before closing it, she glanced up and down the street.

Marc could see she was nervous about something. "Ms. Saylor, my name is Marc LaRose and this is Laura McKay who spoke to you on the phone. I apologize for calling on you at such a late hour, and please, accept our condolences for your loss."

"It's Eleanor, and thank you. As I mentioned on the phone," she glanced at Laura,

"I haven't slept much since the, uh, accident at the plant, but if there is any way I can help, I'll be happy to do what I can."

"Thanks, we appreciate that."

"Can I get you anything? Coffee, something a bit stronger perhaps?" Eleanor asked.

Marc noticed an open bottle of brandy and an empty glass on a stand next to an overstuffed chair.

Marc and Laura exchanged glances. "That brandy looks good," Marc replied.

Eleanor Saylor led Marc and Laura away from the main entrance to the dining room. Eleanor moved the chairs so they could sit close around the massive oak table, then, retrieved two glasses from a nearby hutch and the bottle of brandy. She poured them each a drink.

"How long had your husband been working for Apex?" Marc asked.

Eleanor hesitated, "Let me think. He worked there before we married. Actually, I am, was, Zach's second wife. He started there as a landscape designer, then made his way up to the head of the design staff. That's where he met his first wife, but the marriage didn't last. Zach didn't talk about her much, but I learned she had been running around on him."

"Uh huh. Had he said anything about his work lately? Did he enjoy working at Apex?"

"He did, until about a year or so ago when the company was bought out. The new owners wanted him to do different things. Zach wouldn't say much about it, something about changing his design models. I know he wasn't happy about what they wanted him to do."

"Design models?" Marc asked.

"Zach designed irrigation systems for residential and commercial clients, and his team was well equipped to do that. Just after the takeover, however, when Apex was bought out, he was tasked with re-designing the job at the Savannah River golf course. He told me that what Savannah River wanted and what the new management at Apex told him to do were two different things."

"Why would the owners at Apex do something that the golf course didn't ask for? Besides, I would think that to get the job, the people at the golf course would have to approve the plans."

"Mr. LaRose, I assume you've heard the term, bait and switch?" Eleanor asked.

Marc glanced toward Laura. "You saying the people at Apex promised the Savannah River Golf Links one thing, but delivered something else?"

"That's pretty much it. And when Zach discovered this, he brought it to the attention of the new owners."

"What did they say?"

"'Oh, at first they came up with some excuse, 'that there must be some kind of mistake,' blah, blah, blah. That's when Zach told them, as diplomatically as he could, that someone, preferably himself, had to advise Savannah River of the error.'"

"So, what did they say to that?" Mark asked.

"Simply that they would handle that end of it…that Zach had more important things to take care of and shouldn't concern himself with this detail. Trouble was, Zach knew what they had done was no small item. Besides substituting lesser grade materials, they had retrofitted parts of the system so it could be controlled directly from the Apex office, right here in Aiken."

Marc thought about what Eleanor had just told him. "I wonder why Apex felt they needed to control the irrigation at the golf course? You would think that the golf course superintendent would be in charge of that."

"That's what Zach said, and when he asked management about it, he was told that the main controls were still located at the golf course and that the controls at Apex were simply a back-up system that was an option they were providing the course. Naturally, Zach had never heard of such an arrangement and decided to go to the company's new owner, Sajak Akhtar, and ask him. Mr. Akhtar, who is a recent immigrant from Iran, told him that he shouldn't concern himself with the Savannah River project, that it was completed and he should move on. That was six months ago.

"'So, had Zach 'moved on?'" Laura asked.

"Outwardly, he had to. But he had his reservations."

"What do you mean?"

"He'd heard there were complaints, not about the design, but about the product. The system was not working the way the Savannah River people wanted it to. Sprinkler heads were breaking down, the AIS…automatic irrigation system…was not functioning as it should, sections of new piping were inadequate to handle the load during peak periods, the list went on."

"Did Zach say anything to Mr. Akhtar about what he'd heard?"

"No, not directly. Zach knew Akhtar wouldn't be happy with him making inquiries, especially after previously being told that it was not his problem. So he went to the Golf Course and met the superintendent, Bill Goodspeed. Bill and Zach were old friends. They'd worked together installing the new irrigation system at the course. Zach told Bill what he'd learned."

Marc thought back to when Goodspeed came to The Palm Tree Golf Club a few days before. That was when he first heard that Zach Saylor had been involved in an accident at the plant.

"What did Goodspeed say?" Marc asked.

"According to Zach, Goodspeed told him that it would be best to forget about the Savannah River Golf Links job and concentrate on helping other customers with their projects."

"That sounds a lot like what Akhtar had told Zach." Marc said.

"Pretty much. Then, about a week before the accident, Akhtar told Zach that he no longer had any control over product quality and if he wanted to keep his job, he should concentrate on working with other projects.

"Ms. Saylor, would you mind if I contacted Bill Goodspeed and ask him a few questions?"

Eleanor glanced at her watch, "I have no objection, but it's past ten."

"I know, but we're up against the clock. Every minute that goes by is another minute lost."

Eleanor gave him the phone number. She knew it by heart. "If you don't mind, please don't tell him that I gave you this number."

Marc nodded, then, using his cell phone, he made the call.

The three of them were silent while Marc listened to the puttering sound of Bill Goodspeed's phone ringing through his cell.

Marc was about to give up and end the call when he heard, "Hello," followed by a cough. It was a raspy male's voice, a sure sign he had awoken Goodspeed.

"Mr. Goodspeed, please forgive me for calling at such a late hour. My name is Marc LaRose. I'd like to speak to you about the death of Zachary Saylor."

There was the sound of Goodspeed clearing his throat and the rustling of bed covers. Then, in the background, Marc heard the sound of a female's voice; "Who's that on the phone, hon?"

"Mr. Goodspeed, you still there?" Marc asked.

"Yeah," this was followed by another long cough. "Who'd you say you were again? Rose, or something?"

"My name is Marc LaRose. I understand you were a friend of Zachary Saylor who passed away recently while working at the Apex Irrigation Plant. I'd like to talk to you about what happened."

There was another pause in the conversation.

"Look, I don't know who you are, and besides, other than what's in the papers, I don't have anything more to add," Goodspeed finally replied.

"Yeah, I have the article right here, but it really doesn't say much. When would be a convenient time to speak to you about this?"

"Convenient? For me? Probably never," Goodspeed's voice was beginning to clear.

"Look, Mr. Goodspeed, I understand why you may be reluctant to talk about this, especially with someone you've never met, and I know this is kind of last minute, but I really need to discuss this with you."

"I'm afraid tonight's not good. As you can imagine, tomorrow's our biggest day of the year. It's the final day of the Monarch golf tournament and I have to be there before the sun comes up to make sure everything's perfect for the match."

"I understand. How about we meet up at the golf course then?" Marc said.

"Sure, I suppose. But, if you want to talk, you'll have to get there real early. I doubt I'll have much time to spare."

"I understand. Where can I meet you?" Marc asked.

Marc heard Goodspeed exhale into the phone. "I'll probably be at the superintendent's office most of the day monitoring course conditions. Should be there from five in the morning until the tournament is over," he said.

"Good. Thanks for agreeing to see me, I look forward to talking with you then."

There was a small hesitation, then, Goodspeed asked, "Say, what's your interest in this? You an insurance adjuster or something?"

"No, just a friend. Look forward to seeing you tomorrow. Good night."

"Good night," Goodspeed said and ended the call.

Marc put his phone away and gave Ms. Saylor a look.

"Mr. LaRose, there is one other thing I'd like to give you," Eleanor said. She reached for a small bowl that was sitting on a stand next to the front door. Using her forefinger, she examined a few door keys that had been placed in the bowl and picked one out. She handed Marc the key. "I know I won't need this, but maybe it could help."

Marc looked at it. It was a double-sided key that Marc recognized, the kind commonly used in commercial locks. It was purposely made for a lock that would be difficult to pick.

"This was Zach's work key. He only used it on the days that Apex was closed and he wanted to use the side entrance."

Marc slid the key into his pants pocket.

"Mr. LaRose, if you find out anything, would you please let me know?"

Marc noticed tears welling up in her eyes. "Yes, Eleanor. I will, I promise."

Eleanor Saylor walked Marc and Laura to the door. When they had descended the three steps to the sidewalk, Marc turned. Eleanor was standing with the door still open.

"Until tomorrow," Eleanor said, and then she quietly shut the door.

"Until tomorrow," Marc whispered.

Chapter Fourteen

Marc and Laura were quiet during the short drive back to Rose Hill. When they arrived there, Marc saw that save for a few hangers-on, the hotel bar was almost empty. The clock over the bar showed it was 11:15 p.m.

"I suppose it's too late for a nightcap," Laura said.

"Ordinarily, I'd agree. But the events of late have been anything but. Can I interest you in a scotch?" Marc asked.

Laura shrugged, "Sure, why not."

Marc ordered the drinks and carried them to a small table on the lower level of the lounge, away from the few customers that remained at the bar.

Laura asked, "So you're going to talk with that Goodspeed guy tomorrow at the golf course? With Jake playing in the tournament and you being his caddy, it seems we already have a pretty full day planned. Do you really think you'll have time?"

"Jake doesn't tee off until 10:30 a.m. I figured if we get to the course early, around seven or so, and grab breakfast, that would leave me plenty of time to meet with Goodspeed and still have time to get Jake ready for the tournament."

Laura seemed to consider Marc's plan. "All right, but just as long as you understand, we're here to support Jake. I'm not saying that I wouldn't like some retribution for what those jerks did to me and Ann Marie, but Jake is the reason we're here. His performance on the course has to come first."

Marc took a slow sip as he looked at Laura over the rim of his glass. He set his glass on the table. "I understand. When I tell you that I'll be there for Jake, that's a promise I intend to keep. But I know when something doesn't feel right. I've experienced that in the past and this is one of those times."

Laura studied her glass. "Marc, have you thought about sharing our concerns with the police?"

"Of course I have. The problem is, what do we tell them? We were nosing around the Apex plant pretending to be police officers because we suspected there's something going on that they failed to see during their investigation?"

Laura hesitated, "Yeah, I see what you mean."

"Look, I don't intend to jeopardize Jake's chances of a good showing in the tournament on a hunch that something nefarious may or may not be happening there. He has too much riding on this. But with everything we've seen so far, things don't feel right. I'm sorry, but I can't rest until I'm satisfied that either there's something there, or that everything we've experienced is just a string of coincidences that doesn't warrant wasting any more of our time."

Laura appeared to accept Marc's explanation. She took a deep swallow of her drink, "Fair enough. Our rooms are reserved through tomorrow night. Hopefully we won't need them and we can leave Aiken right after the tournament."

Marc raised his half empty glass, "Here's to Jake, and to tomorrow."

"To Jake," Laura said. They clicked glasses and finished their drinks.

Marc paid the bill and walked Laura to the elevator. Although they rode up in silence, Marc sensed that Laura had something else on her mind as she had become unusually quiet. When they approached her room, she suddenly leaned into him, slowly wrapped her arms around him and held him in a tight embrace.

"What?" was all he could manage as suddenly her lips searched for his. Marc's immediate reaction was instinctive. He returned the kiss, but worried her intentions were becoming more serious.

Before Marc could break it off, there was the heavy metallic sound of a room door's locking mechanism disengaging from across the hallway. As the door swung open, Marc pulled back and held Laura at arm's length. An older gentleman appeared from around the door and, with little more than a glance at Marc and Laura, he let the door swing shut. "If you need a room, mine's free, at least for a few minutes. I have to go out for awhile." He proffered his room key.

"Uh, no, thanks we were just, uh, talking," Marc said.

The old man turned, shook his head and hobbled toward the elevator. "From my vantage point, your lady friend appeared to be giving you quite a tongue lashing," he said over his shoulder.

Marc looked back at the man's closed door and noticed the door's peephole. He'd apparently seen them kissing from inside his room.

Marc whispered to Laura, "If it's all the same to you, I think we'd better turn in."

Marc heard the chime of the elevator door opening for the man to enter.

"I suppose," she said reluctantly. She stared in the direction of the gentleman as he disappeared into the elevator. "Thanks for nothing, you old fuck," she whispered.

Marc walked the few steps to his room. "Goodnight, Laura," he said without turning. But all he heard was her door closing. She was gone.

****

Early the following morning, along the southern banks of the Savannah River six miles south of the Augusta Regional Airport, five men dressed in black wet suits strapped on scuba gear that had been stashed in a nearby hunting camp. The Savannah River is relatively shallow at this point, but deep enough to swim below the surface as it flows lazily toward the City of Savannah and the Atlantic Ocean some 95 miles to the southeast. Under the cover of darkness, the men, using three battery-powered underwater tugs, slowly and methodically made their way across the river to the other side.

The Savannah River Site is a sprawling 310-square-mile government-run facility. The Bomb Plant was originally built in the early 1950's to combat the threat of the USSR's atomic capability during the Cold War.

Out of reach of Soviet bombers and away from large urban city habitation, the Savannah River Site, or SRS, as it would eventually be called, was ideally located. The River, forming a natural border between South Carolina and Georgia, was another consideration for the plant's location. A reliable supply of fresh water would be needed to cool the huge nuclear reactors planned for the facility. The river's water also met the government's need for the production of heavy water, a necessary component in the production of nuclear energy. Although most of the Site's nuclear reactors had long been dismantled, one reactor, known as C reactor, had been held in cold storage, where, under cover of top secrecy, it was slowly refurbished in the possible scenario that it may be needed sometime in the future. With other world powers beginning to flex their nuclear capabilities, the decision had been made to recall C reactor's plutonium producing capability.

The five men silently made their way across the river toward their destination, the Savannah River Site's main water intake pipes. Aware that security at SRS was highly sophisticated, a well-organized plan had been developed for the surreptitious deployment of a thick rubber barrier to block the plant's water intake from the river. An estimated 900,000 gallons a minute would be needed when the long dormant C reactor would be reactivated the following day. In attendance would be the U.S. Secretary of State, Secretary of Energy and a third guest, the Prime Minister of Israel.

Months of surveillance, as well as paid informants planted inside the over 10,000 person workforce at the Site, had provided the intruders with intelligence on how to best carry out their plan undetected. Just before dawn the following morning, with the barrier successfully installed, the men returned to the hunting cabin on the Georgia side of the river. They ate a full breakfast, then turned in for a few hours of sleep, in preparation to attend the Monarch Golf Tournament shortly after noon. Their partners in the plot would be waiting for them. There was still much work to do.

Chapter Fifteen

Understanding the need for an early start, Marc was first in the shower at 5:30 a.m. Jake was up shortly afterward and thirty minutes later the two men were ready to start their day. Jake seemed to have shaken off the events of the previous evening and appeared psyched with the prospect of a good showing in the tournament. Marc was not about to spoil Jake's exuberance by mentioning that he suspected something else might be brewing at the Savannah River Golf Links besides great playing from the top ranked golfers in the world.

There was a soft knock on the door. Marc saw that Laura and Ann Marie appeared ready to go. "Did you ladies sleep well?" Marc asked as they entered the room.

Ann Marie gave Jake a quick glance, "Pretty well, I guess." The two appeared to exchange the hint of a grin. Marc suspected the kids may have taken advantage of the time they were alone while he and Laura were meeting with Eleanor Saylor. Laura, however, had dark circles under her eyes. "You guys can grab a bite when we get to the course. I have a few things to check out."

"Dad, what can be so important that you have to leave us, even for a few minutes?" Ann Marie looked confused.

"There's a guy at the golf club I need to talk to. I won't be long. While I'm gone, Jake can use the time to warm up. Don't worry, I'll be back well before Jake's tee time."

"Maybe I can be Jake's substitute caddy until you return from your meeting," Ann Marie flashed another grin.

"Let's not get ahead of ourselves. Jake needs to be concentrating on his game, not his caddy," Marc said as he tossed her a wink.

"Oh Daddy "

Laura cut her off. "I think your father is right on this one. I'll stand in for Marc while Jake is at the range. I'm sure Jake will feel good just knowing you're close by."

"I guess," Ann Marie said.

Marc opened the door, "Okay, it's time to get started. I know we're a little early, but better to be safe than sorry."

Even with the early start, they found the Augusta traffic was backed up with lines of cars leading to the golf course. Marc maneuvered around the backup and turned into the entrance reserved for the players. "Looks like another sell-out crowd," he said.

Once through the security gate, Marc found a spot in the player's parking area.

"Laura, would you mind accompanying the kids to breakfast?" Marc asked.

She gave Marc a look, "Uh, I thought you'd want me to go with you when you meet up with mister what's-his-name?"

"I appreciate the offer, but someone should stay with the kids. I shouldn't be long."

"Dad, what's going on? You guys are acting a little strange this morning. Something happen that we should know about?" Ann Marie asked.

Marc and Laura gave each other a quick look. "Nothing important" Marc said. "We met someone last night who works here at the course. We got to talking and I let on that I was caddying for Jake. He asked if I could stop over and see him before Jake teed off, that's all," Marc said.

"Aren't there rules against getting inside information regarding course conditions?" Jake asked.

"I'm sure there are," Marc replied. "Don't worry, I promise we won't be discussing anything that we shouldn't be."

"I suppose we should be going then," Laura said, glancing at her cell phone.

Marc watched as Laura and the kids trundled off toward the bag storage to retrieve Jake's clubs. Getting directions from a passing groundskeeper, Marc made the ten-minute walk to the course superintendent's office. It was located in a large building out of view of golfers and patrons near the perimeter of the golf course property. It even had its own entrance gate that opened onto one of the city's thoroughfares, now closed to traffic for the tournament. Entering through an open overhead door, he saw that the building housed a variety of mowers, backhoes, tractors, trimmers and various pieces of equipment necessary to keep the golf course in pristine condition. A corner of the structure had been partitioned off forming a closed office space. A sign above the entrance door read, "Bill Goodspeed, Course Superintendent." Marc tapped on the door.

"Come in," came a voice from inside. Marc recognized the voice from his phone conversation the evening before.

Bill Goodspeed's eyes were puffy, probably from the stress of getting the golf course in shape for the tournament and lack of sleep.

"If you're looking for the first tee, you passed it on the way in."

"Actually, I'm looking for Bill Goodspeed."

"Yeah? Well, you got him," he answered in an irritated tone. "You must be the guy who called me last night." Goodspeed leaned back in his chair and stifled a yawn.

"Yes. Name's Marc LaRose."

"Shit. I was hoping that conversation was just another one of my weird dreams. You're here, so obviously, it wasn't." He yawned again, dropped his pen on a pad, and motioned to an empty chair in front of his desk.

Glancing around, Marc noticed there was a bank of TV monitors along one wall that showed different parts of the golf course. "Looks like you have the course pretty well monitored right from your vantage point at the superintendent's desk."

"It helps, but look, I'm sure you're aware, today is our biggest day of the year. What can I do for you?"

Marc thought how to answer. "Got a little situation. Like I mentioned last evening, it concerns Zach Saylor."

"Yeah, and like I mentioned, I've known Zach for years, even worked with him when he installed some of the irrigation here at the Savannah River Golf Links. Felt really bad when I heard about the accident. So, what's up?"

"Right before I spoke to you last night, I had a conversation with Eleanor Saylor. She gave me your phone number. She's not convinced her husband's death was accidental."

Simmons rubbed his eyes. He started to speak, but before he could answer, his phone rang. He looked at the caller ID. "I have to take this."

As Marc waited, he listened to the one-sided conversation. Apparently there was a problem with a water sprinkler somewhere on the eighteenth fairway.

"Have you checked the timer?" Goodspeed's brow furrowed as he listened to the response. He glanced at his wristwatch. "Okay, Jimmy, we only have about four hours or so before the first player reaches that area, so we can't wait. Try resetting the timer and let me know," he said and ended the call.

"Problem with the irrigation?" Marc asked.

"Yeah. The entire system was overhauled this past winter, and it just so happens that Zach Saylor designed it. Up to this point, it's been functioning well, but as you're probably aware, with anything new there's bound to be a few glitches. I doubt this is anything that can't be managed. So, tell me, what's your connection with Eleanor and Zack Saylor and his apparent accident?"

"None, really, other than the fact that my future son-in-law is playing in the tournament today."

"Let me get this straight," Goodspeed said. "Your future son-in-law's made the cut and you decided to come and talk to me? You know I can't talk to you about course conditions."

"I'm not here for that, I'm here to talk about Zach Saylor's death, accidental or otherwise."

Goodspeed stared up at Marc. "Alright. But why are you so interested in Zach's death?"

"We're staying at the Rose Hill in Aiken. Last Tuesday I made the short walk to The Palm Tree Golf Club and while I was there, I heard about Zach's accident, or whatever it was.

Goodspeed reached into his desk and retrieved a fresh pack of Marlboros, shook one out and offered it to Marc.

"No thanks, gave them up years ago," Marc said.

Goodspeed lit the cigarette and took a deep draw. He turned his head and blew out a cloud of blue smoke. "Yeah, that was quite a shock when I heard about it. Quite frankly, at the time, I didn't think his apparent accident was anything serious, but obviously I was wrong. Zach was a good friend."

Bill Goodspeed looked genuinely saddened.

"So, Mr. LaRose, you still haven't told me how – and why – you got involved with this."

Marc's eyes wandered toward the monitors as he thought how to answer. "In the days since Zach's death, a few things have piqued my interest, including a couple of run-ins with the people at the Apex Irrigation Company."

"Run-ins? What are you talking about?" Goodspeed asked.

"I'm not a professional golf caddy. I run a private detective agency in upstate New York. I've been asked by Zach's widow to ask around, see what I can find out. She has her doubts about her husband's death, and quite frankly, so do I."

"I see," Goodspeed said. "So your New York State PI license allows you to conduct investigations in South Carolina?"

"No, of course not. I'm doing this as a courtesy for Eleanor Saylor."

"Uh huh," Goodspeed grunted.

"Mr. Goodspeed, I noticed you've referred to Zach's death as an apparent accident. Sounds like you're not convinced that it was an accident either."

Goodspeed exhaled deeply, then glanced at the monitors again. "Zach's been...had been...working at Apex for years. He knew the irrigation business forward and backward. Like I said, he redesigned the irrigation for this golf course. Took him over a year. They say he died of chlorine gas inhalation."

"You don't think so?" Marc said. He noticed Goodspeed's face begin to redden.

"Total bullshit. Zach may have been a lot of things, but when it comes to irrigation, he was the best. It takes an accomplished agronomist to know what chemicals and fertilizers to apply, when to apply them and in what quantity to keep golf course fairways looking green and lush, especially for a tournament such as the one your future son-in-law is playing in. He knew the effects of chlorine and how to use it. I seriously doubt that Zach accidently inhaled chlorine gas."

"So, are you saying that he intentionally inhaled the gas?" Marc asked.

"Hardly. In the first place, chlorine gas is an irritant. One whiff and you'll choke, gag and run for fresh air. No, I tend to agree with Eleanor's suspicions. I can't prove it, but I think Zach had some help."

Marc let Bill Goodspeed's statement settle in. "Okay but who would do that to him, and why?"

"You are aware that Apex was recently bought out?"

"So I've heard. Understand a guy named Akhtar bought the company a couple of years ago. The way it was explained to me, sounded like it was more of a hostile takeover."

Goodspeed took another deep drag on his cigarette. The ash lengthened and turned downward like a gray worm. He tapped the ash onto the floor. "Apex was on the ropes. It was a successful family business, had a good customer list, including the Savannah River Golf Links. But over the past few years, the family seemed to have lost interest. Debts were piling up. They lost their line of credit with the bank. Then, a little over a year ago, Akhtar appeared out of nowhere with money to burn. The banks like local business, but they love a healthy balance sheet even more."

"So why do you think Zach was killed?"

Before Goodspeed could answer, his desk phone rang again. He glanced at the caller ID, then back up at Marc, "Shit, I got to take this one too."

Marc nodded.

"Yeah, Bill. That sprinkler still giving us fits?"

Goodspeed glanced up at Marc, but continued with his call, "Damn it. Okay, look, I'll be right out there. Take me about ten minutes."

Goodspeed hung up the phone, rose from his chair and again glanced at Marc, "Sorry, Mr. LaRose, we'll have to continue this conversation another time. Today, of all fucking times, that sprinkler head doesn't seem to want to cooperate."

"I understand," Marc said, "Just one last question. How was the relationship between Zach and the new ownership?"

Goodspeed took a few steps, then, after taking one last draw, dropped the remains of his cigarette on the cement floor and ground it out with the sole of his shoe. "Oil and water. Zach only had another year remaining on his contract with Apex. He disliked Akhtar and, from what he told me, the feeling was mutual. I wish your future son-in-law all the best with the tournament, but if you'll excuse me, I've got a golf tournament to attend to."

"Good luck with your sprinkler problem," Marc said.

With one last glance and a wave, Goodspeed was out the door.

Marc looked up at the TV monitors. He located one showing the practice range and saw Jake and Laura at one end of the line of golfers. Jake was hitting his driver which, as it is for most golfers, was the last club in his warm-up routine. Marc glanced at his watch. Jake's tee time was about forty minutes away, barely enough time remaining for a few practice putts, then the short walk to the first tee. It was time to go.

When Marc got to the practice putting green, he found Jake and Laura in the middle of the green, standing about ten feet from the nearest hole. There were a number of golf balls around the hole.

"There you are, Marc. Is everything alright?" Laura asked.

"Funny, I was going to ask you the same thing."

She looked at her son. "I'm not sure. You'll have to ask him."

Jake looked up with a nervous grin, "Glad you're here, Marc. For some reason, I seem to be pulling the ball a little more than usual."

"Yeah, I can see that," Marc said, glancing at the balls lying around the hole Jake was motioning toward.

An awkward silence fell over the trio.

"Well, I'll leave you two to figure it out," Laura said. "Besides, I think Ann Marie would like some company." Laura left to join Marc's daughter who was waiting just outside the ropes.

Marc watched as Jake dropped two balls on the green, then methodically putted them in, center cut each time. "Your putting stroke looks good. So, what brought all this on, pulling the ball?"

Jake glanced at Marc. "It's not what, it's who." His glance then shifted toward his mom who was standing next to Ann Marie at the far side of the practice putting green.

"Sounds like your mom's pressuring you to succeed."

"Always has. You think I'd be used to it by now, but I've never been in this position before in a professional golf tournament."

"I doubt she has either," Marc said. "You know, Jake, I think she sees your success as an extension of her own desire to succeed."

Jake sighed. He recovered a few of his golf balls and dropped them on the green, this time a few feet back from where he putted them before. Once again he smoothly stroked each of them into the back of the cup.

Marc glanced at the time clock near the first tee box. Jake's tee time was fifteen minutes away.

"Tell me, which clubs were giving you problems on the driving range?"

"Most all of them, especially the long irons."

"Probably some tension. It's natural on the final day of a tournament. Sorry I wasn't there to watch. Let's try and take it easy for the first couple of holes and see how it goes. Maybe I can pick up on something."

"Okay, but Mom said—"

Marc cut him off. "Jake, let me handle your mother. Right now, I think it's time for us to be heading to the first tee."

"You think you can handle my mother?" Jake picked the balls out of the hole and handed them to Marc. "My father tried. He got mauled."

Marc flashed a small grin. "You concentrate on playing golf and leave the lion taming to me. Believe me kid, this isn't my first wild animal act."

As Marc and Jake left the practice green, they heard the announcer introduce the next pairing. A moment later, Jake and his playing partner, Teddy Doubles, were called to the on-deck circle. They were second in line to tee off. Marc felt he could use this time to get Jake settled down and help him to put aside a lifetime of pressure his mother had laid on him to succeed.

"So, it sounds like your feelings for Ann Marie are pretty sincere."

Jake hesitated a moment before answering. "I've never met anyone like her. She's a serious person, but doesn't take life too seriously. She's optimistic, but knows the risks. She's beautiful, but doesn't think so."

"Those happen to be her mother's traits as well," Marc answered.

"You would know that better than I do, but Ann Marie really looks up to you."

As Marc thought about what Jake had said, he heard the announcer calling Jake and Doubles to the first tee.

"You ready to do this?" Marc said.

"It's what we came here for," Jake answered.

Doubles, the experienced champion of several professional tournaments, seemed relaxed, though Marc could tell there was an anxious air about him. After all, Marc thought, Teddy Doubles was closing in on his forties. How much longer could he remain competitive in this ever-evolving game where youth had the advantage of hitting longer tee shots and using shorter, more accurate irons into the greens?

Doubles won the coin toss and chose to tee-off first. Marc knew this was the smart play, setting the pace right from the start. Trouble was, Doubles' swing was too quick, and he pulled his tee ball to the left toward a stand of pine trees.

"He must have been talking to your mother," Marc whispered with a grin and handed Jake the driver. Jake returned the grin and Marc noticed how this had an instant calming effect on his young player.

Jake followed his routine of standing behind his tee-ball to line up his drive. He then moved over the ball and with a smooth, languid swing, sent the dimpled sphere carrying his initials "JM," well over 300 yards down the middle of the fairway. The gallery announced their approval with a chorus of "Ahs," followed by polite applause.

Jake handed the driver to Marc, who slid it into its place in the golf bag. As the two started off toward Jake's ball, Marc said, just loud enough for Jake to hear, "Nice shot, son."

With a grin and a wink, Jake replied, "Thanks, Dad."

Not unlike the days before, Marc couldn't help but notice the extra security mixed in with the throng of golf fans lining the fairway. Almost as disconcerting was the appearance of a small group of young girls that seemed to have gained a particular interest in Jake. Whenever he hit a shot, the girls erupted in a chorus of applause and giddy cheers. Although Jake didn't seem to pay much attention to his newfound admirers, Ann Marie appeared keenly aware and kept herself and Laura between Jake and his new fan club.

Reaching the area where Doubles' ball made its exit from the fairway, Jake and Marc assisted in the search. About a minute later, his caddy located the ball laying partially covered in some loose pine straw. Doubles managed to chop it out, sending it back to the middle of the fairway. Then, with practiced precision, he chipped his ball onto the green, five yards short of the hole.

"Got to hand it to him," Jake said. "He doesn't get rattled, even when he's hit his drive into trouble."

"That's how he got to be a champion. He plays the game one shot at a time," Marc replied.

Jake grinned again. "Where've I heard that before?"

After making a birdie on the first hole, Jake continued to maneuver through the next few holes well, leaving no blemishes on his card while adding another birdie. The angst that he had demonstrated on the practice tee with his mother had apparently subsided.

At the long dogleg par five, sixth hole, both Jake and Doubles hit their drives straight down the middle of the narrow fairway.

"Looks like we may have a mini-contest on who can reach the green in two," Marc said.

When they turned the corner toward the hole, they could see the players in front of them were still in the fairway, having hit their second shots short of the green. This, coupled with the fact that the players in front were just leaving the green, was contributing to a small back-up. All Jake and Doubles could do was to wait for the pair in front to finish the hole and move on. Of course this pause in the action gave Jake's newfound fan club a chance to inch ever closer, much to the chagrin of Ann Marie.

"This is like watching paint dry," Doubles exclaimed, obviously anxious for play to resume.

Jake knew there was nothing they could do and simply shrugged his shoulders.

Marc nodded in agreement. There was nothing more to say. While monitoring the activity in front of them, Marc heard a rhythmic thumping coming from somewhere in the distance. As the noise grew louder, he spotted a large helicopter beyond the pine trees over the city of Augusta. From his vantage point, he could see the familiar dark green color of the U.S. President's helicopter, Marine One. Marc knew when it was used by the Vice President or the Secretary of State, it carried the moniker, "Marine Two."

"Bet you that's the Secretary of State," Doubles said. "Looks like he's landing over at Daniel Field."

Marc was aware that the public airfield was located about three miles from the Savannah River Golf Links. "Yeah, I didn't realize he was a big golf fan."

"I'm not sure he is," Doubles replied. "Rumor has it he's attending the golf tournament with the Secretary of Energy and the Israeli Prime Minister as a run-up to some announcement concerning the Savannah River Nuclear Site. Something about a partnership with the State of Israel, I think."

As Marc was pondering this bit of news, he heard a smattering of applause from the crowd around the sixth green. The twosome in front of them had finally putted out and were heading for the next tee box.

Since Doubles' drive was a few yards shorter than Jake's, he was first to hit. Marc estimated they were about 285 yards from the green. With a light breeze blowing from their left, it was a challenging shot, even for an experienced professional. Doubles pulled his three-wood from the bag. Employing a smooth swing with his trademark short pause at the top, he made a solid connection. The ball started out a little to the right, then drew back to the left. It landed a few feet short of the green, took one bounce and came to a stop about twenty feet short of the hole. It was a marvelous shot that brought hearty applause from the gallery.

Jake nodded his approval, then addressed his ball. Using his five iron, he launched his ball high, directly toward the center of the green which would have been perfect if it hadn't been for a sudden gust of wind that seemed to come out of nowhere and pushed his ball off to the right. Marc watched as Jake's ball bounced off the side of the green, then took a bad hop toward a stand of pines. A chorus of "ooh's" could be heard from the collection of onlookers around the green.

Marc knew the gallery's response meant that Jake's ball had landed in some trouble.

"That was a good shot, Jake, just a little bad luck. All we can do is hope we're not blocked out by those trees." Marc said, trying to remain positive.

Although Jake was up on Doubles by three shots for the tournament, Doubles was a fan favorite, having won the Monarch Championship twice in the past. He received a lively round of approval as he stepped onto the green to mark his ball. Marc and Jake peeled off to the right and with the "assistance" of a few exuberant fans, located his ball on a flattened bed of pine straw among a stand of mature trees, about twenty yards from the center of the green.

Marc politely motioned for the fans to move away so he and Jake could determine their best option. His immediate goal was to get Jake's ball back into play in an attempt to save par for the hole. Although it was late morning, Marc noticed that several of the fans were in different stages of inebriation, casually holding plastic containers of frothy brew while freely offering advice for 'the best way' to recover from Jake's errant shot. One fan, with a noticeable slur, shouted that Jake "should launch his ball over a few of the pines," even though the closest one was five feet away and about 40 feet tall.

As Marc was assessing what to do, he heard a roar from the gallery on the opposite side of a grove of pine trees near the eighteenth fairway. Glancing toward the noise, Marc caught a subtle movement in the trees. There were a couple men standing behind a cluster of trees near the fairway. They appeared to be looking in the direction of the noise.

Probably the groundskeepers working on the faulty sprinkler head that Bill Goodspeed had mentioned earlier that morning.

"Hello, Marc? Little help here?" It was Jake.

"Oh, sorry, I didn't hear you." Marc replied.

"I could take a chance and cut the ball around the trees in front of us which could bring it close to the hole, or maybe, I should just pitch it out and land it somewhere in front of the green," Jake said, pointing out the two options. "That would leave me either a short pitch, or a long putt and a chance for a birdie."

Marc studied Jake's quandary. "Cutting the ball around trees sounds great, but it's the low percentage shot, probably one out of ten. Let's pitch it out and take our chances on a long birdie putt. Worse you could do is settle for a par."

After a moment of consideration, Jake said, "Yeah, suppose you're right." He seemed a bit disappointed with Marc's suggestion, but using his nine iron, Jake chipped his ball under a few branches and onto the center of the green. Marc watched as the ball stopped about ten feet from the hole. Jake then putted it in for an amazing birdie. Doubles missed his eagle putt and settled for a birdie as well.

As the four of them walked off the green toward the next tee box, Doubles said "Where'd you find your caddy, kid? I'd have taken my chances and cut a shot around those trees. The pitch-out was the smart play."

"'I was tempted but someone told me not too long ago, that 'the game of golf is played one shot at a time.' It's taken me awhile, but I've come to appreciate that bit of advice.'"

Marc smiled, "It's one thing to offer up some counseling. It's quite another when someone actually appreciates it."

The next two holes were more tricky than difficult. It took all of Jake's skills just to hold steady with pars on each. Completing the par 3 ninth hole brought them back to the clubhouse where they would begin the difficult back nine.

The backup they had experienced before was still with them on the tenth hole. This gave Jake a chance to run to one of the portable restrooms reserved for the players for a much-needed break.

"Oh, where are you going, Jake," cried one of his female fans. Another yelled, "Oh, Jakey, let us know if you need any help!" This was followed with a chorus of giggles from his "fan club."

Ann Marie seemed to be warming to Jake's new-found attention, and stood nearby with a strained smile.

While Jake was gone, Marc noticed the crowd around the eighteenth green, located not far away, had swelled in anticipation of seeing some of the early golfers finish their rounds. A large scoreboard next to the green showed the tournament's leaders and, much to his surprise, Jake's name was listed. He was near the bottom of the board of the top twenty players, but Marc knew that Jake's inclusion was no mean feat.

Can't get too far ahead of ourselves. This is only the half-way mark.

As he dug a sandwich out of the golf-bag, Marc noticed a bit of commotion coming from one of the outdoor eating concessions near the clubhouse. A small army of security officers, including several men and women in dark suits wearing sun-glasses had formed a not-so-obvious circle around one of the tables. One of the plain-clothed men seemed to be talking into his sleeve.

Could this be the U.S. Secretary of State and his entourage that Doubles had mentioned?

A moment later, Jake reappeared at Marc's side.

"Hungry?" Marc asked.

"We have any snack bars? I really don't want a sandwich. Could upset my stomach."

Marc dug into the bag and found a couple of Kind bars. He handed one to Jake.

"Oh, man, where you been hiding these? Jake asked, eagerly unwrapping one.

"Been in the bag all along. They're one of my favorites."

"Mine too," Jake replied.

Marc wiped his mouth with a paper napkin, "Jake, did you happen to notice if the U.S. Secretary of State is sitting over by the club house?" Marc motioned toward the circle of security officers.

Jake glanced back toward the club house. "I wouldn't know the U.S. Secretary of State if he hit me over the head. I did notice a bunch of suspicious looking characters standing around a couple of old men eating and talking under an umbrella table over there." He nodded in the direction of the table.

"That's probably them," Marc replied.

Jake took a sip of water. "One of them seemed to be speaking a foreign language. Sounded like Yiddish, or something. I think there was an interpreter. Couldn't tell for sure. I was in a hurry to get back here before they called us to the tee box."

Marc was thinking about Jake's comment when the announcement was made for Jake and Teddy Doubles to proceed to the tenth tee. Lunch was over.

Retaining the honors from the ninth hole, Jake was first to tee off. Both men hit good drives, then proceeded down the fairway. As they strode along, Marc allowed his mind to wander. He thought of this glorious day and what had brought him to Augusta. Whatever the outcome of the tournament, Marc was thinking that the blessings of being on one of the finest golf courses in the world while caddying for his daughter's future husband was more than he could have ever hoped for. At this moment, he knew there was no better place on earth for him to be.

Jake's steady play continued. He birdied the eleventh hole, and although he bogeyed the treacherous thirteenth, he parred holes fourteen and fifteen. Doubles, however, had found renewed spirit in the game and poured in five birdies in a row. The past champion seemed intent on another repeat performance.

The eighteenth hole was a long par 5 and Marc knew it set up nicely for Jake's right to left draw. Although both men hit good drives, Jake's had gone at least twenty yards beyond Doubles' ball. Trouble was, Doubles' ball seemed to have disappeared somewhere in the middle of the fairway. When they reached that point in the fairway, Marc noticed the ground was soft and wet.

Indeed, Doubles' golf ball had plugged in the wet ground and was barely visible. After assessing the situation, Teddy called for an official to ask for a ruling. About three minutes later, the official arrived.

"Yeah, we've had a few players with the same problem today. Malfunctioning sprinkler head. Go ahead and retrieve your ball, then drop it near the plug mark."

Doubles shook his head. "You'd think someone would've fixed this. I mean, this is the Monarch Championship. A fucked-up sprinkler head has cost me at least twenty yards, maybe more."

"Sorry, Mr. Doubles. That's the ruling. Best I can do."

Marc felt Doubles was right, but he also knew there wasn't much that could be done about it.

Doubles, still obviously miffed about the situation, dropped the ball, then proceeded to hit his second shot. Not unlike his drive on the first hole, he again pulled his shot to the left. This time he found a fairway bunker about fifty yards short of the green.

Doubles was clearly having a tough time controlling his anger as he firmly shoved his club back into the bag.

They moved ahead. Marc estimated Jake's ball was about 275 yards from the center of the eighteenth green, which was surrounded on three sides by a throng of patrons at least ten rows deep. A TV camera tower loomed above the crowd toward the back of the green. The pairing in front of them were still lining up their putts.

"What do you think, Marc? Three wood?"

Marc considered the situation. "275 yards is certainly reachable. The only hazards are the two sand bunkers on either side of the green. Sure, why not? We'll just have to wait for the green to clear."

Glancing off to his right, Marc saw Bill Goodspeed sitting in one of the course's utility vehicles. Marc gave him a small wave. Goodspeed nodded in return.

Marc suspected Goodspeed was monitoring the watering problem he had mentioned while visiting with him earlier that morning. Unfortunately, the malfunctioning sprinkler head had already soaked the fairway, much to the dismay of Teddy Doubles.

Hopefully, Doubles won't notice him sitting there or there could be a scene.

The green cleared a few minutes later, allowing Jake to hit. Using his three-wood, he launched his ball high into a slight breeze blowing directly at him. Marc watched as the ball landed just short of the green, then, after a couple of hops, it came to rest a few yards left of the hole. A loud roar erupted from the crowd around the green and Marc knew Jake's ball was close. Doubles then hit a fine shot out of the bunker, his ball landing on the center of the green.

Jake closely watched Doubles putt as his ball was on a similar line. Doubles went on to two-putt for a disappointing par.

"What do you think, Marc? Doubles' first putt looked really good, but it veered to the left at the end, away from the hole. It should have gone in. It must have hit something."

Before answering, Marc's mind flashed back to his conversation with Ned, the proprietor at The Palm Tree Golf Club and what he had mentioned earlier in the week. He remembered the advice Ned had offered him.

If there is any one thing I can say that might help, it would be that if you and Jake are unsure which way a putt will break, nine out of ten times, it will break toward the Savannah River.

Marc remembered crossing the river on the way to the course. From where they were standing, it was definitely off to their left. "Jake, play it to go slightly to the left."

"Okay, Marc, but it sure looks like it could go either way."

"Trust me on this, Jake. It's going to go to the left."

Jake took his time lining up his putt. He then stood over the ball and with a smooth stroke, started his ball a little to the right of the hole. Then, just when Marc thought it would miss, it veered back to the left and found the bottom of the cup for an eagle. A gain of two strokes in one shot. This resulted in a thunderous roar from the gallery. Jake's all-girl fan club screamed and jumped up and down with a chorus of cheers. Ann Marie met Jake at the edge of the green with a wide smile, and gave him a big hug and a peck on his cheek.

She then glanced over at the cluster of young girls that seemed to have grown with each passing hole.

With about half the field yet to finish, Jake was now in third place for the tournament championship.

Marc walked with Jake back to the scorer's tent to sign and attest his score card. Ann Marie and Laura knew they weren't allowed inside the tent and followed at a discreet distance.

Jake learned that not only was he in third place, he was also the leading amateur in the field. Teddy Doubles, the former champion was now eight shots off the pace.

Ann Marie and Laura jumped and shrieked for joy, obviously elated with Jake's standing. They cheered and hugged each other, something that Marc had not seen them do before.

"Half the field is still out on the course so anything can happen," Jake said in an apparent effort to tamp down their exuberance.

Although Marc could tell the young man was thoroughly elated, he knew that Jake's final standing was out of his hands. It was now a waiting game to see how the rest of the players finished.

Chapter Sixteen

The crowd of fans surrounding the eighteenth green was huge and growing larger as each of the competing pairings ended their rounds. Marc found a space for his group along the fairway giving them a decent view of the action on the green. As each pair of contenders finished, Marc noticed Jake glancing at the leader board, anxiously looking for any change in his standing, even though he knew he had the low amateur title in his pocket.

As more players finished, Jake found himself tied for sixth place overall. "Darn it Marc, if I had made that par putt on thirteen, I'd be in fourth place right now."

Marc gave Jake a serious look. "And your drive on the last hole could just as easily have plugged in the fairway, like Doubles' did. That would have made your second shot to the green much longer, putting you in a more difficult situation. There are still two groups yet to finish, and they're ahead of the leaders, so, there's bound to be a change."

Marc noticed Jake was quiet, apparently still brooding about his efforts.

"Jake, look at it this way, you're the lead amateur in the clubhouse. That position will not change. You know what that means?"

Jake shrugged his shoulders and bit his lip. "Yeah, I get an automatic invitation to next year's tournament. Big whoop!"

"That, plus you'll be invited to a number of other professional tournaments. With your performance today, you've punched your ticket for a chance to play with the pros. I'd say you have quite a career ahead of you," Marc said.

Jake exhaled, "I suppose you're right. Guess I should count my blessings."

"Rather than looking back at a few missed hits and wishing you'd done better, it's best to concentrate on what you did right. That will be key to future improvement."

Jake nodded thoughtfully.

"Bet you didn't know that you not only had a good caddy, you had a philosopher on your bag as well," Laura said.

They quietly watched as another set of players finished their round.

Marc broke the silence. "There's just one pair of golfers yet to finish, and they're a few minutes behind, probably delayed by that sprinkler problem on the fairway." Marc motioned back toward the area where Teddy Doubles' ball had plugged. "If we head over to the concession stand, maybe we could celebrate with a nice craft beer?" Marc said with a broad grin, hoping to raise Jake's spirits.

"Good idea, my treat, but we better hurry, I believe the concessions are about to close," Laura said, glancing at her watch.

When they reached the beer tent, they noticed the attendants were in the process of packing up. Laura, however used her feminine powers of persuasion and got them to pour four cups of beer. She left a hefty tip for their trouble, then, the four of them rejoined the crowd heading back toward the eighteenth green. Along the way, Laura suggested they stop under a lone shade tree.

She raised her cup. "To my son, whatever your future holds, I hope this day will always stand out as special for you as it was for me. I'm so proud of you."

"Hear, hear," Marc said. They all raised their plastic souvenir cups and offered a faux clinking gesture before taking a swallow of the frothy brew.

Ann Marie, wearing a foam moustache, threw her free arm around Jake and gave him a kiss. "My Jake, the golf champion."

"'Excuse me, 'your Jake?'" Laura said.

"Um," Ann Marie started, but their attention was interrupted by a sudden roar from the crowd around the green.

"Sounds like someone's made another birdie," Marc said. "They should be announcing the winner of the tournament soon. Let's get down closer to the green. "After all, Jake is the low amateur winner, and I think we'd all like to see him raise his trophy!"

"I have all the trophy I need right here," Jake said, one arm wrapped around Ann Marie.

Marc could see Laura's ire was rising on hearing her son's intentions for Ann Marie. "Let's get a move on. It's customary for the president of the Savannah River Golf Links to present the trophies," he said.

"I guess," Jake said, with feigned reluctance while avoiding eye contact with his mother. A moment later, the four of them blended in with the sea of fans moving in the direction of the eighteenth green.

As they got closer, Marc saw that the crowd around the green had more than doubled in size. The large leaderboard behind the green listed the professionals who had finished in the top three places. Under those names it read, "Low Amateur, Jake McKay, CA."

Eyeing the crowd, Marc said, "Why don't we head in the direction of the scorer's tent. No sense fighting this crowd to get near the green."

He led the way to the roped-off path they had taken earlier, except now, even that was blocked with golf fans standing eight deep to get a glimpse of the leaders.

Using a string of "excuse me's" and "sorry's," Marc got them to the tent.

When they arrived there, Marc spotted a rather distinguished looking gentleman wearing a bright gold jacket and green tie, the customary dress allotted only to members of the club and past champions of the Monarch Golf Tournament.

"Ah, there you are," cried the Club President, motioning to Marc and Jake. "Thank heavens y'all are still here. We thought maybe you'd forgotten about the presentation and left us."

Marc introduced Ann Marie and Laura.

"So nice to meet y'all. This is quite an accomplishment for Jake and I'm sure y'all are very proud of him."

Laura started to interject, but the man raised his hand. "Sorry to interrupt, ma'am, but we're short on time. If you'd all be so kind, please follow me."

When they arrived back at the eighteenth hole, Marc noticed the three top finishers were already standing behind a table that had been set up at the center of the green. The table held three trophies and a large gold cup.

Marc noticed the event's emcee was also the Club president and a long-time member. Using a microphone, the president thanked the gallery for their support, then proclaimed in a rich voice laced with an educated Georgian accent, "Ladies and gentlemen, the tournament is complete, and we have a winner!" One by one, he introduced the third and second place finishers, then the winner of the tournament. Lastly, he introduced Jake as the Low Amateur Champion of the event. There were handshakes all around. Afterwards, a group photo was taken of the four men together.

The Club President hinted at the prospect of "some very special guests," who would be assisting in awarding the champions' trophies.

This announcement resulted in a low hum of "ooh's" followed with muted applause.

The president continued, "But first, as is tradition at the Savannah River Golf Links, it is my honor to present the low amateur winner of this year's Monarch Golf Championship, Mr. Jake McKay of Ontario, Canada." He went to the table holding the trophies and grabbed the golden cup, raised it over his head, and with theatrical poise, presented it to Jake. This brought a polite, if not a subdued round of applause from the gallery. There were also a few shouts of "Oh Canada" from the crowd.

Nice to see that a few Canucks made the trip, Marc mused.

The President/emcee stood next to Jake as the club's photographer snapped a few photos of the two with Jake holding the cup up with both hands. He then motioned for Marc, Laura and Ann Marie to come for a group photo, guiding them to stand on either side of himself and Jake as the photographer captured another shot.

"We're always happy to see our friends from north of the border. Isn't that right folks?", the Club President announced to the crowd. This elicited another polite round of applause.

The President brought the group in for a huddle, and in hushed tones, said, "If you would be so kind as to exit back toward the scoring tent, that way you won't have to fight the crowd. Congratulations again, and thanks for coming."

Holding his arm out toward the exit, he announced, "Folks, how about another round of applause for this year's amateur champion."

Jake and Marc waved to the applauding gallery as they led Laura and Ann Marie between the two lines of yellow ropes.

Making their retreat toward the scoring tent, Marc noticed more uniformed security officers lined up along the ropes on both sides of the path.

"Wow, this is quite a send-off for being the low amateur," Jake said.

"I doubt this security is for us," Marc said.

When they arrived near the scoring tent, a husky young man in a suit and tie ushered the four of them off to one side. "Sorry folks, U.S. Secret Service. If you could please hold still for a moment." Just then, Marc saw a cadre of security officers dressed in black suits and ties, equipped with mirrored sunglasses, earpieces and red lapel pins leave the scorer's tent and move past them back toward the green. In the center of the group, Marc recognized a white-haired gentleman dressed in smart golf attire walking with another man, the apparent mystery guests the Club President had alluded to earlier.

"Who the hell was that?" Laura asked.

"I believe one of them was the U.S. Secretary of State," Marc said.

"Yeah, so why's he here? He a big fan or something?"

"It's called politics, playing to the crowd," Marc said, thinking back to the conversation he had with Sammy, the shoeshine guy he'd met at the club three days before. "From what I understand, he's in the area for a meeting at the Savannah River Site. Something about a collaborative agreement with the Israeli government. But I don't know who the other guy is. Let's hang around a few minutes and see what's going on."

"Dad, I'm bushed. Would you mind if Jake and I head back to the SUV? We'll wait for you there."

Figuring his daughter really wanted to be alone with Jake, Marc handed her the keys, "Don't do anything I wouldn't do."

"Dad, really?" she said, rolling her eyes. She then turned toward the parking lot holding Jake's free hand. His other hand held the cup he had just won.

Marc and Laura turned their attention back to the Club President's announcement. "Before we get started with the presentations of the winners, we have not one, but two, very distinguished guests on hand who hardly need introduction. First is our own U.S. Secretary of State, and, as an added surprise, we also have the Prime Minister of Israel."

This statement was followed by a roar of approval from the gallery. There were also a few shouts of "Mazel Tov."

The Secretary of State was introduced, and said a few words of appreciation to the course committee for inviting him. After a brief explanation of what brought the men to the course, he returned the microphone to the Club President.

"Well, this is quite a surprise," Laura said. "It's one thing to have your Secretary of State on hand, but quite another for the Prime Minister of Israel to attend. Just seems a little unusual for a golf tournament though, don't you think?"

"Makes sense, in a way. I believe they're both in town for the nuclear collaboration agreement out at the Site. Looking at it from their point of view, why not take advantage of a photo-op at the tournament? Kind of a twofer for both men, I'd say,"

Laura and Marc listened as the Club President started to speak. "Mr. Prime Minister, it's an honor to have you visit us and we want to wish you a warm welcome to the Savannah River Golf Links and the Monarch Golf Tournament. Would you like to say a few words?"

Marc heard microphone noises as it was passed from one man to the other, then the sound of heavy breathing. The old guy apparently hadn't quite recovered from the brisk walk to the green.

"Thank you for that kind invitation. As some of you may know, I am here in the United States to participate in our country's first nuclear collaboration with the U.S. government at the Savannah River Site. However, upon learning that our own Eli Cohen had finished in the top ten at this, the prestigious Monarch Golf Tournament, and being the first Israeli to do so, I could not pass up the opportunity to be on hand to congratulate him for this achievement. As you know, the sport of golf in Israel is just getting started, and with Eli's performance these last four days, I am hoping that Israeli players will be a force in the PGA in the years to come. Mr. Eli Cohen, would you please come to the center of the green?"

Marc heard the galleries' approval of this announcement with polite applause. There were more rustling noises as the microphone was passed to Cohen. Just then however, Marc heard a few shouts, then a scream from someone in the gallery. Somebody yelled, "It's the sprinklers!"

"Marc, what the hell is going on down there?" Laura asked.

Mixed in with the colorful golf shirts of those in the gallery, Marc detected a faint yellow haze begin to billow up from the area around the green.

Again, there were more rustling noises from the microphone.

"Sorry folks, we seem to have a problem with the sprinkler system," the emcee was saying when he too began coughing uncontrollably.

The sounds of people coughing and gagging increased. The huge gallery began to move in a wave, slowly at first, then Marc could see people running and stumbling, attempting to get away from the eighteenth green.

Marc caught a whiff of something peculiar. It smelled like bleach.

"Chlorine gas," Marc whispered.

"Marc, did you say something?" Laura asked.

"Someone's piping chlorine gas through the sprinkler system. Those people have to get upwind, it's their only chance. Get to the SUV and get the kids off the course!"

Marc removed his handkerchief from his back pocket and soaked it in his cup of beer, then quickly wrung it out.

"Marc what are you doing? Laura asked.

Ignoring Laura's question, Marc covered his nose with the handkerchief and started off in the direction of the green. "Get the kids back to Aiken, I'll see you there," Marc shouted over his shoulder as he ran.

Chapter Seventeen

Heading down the slope toward the green, Marc ran headlong into the crowd of spectators trying to escape the gas. Above the tide of screaming patrons, he sensed a distant thumping that seemed strangely familiar. After successfully dodging the onslaught, Marc arrived at the backside of a set of bleachers set up next to the green. Although his eyes were stinging from the gas, he was able to make out the shape of a large wind fan that had been stored under the bleachers. Marc knew fans were used to keep the bentgrass greens from overheating and figured the fan had been stored there for that purpose.

Afraid the effects of the gas could soon overtake him, he frantically searched for a way to activate the fan in an attempt to blow the gas away. Masked by the screams and shouts of the fleeing gallery, the persistent thumping sound continued to occupy a corner of his mind.

Could be the effects of my beer-soaked handkerchief, or the chlorine.

Then the air around him began to swirl, slowly at first. The thumping grew steadily louder as discarded brochures, paper cups, sandwich wrappings—anything that wasn't tied down—flew past. As the noise intensified, Marc saw the table that had been set up to hold the winners' trophies, the speakers, the microphone and wires that just moments before were used to announce the tournament winners, had been caught up in the wind's swirl. He felt he was in the center of a tornado.

Golf spectators, attempting to flee the now dissipating gas, were running in all directions, many holding onto their caps and sunhats, a few successfully. But, with the swirling winds, the cloud of offending gas appeared to dissipate. Wiping away more tears, Marc glanced upwards toward the noise. Although his eyes were burning, he could make out the now familiar sight of the green Sea King helicopter, the one that he suspected had transported the Secretary of State to the airfield earlier in the day.

Shielding his eyes from the wind and flying debris caused by the helicopter's rotary downwash, he glanced toward the center of the green where the club's president had addressed the throng of spectators moments before. The green was now empty, save for the figure of a man lying motionless in its center along with another man who looked to be attending to him. Marc ran to where the body lay and instantly recognized the fallen man. It was the Israeli Prime Minister. He recalled that the short walk to the green had left him labored moments before the gas attack. Marc recognized the man with the PM was a member of his security team. The air around the green became calmer as the helicopter continued to move away, back toward the fairway.

Marc knelt next to the man. "Can he get up?" Marc yelled over the noise of the helicopter.

"He's been overcome by the gas," the security man replied. "He has chronic COPD. We need to get him to a hospital. I found a pulse, but it's weak."

Marc pulled his phone from his pocket and dialed 911. There was no answer, only a recorded message indicating there were no operators available.

Calls for help at the golf course had overloaded the system.

Marc glanced upward again. The helicopter had moved well away from the green and was hovering over the fairway. He stood and ran toward the aircraft. Waving both arms, he frantically motioned for the pilot to land the helicopter.

It seemed to take the pilot a few moments to translate Marc's intentions before the craft slowly descended. Shortly after it landed, a side door opened and a short flight of steps unfolded, extending to the fairway. One of the crewmen met Marc at the bottom of the steps.

"What the hell's happened?" The crewman asked, apparently unaware of the cause of the melee.

"There's been a gas attack. The Israeli Prime Minister is down!" Marc yelled over the noise of the helicopter's engine and pointed to the man lying on green. "He's having serious respiratory problems and needs immediate medical attention. We need to get him to the hospital, now."

The crewman, using his helmet intercom, relayed the information to the pilot. Marc could see one of the men behind the controls signal that he had received the message. A moment later, another crewman carried a stretcher down the helicopter's stairway.

Laying the stretcher next to the stricken diplomat, Marc, the security man and a crewman lifted the still unconscious Prime Minister onto it and secured him with tie-down straps.

As the Prime Minister was being lifted into the helicopter, two more men dressed in suits and dark sunglasses came to where Marc was standing. Both wore ear buds and were holding their handkerchiefs over their noses. Judging by the bulge under their jackets, Marc guessed they were armed.

"Where are you taking him?" One of the men asked through his handkerchief.

"Doctors Hospital. They have a helipad close by," the security man replied.

"You with the Secret Service?" Marc asked.

The suited man glanced at Marc, and behind his darkened sunglasses, seemed to notice him for the first time, "State Department Security. Who are you?"

"Nobody, just a bystander trying to help," Marc answered.

He watched as another serviceman appeared at the helicopter's door. The stretcher was hoisted up, then pulled inside. The Prime Minister's security man followed the stretcher into the helicopter. A few seconds later, the stairs folded back and the craft lifted off.

Marc and the remaining security men ducked and turned to shield their faces from the swirling wind and debris caused by the downwash.

Shortly after the craft had left and the noise dissipated, the State Department Security man approached Marc again and asked for some ID.

Marc reached in his back pocket and produced his New York State Police retirement ID and shield.

"Little out of your territory, aren't you, Mister LaRose?" He compared Marc's face to the photo on his ID.

"My daughter's boyfriend was playing in today's tournament."

The man returned Marc's ID. "So, what the hell happened?"

"We were watching the awards ceremonies from the top of that knoll," Marc said, pointing to where he had been standing just a few minutes before. "The Club's President had just introduced Eli

Cohen, an Israeli player who played and finished in the top ten. About then I saw a yellowish cloud coming from the sprinkler heads around the green. I believe it was chlorine gas. That's when people started feeling its effects. Many panicked and ran. Luckily that helicopter was close by, or things could have been much worse."

"Actually, the helicopter's stop here was pre-planned. The Prime Minister and the Secretary of State were scheduled to mark the U.S./Israeli coalition at the Savannah River Site. But I doubt that's going to happen now."

Although the gas had mostly dissipated, the distant sound of the receding helicopter could not mask the coughing and gagging of the golf fans still in the area.

"Yeah, it looks like a lot of things aren't going to happen now," Marc said.

The agent gave Marc his card. "We may need to talk with you some more. You staying in the area?

"We're at the Rose Hill in Aiken, but we plan on heading back to upstate New York tomorrow."

"What's your cell number?"

Marc gave the agent his business card. The agent entered the number into his cell. "We need to get to the hospital and check on the PM's condition. We'll be in touch."

With that, the two agents left, heading back the way they'd come.

Suddenly, Marc was standing alone in the middle of the green, where just moments before, a grand ceremony had taken place, followed by what appeared to have been a terrorist attack.

He wiped the remaining tears from his eyes.

Nothing more to do here. I better go find Laura and the kids.

As he turned to leave, he saw Bill Goodspeed pull up in the course maintenance vehicle and stop next to a sprinkler head that just minutes before had emitted the cloud of noxious gas. Goodspeed appeared haggard as he got off the cart. He pulled his handkerchief from his back pocket and covered his nose. Getting down on his knees he commenced to inspect the offending sprinkler.

Marc went to where Goodspeed was kneeling. "Bill, what happened?"

"Beats the fuck out of me. I was dealing with that sprinkler back in the fairway," he said, motioning toward the area where Teddy

Doubles' ball had plugged, "and just like that, I saw all hell break loose. Somehow the sprinklers around the eighteenth green were activated, not by me, or anyone else working here."

"Okay, so how do you think chlorine gas got into the irrigation system?" Marc asked.

Goodspeed coughed. "Can we talk somewhere else? I have to get away from here. This gas is nauseating."

Marc got in the maintenance vehicle's passenger seat. "Let's go upwind." He pointed toward the eighteenth hole tee box.

Goodspeed turned the vehicle into the wind and stopped a couple hundred yards away. He scratched his head and looked down the fairway at the now empty green. "To answer your question, we use injectors to regulate the flow of fertilizer to each area of the golf course. The only thing I can come up with is someone tampered with one of the underground tanks that feeds that green, replacing the fertilizer with something else."

"Yeah, chlorine and acid," Marc replied. "I believe that's the combination that produces chlorine gas."

Goodspeed seemed to think about Marc's words. "Now that you mention it, I remember one of the tanks feeding this green was replaced recently."

"One of the tanks?" Marc asked.

"We often mix the fertilizer with acid at different rates. This is done to regulate the PH of the soil."

"So, who fills the tanks? Marc asked.

Goodspeed hesitated. "Well, I do. Not personally, but I instruct my fertilizing team to inject the fertilizer/acid combination based on the soil tests that are conducted periodically."

"Going back to the fertilizer tank that was replaced, who replaced it?" Marc asked.

"Well, Apex Irrigation, of course. Zach and his crew came over to work on it a couple months ago."

"Zach Saylor?" Marc asked.

"Uh, yeah. I sent Zach a work order to replace the tank that was leaking. It took a few weeks for the new tank to arrive, then Apex dug up the old tank and fitted the system with the new one."

"Have you had a chance to use it?"

"Of course. It's been working fine, up to now."

"Okay, so who activated the sprinkler at the eighteenth green today?" Marc asked.

"I have no idea. The system can be controlled here at the course, or at the Apex office in Aiken."

"Yeah, I remember hearing that. I thought it sounded kind of unusual. You know, for an irrigation supply company to control an off-premises system. But I was never in the irrigation business, so what do I know?"

Goodspeed shrugged his shoulders. "Supposedly, it was an option that the club purchased with the system. Kind of a back-up, I guess."

"So let me get this straight, your watering system can be controlled by yourself, or by someone at the Apex Company in Aiken."

"That's pretty much it. Naturally, the system is usually turned off while there are players on the course. It doesn't make for good TV to have water sprinklers come on in the middle of a player's back swing," Goodspeed said.

While Goodspeed was talking, Marc noticed a few more uniformed sheriffs' deputies as well as several EMTs had arrived in the area. They immediately went about the job of attending to the remaining members of the gallery still experiencing the effects of the gas.

"Do you think it's possible someone on the premises accidentally activated the system?"

Goodspeed seemed to give Marc's question some thought. "I suppose anything's possible. The main controls are in a panel in my office, but, when I'm not there, my door is locked. I have the only key."

Marc's gaze drifted to where the police were stringing crime scene tape around the eighteenth green. He thought about what Goodspeed had told him.

"What can you tell me about the problem you had with the sprinkler back in the middle of the fairway?" Marc motioned toward the area where Teddy Couples ball had plugged.

"Looks like that was caused by a busted pipe. One of the lines that run under the fairway broke under pressure during the night. We found it early this morning, about the time we were talking in my office. We drained off as much of the standing water we could and notified the tournament committee, but the ground was already saturated."

"You think someone tampered with the system overnight?" Marc asked.

"We had security on the premises all night, but like I said, anything's possible. The system was completely overhauled this past winter. That's when Apex installed the new fertilizer tank. It could have been caused by a loose connection. When I dig it up, I'll know more."

Marc thought about what he had learned. "Talking about Apex, I saw one of their workmen here on the course the other day."

"That's routine, especially during a tournament like the Monarch. We like to have one of their techs on hand for things like that busted pipe."

Marc looked around. "So where are they now?"

"Funny you should ask. The tech that was supposed to be here got into a car accident yesterday on the way home. He's in the hospital. I called Apex to get another tech to cover for him, but Mr. Akhtar, the owner, said he didn't have anyone else to send."

Marc hesitated. "So, the night before the final day of one of the biggest golf tournaments of the year, an irrigation service tech that was supposed to be here was injured in a car wreck, and Apex didn't have anyone else?"

In the background, Marc heard multiple sirens coming from different directions. Probably more first responders dispatched to the course, he figured.

"That's what Akhtar told me. Sounds like bullshit, I know."

"I guess the only way to find out is to dig up the holding tank," Marc said. "But I'm sure the police are going to want to talk to you first. They'll probably want to check that out for themselves."

"Yeah, looks like this is going to be a long day," Goodspeed said.

"Yeah, probably for all of us," Marc said. "I've got to go and find my daughter and the other people I came with."

"Want a ride?" Goodspeed asked.

"I'd love one, but I think this guy's looking to talk to you." Marc motioned to the security man that he'd spoken to earlier. The man was approaching them at a brisk pace.

"Okay, talk to you later," Goodspeed said. "Remember, if the patrons' gates are backed up, use the maintenance vehicle gate. It's around back of the maintenance barn. And, let me know if you find anything."

"Will do, Bill, and thanks for the heads-up on the gate."

On the way to the parking area Marc noticed the remnants of the chlorine gas lingering in the air. There were still a number of people in different stages of recovery from the effects of the gas lying about. Although most were upright, a few were still on the ground, sitting, or kneeling. Some were being attended to by emergency responders, but most by friends or passers-by.

"Daddy, Daddy," Over the sound of the sirens, Marc heard Ann Marie calling to him. She and Jake were standing next to the SUV, six rows deep into the vast parking lot. Marc could see that the exits had been blocked by the incoming emergency vehicles caught up in the crush of cars trying to leave. Nothing was moving.

Marc waved to her. "Stay there, I'll come to you!"

It took him a few minutes as he dodged several rows of motorists, intent on escaping the melee, to reach the SUV.

"Daddy, what's going on? We heard people screaming and we saw a helicopter. What's with all the emergency vehicles and what's that awful smell?"

"I'll tell you later. But right now, we need to get out of here."

Laura and Jake were already in their seats. Laura glanced at Marc, then rolled her eyes.

"Good luck if you think we're going to get out of here anytime soon," she said.

Marc remembered seeing signs for the Maintenance Personnel Entrance Gate when he'd visited Goodspeed earlier in the day. But to get there he would have to maneuver around the course to the other side of the property, bucking the lines of cars attempting to exit through the patrons' gates. The horns from impatient drivers were being drowned out by the sirens of the first responders coming onto the property.

"Buckle up," Marc said and pulled out of the parking space. He got behind a police car that was heading in the direction of the eighteenth green. Cars heading toward them veered off to the side to allow the police car through. Marc saw the road that he remembered would take him toward the maintenance barn coming up on his left. When the police car passed the intersection and continued straight, Marc, ignoring a chorus of car horns, veered left and headed for the barn.

As he passed the maintenance barn, he noticed a couple of nondescript cars were parked next to its open door. Marc recognized them as police detective cars.

Probably looking to talk to Bill Goodspeed. No doubt, he will have some answering to do.

Chapter Eighteen

Marc followed the narrow road past the barn to the gate that Goodspeed had suggested, but the gate was partially blocked by an SUV with the name of a security company on it. A female security officer was standing next to the vehicle. Marc stopped behind the SUV.

When the guard approached Marc's SUV, he recognized her. She was the K9 officer he'd seen at the Billiards Room Restaurant the night before, and on the golf course with the Belgian Malinois K9 earlier in the week.

"Why is this gate closed?" Marc asked.

Ignoring Marc's question, she said, "I need to see some ID, sir."

Marc noticed that she took note of his vehicle's license plate. He handed her his State Police retirement identification. Like the State Department Security man had done twenty minutes before, she compared his face to the ID.

"Enjoying retirement?" she asked.

"It's okay. But I still work." Marc handed her one of his business cards.

She examined it. "Why are you exiting through this gate, Mr. LaRose?"

Marc noticed her name tag, Rebecca. "The other gates are jammed. Mr. Goodspeed, the course superintendent, suggested that we use this one."

The guard returned Marc's ID, but held onto his card.

"All right, can you get around my car?" she asked.

"I think so," Marc replied.

She went to the gate and started to open it, then hesitated, "You know, you look sort of familiar."

"Yeah, I saw you last night at the Billiard Room Restaurant, as well as on the course. My daughter's boyfriend was playing in the match. I was his caddy." He motioned with his thumb toward Jake sitting in the back seat next to Ann Marie. "I remember you were working security on the fourth hole."

"Oh yeah, the Canadian amateur."

Then, looking toward Jake, she said, "Understand you did pretty well. Congratulations."

"Thank you, ma'am," Jake said.

"Too bad the tournament had to end like this. But we'll figure it out, eventually," she said, glancing at his business card again. "Have a nice day, uh, Mr. LaRose."

When Marc cleared the gate, he looked in his rearview mirror. The guard had swung the gate closed. The short road from the course emptied onto a main thoroughfare. It was busy with traffic, including an abundance of first responders heading toward the main gate.

"Nice job getting us out of there," Laura said. "For a while, I thought we were going to be stuck there the rest of the afternoon."

"I'll take that as a compliment," Marc said. "But, as you can see, we still have some maneuvering to get across the river and back to Aiken."

Rather than take the interstate, the way they'd come, Marc followed the SUV's GPS and found a two-lane highway that brought them through an area called Beech Island on the South Carolina side of the river. Several of the local businesses had steel cages strung across their front windows. When he hit the button to lock the doors, no one commented.

It took another half hour to get back to Rose Hill. It felt good to return to the relative serenity of Aiken and their hotel. Marc noticed that the parking lot was mostly empty. Many of the inn's patrons were probably stuck at the golf course, he figured.

Marc parked the SUV. "What time does our flight leave tomorrow?"

"We fly out of Columbia at 2:30 in the afternoon," Laura said.

Marc glanced at the dashboard clock. It was almost 4:00 p.m.

Everyone piled out of the car and headed toward the Inn's front entrance, Jake proudly carrying his trophy in one arm while clinging to Ann Marie with the other.

"I don't know if anyone has any plans for this evening, but first thing I'm doing is taking a shower and wash this chlorine stink off my body," Marc said.

"Good idea, Dad," Ann Marie said. "The inside of that car smells like an old laundromat."

Laura was noticeably quiet.

A half hour later, Marc was out of the shower and dressed in a change of clothing. Jake and Ann Marie had wandered off, apparently to be by themselves. He picked up his phone and hit the number he had for Bill Goodspeed. He was curious to find out what was happening at the golf course. The phone rang several times. Just as it was going to voice mail, Marc heard a tired voice answer, "Hello." It was Goodspeed.

"Bill, Marc LaRose. What's happening?"

"Who? Oh yeah, the investigator. You still here, on the course somewhere?"

Marc could hear the tension in Bill's voice, "No, I took your suggestion and left through the Maintenance Gate. We're back in Aiken. Just thought I'd give you a call and see how things are going, but by the tone of your voice, it doesn't sound so good."

Marc heard Bill exhale into his phone. "It's a giant cluster-fuck is how it's going. Every federal police agency you can think of has been called in. The news people, CNN, Fox, MSNBC, and the locals are crawling all over the place. The Feds won't let anyone get close to the eighteenth hole; it's all roped off and ringed with security. It's a wonder they let you leave the property. They're taking statements from practically everyone who was near the hole when the attack went down."

Marc thought about Bill's revelations. "Just thinking. The chlorine gas that was emitted through the sprinkler system had to come from somewhere, and probably not the Augusta Water and Sewer Department. That leaves the underground fertilizer tanks as the most probable source of gas. Those tanks were recently replaced by Apex Irrigation, and apparently, Apex has control of the irrigation timing, right?"

After a brief silence, Bill asked, "You thinking what I'm thinking?"

"That someone at Apex could be a suspect in this scheme? Yeah," Marc said. "Bill, how familiar are you with their facility?"

"The one in Aiken? Why, you thinking of breaking in there and rummaging around?"

"Breaking into a building without the owner's permission would be against the law; I think it's called burglary," Marc said. "And rummaging around sounds kind of amateurish. I was thinking something more in the lines of conducting some field research. Besides, we wouldn't be breaking in if we used a key."

"You have a key to the Apex building? How did you—"

Marc cut Goodspeed off. "What time can you meet me tonight?"

"Mr. LaRose, I want to get to the bottom of this as bad as anyone else, but…" his voice trailed off.

Marc could tell that Bill would need some convincing, "Look, I think the people at Apex killed your friend, Zach Saylor. It appears that Zach suspected the new owners were up to something and weren't going to stop until they succeeded."

"Wouldn't it be prudent to take your suspicions to the police?" Goodspeed asked. "I mean, that is their job."

"Why would they listen to me? I'm just a stand-in caddy from upstate New York down for the tournament. You're the club superintendent. You know the irrigation system forward and backward and how your course is tied to Apex. All I'm asking is for you to accompany me and show me how they can control the irrigation at the Savannah River Golf Course from the Apex office."

Through the silence that followed, Marc could hear Goodspeed breathing into the phone. He suspected Bill was still unsure.

"Bill, what occurred today was a case of international terrorism. You know more about that irrigation system than anyone else. I need your help."

After a long pause, Bill spoke, "Alright, I just have to get away from here sometime before dark," he said. "What time you want to do this?"

"How about ten this evening? Where can I pick you up?"

"I'll pick you up. You said you're staying at the Rose Hill Hotel?"

"I'll be sitting in one of the rocking chairs out front," Marc said.

"See you then." Goodspeed said, and cut the connection.

After showering, everyone agreed that because this was their last night in Aiken, they would all go out to dinner together. Marc suggested a family restaurant on Whiskey Road near the city's south end of town. No one objected, not even Laura.

The atmosphere at Applebee's was pleasant enough. Marc overheard several patrons discussing the terrorist attack that had occurred earlier. A few even recognized Jake from his appearance on one of the many suspended TV's positioned around the restaurant.

An elderly couple stopped by the table to congratulate Jake, while a few others acknowledged his presence with a friendly wave.

As Marc was finishing his salad, he felt his cell vibrate. He glanced at the phone. He excused himself and walked toward the back of the restaurant where there were fewer patrons present.

"Hello."

"Mr. LaRose, hope I didn't catch you at a bad time."

It was a female caller. Her voice was familiar. As he was about to answer, the caller continued, "If you're available later this evening, I'd like to meet up. I think I have some information that you might be interested in hearing."

"Is this Rebecca?" Marc asked.

"Good to know the chlorine gas hasn't affected your memory," she said.

"Look, Rebecca, we're leaving tomorrow to return home. What's so important that you have to see me this evening?"

"I saw you helping the Israeli Prime Minister on the course today, then motioning for the helicopter to land. Afterwards, you were talking to members of the State Department Security team. What you probably didn't see were the others, men who had arrived earlier and were watching, waiting for something to happen."

Marc glanced back at the table. Laura and Jake were talking about something. Ann Marie glanced over at him.

"Rebecca, if you have information regarding the attack at the golf course, you should report it to the police. Why are you calling me with this?"

"Already tried that. The locals said to call the Feds, but between the FBI, ATF and the DEA, it's alphabetic hysteria as to which agency should take the lead. With the tournament over, the private security company has pretty much washed their hands of the whole affair."

"So again, why are you calling me?"

"I got your card and did some checking. Terrorism seems to follow you around, even on the golf course."

Marc thought a moment. "Can you give me a quick rundown of what you saw?"

"Maybe, but not over the phone," she said.

"Alright, are you familiar with the Rose Hill Hotel in Aiken?"

"Sure, who isn't?"

"Meet me there, tonight, 9:30. I'll be out front, sitting on the porch," Marc said, remembering he was also meeting Bill Goodspeed there a half hour later.

"See you then," she said. There was a click, and the line went dead.

"Everything alright, Dad?" Ann Marie asked when Marc returned to the table.

"Yeah sure, no problem," Marc said. Noticing she wasn't convinced, he continued, "That was just some guy from an insurance company back home. He called looking for my charges to conduct a slip and fall investigation at the Plattsburgh Mall. They're going to email me the particulars tomorrow."

"Uh huh," she said.

Apparently, she's unconvinced. Wonder where she gets that from?

Attempting to change the subject, Marc ordered a carafe of wine to celebrate Jake's success on winning the low amateur trophy.

An hour later, Marc returned to his room and turned on the TV. Not surprisingly, all local programming had been overridden by the events at the Savannah River Golf Links earlier in the day. According to the newscaster, there were no fatalities reported; however, several people had been transported to area hospitals and were recovering from the effects of chlorine gas exposure. A spokesman for the Israeli Prime Minister said only that he had been treated at the Doctors Hospital, was released and recovering at an undisclosed location.

There was no mention of the impending meeting between the Prime Minister and the U.S. Secretary of State.

Marc heard a light tap on his door. Through the peephole, he saw it was Laura.

Figuring that she had overheard his TV, he opened the door.

"The kids are off somewhere, and I thought now would be a good time for us to talk. May I come in?"

Marc opened the door and moved to one side. "Sure, what's up?" he asked, as she entered. He closed the door and pointed to a chair that was positioned in front of the room's desk, then he muted the TV.

She sat, exhaled and crossed her legs. "Before we leave Aiken and head for home, I'd like to clear the air about my behavior the other night."

She must be referring to the incident that had been witnessed by the gentleman in the room across the hall, he figured. "If you're referring to our little episode in the hallway, no explanation is necessary. Remember, we'd been drinking."

Laura sat quietly for a moment. "So that was all it was, just a 'little episode'?"

"Alright, my bad. Poor choice of words." Marc paused. "Look, I appreciate all you've done for Ann Marie and me. However, my plate has been pretty full lately, caddying for Jake and getting my head wrapped around the news of my daughter's impending marriage to your son. Not to mention what I suspect has been happening at the Apex Irrigation Company, then today, with the attack at the golf course. Maybe I haven't been as attentive to your feelings as I should have been."

"Well, for what it's worth, I want to thank you for your understanding."

"Sorry. Are we talking about two different things?" Marc asked with a confused look.

"No, I don't believe so. You have to understand that my life has taken a few turns in the past couple of years. It started with my husband leaving me, then Jake going off to college in Plattsburgh, and now with his intentions of marrying Ann Marie, I guess I'm feeling somewhat abandoned."

Marc could see her eyes begin to well-up. He reached in his drawer and retrieved a fresh handkerchief and handed it to her. Laura dabbed the tears.

"I see the relationship you and Ann Marie share," she said. "I don't have that with Jake and don't know how to make it happen. What I did, in the hallway was wrong, and I apologize. Sometimes I just feel so alone, and of course, the alcohol didn't help." She snuffed back more tears.

Marc hesitated, giving her a moment to recover. "Honestly, thinking back on it, it's probably a good thing that old guy showed up when he did, or, who knows, maybe we'd both be apologizing. I think your feelings are normal. You have a lot going for you, a fantastic son who happens to love my daughter, a great business that I understand is doing very well, and to be candid, you're a bright, attractive woman. I'm probably the last person to give matrimonial advice. After all, I've had more than my share of problems in that regard. The best thing I can say is to be yourself. Good things happen to good people."

Laura dabbed her eyes again, then sighed deeply. She seemed to study the wallpaper pattern for a long moment. "You know something, Marc LaRose?"

"What's that?"

"That's probably the nicest thing anyone has ever said to me. Thank you."

"Don't mention it. So, what time should we leave tomorrow? It's about an hour or so to Columbia. It's a small airport. We shouldn't have much trouble checking in and—what?

He noticed Laura was giving him a look,

"Do you always act so flippant when praised?"

"Sorry. I didn't mean to sound superficial. Guess I have a few things on my mind, and, well, I meant what I said."

Laura stood. "Thank you for listening and for your advice. I just wanted to clear the air before we left."

Marc rose from his chair. "Look, Laura, with what's happened today, there's a little unfinished business I should attend to this evening. But, if there's anything I can do for you, please let me know."

She gave him a doubtful look. "No problem, Marc. I have some packing to do myself. Besides, I need some time to reassess my plans for the future. Good luck with whatever you have in mind. I'll see you in the morning, then."

"Till then," Marc said, and opened the door as Laura left the room. A moment later the door clicked shut and she was gone.

Marc looked at the clock on the nightstand. It was just after 7:00 p.m. He made his way to the lobby where several people had gathered. By their dress and haggard appearance, he suspected they had just returned from the golf tournament.

Marc passed through the main entrance onto the long front porch. A few people were already sitting in the line of rocking chairs, facing the street. He chose a seat at the far end, wanting to be alone with his thoughts. As he was contemplating his upcoming meetings with Rebecca and Bill Goodspeed, he felt the presence of someone close by. When he looked at the chair beside him, he saw that a gentleman had taken the seat. He was busy lighting a Meerschaum pipe that appeared to have been carved in the likeness of a bearded man. Although Marc's initial desire was to be alone with his thoughts, the pleasant aroma of pipe tobacco that drifted in his direction had its benefits. Shortly after, Marc felt the man's gaze. He glanced over at him.

"Sorry. If the smoke offends, I'll—."

"No, not at all," Marc interrupted. "Actually, I used to smoke a pipe, but gave it up years ago. My wife didn't approve."

"Too bad, but I understand. Sometimes it's prudent to surrender a passing desire rather than incur the wrath of someone whose presence is dear."

Marc estimated the man to be in his late 60's. His unruly mane of grey hair covered the tops of his ears and was accompanied by an equally unruly moustache. Despite the unseasonably warm weather, 80 degrees or so, the man wore a tweed jacket over a long-sleeved shirt.

"You sound like a philosophy instructor I once had in college," Marc said.

The corners of the man's mouth turned upward, but only for an instant. He drew deeply on his Meerschaum, and while tilting his head slightly upwards, he released a long plume of the mellow essence. "I've been accused of many things, but this is the first time I've been called a philosopher."

"Sorry, I didn't mean to—,"

"No apology necessary. Actually, I'm into politics," the stranger said.

"So, you're a politician, then?" Marc said.

"Well, not exactly. I'm a consultant for a local project. And, as with many projects, especially with those that may be viewed as somewhat controversial, people need to be persuaded that the long-term benefits of a particular endeavor usually outweigh the initial or immediate costs."

Marc's defenses went up as he again watched the man draw deeply on his pipe, this time holding the smoke inside his lungs for a moment, seemingly lost in thought.

"That's ironic," Marc said.

After releasing the pent-up cloud, the man asked. "How's that?"

"Just that, the fellow that I mentioned, the philosopher? Well, come to find out, he wasn't a philosopher, or a teacher. He was actually a defense contractor."

The man appeared unfazed by Marc's unsolicited evaluation. After another slow draw on his pipe, he slowly exhaled and watched the plume drift toward the street in front of them. "It appears your reputation as a quick wit is only slightly diminished by your grasp of reality, Mr. LaRose."

Marc studied the man's profile. "So, you know my name. What do I call you?"

"Call me what you like. The question you should be asking is: Why am I talking to you at all?"

Marc felt the hair on the back of his neck stand up. "I suspect I know. How is the Israeli Prime Minister doing, by the way?"

"A bit better than we'd hoped for, but the long-term prognosis has not yet been determined."

"Apparently, the attack at the golf course was a failure then," Marc said.

The man again drew on his pipe, but the flame appeared to have extinguished. He gently tapped the spent ash into the palm of his hand and dropped the ashes on the concrete next to his chair. "A momentary setback. More importantly, you have a decision to make, Mr. LaRose. You can leave Aiken, while your family and friends are still in good health, or stay, and risk losing what is dear to you."

Marc glared at the stranger. "That sounds like a threat."

The man slowly slipped his pipe in his jacket side-pocket. "To threaten would imply the possibility of future harm. Please do not take my words as an idle threat. They are meant to provide you with ample warning. Return to where you came from, sooner rather than later. It would be the sensible thing for you to do. What happens here, in Aiken, is none of your affair. Your life, your ex-wife and your on-again-off-again amours, are all located in upstate New York.

The prudent thing for you to do would be to gather your loved ones and simply leave, while you can."

Marc remained silent as the stranger stood. "I understand your flight from Columbia leaves at two o'clock tomorrow afternoon. The traffic in Columbia can be a bear at any time of the day. I'd suggest you leave early."

As the man turned to leave, Marc got up from his chair. The stranger hesitated.

Marc stepped close to him, and glared down into the man's rheumy eyes. Marc was a good three inches taller. "Before you slither back to your library or tobacco-soaked den or wherever the fuck you hide out, listen, because I will not say this again. If anything should happen to anyone I care for, I will find you and whoever else is accountable. I will not contact any authority. It will not be necessary. Not unlike the COVID pandemic, I will quietly remove you and your kind from existence. If you believe your veiled threats will, in any way, impede what I think should be done, you will soon find that you're fucking with the wrong man."

The man looked up at Marc. His smug expression had not changed. "Have a pleasant evening, Mr. LaRose."

Then, as if on command, a black sedan pulled up to the curb. The man got in the back seat and firmly shut the door. The car's windows were lightly tinted, barely distorting the man's image. He did not look at Marc. The car pulled away. It turned left at the end of the street and was gone.

Chapter Nineteen

Although Marc had warned the man with the Meerschaum pipe about messing with his family, he had to assume everyone was exposed and being watched. He needed to inform Ann Marie and Jake to remain in the hotel for the evening, which, he figured would be an easy sell. Laura, on the other hand would be a challenge. Marc was pretty sure that Ann Marie and Jake were still in his room. Through the door he could hear the sound of the TV playing. Not wanting to interrupt, Marc knocked before entering. It was the prudent thing to do.

"Oh, hi Daddy! We didn't expect you back so soon," Ann Marie said, rearranging her hair, then straightening her blouse.

Jake's face was flushed.

"Sorry, didn't mean to interrupt. But, I have a favor to ask," Marc said.

"Yeah, sure. What's up?" she asked.

"Would you mind staying in the hotel this evening? I have to go out in a while and I'd feel more comfortable if I knew where you were."

The two kids exchanged glances.

"Marc, is there something wrong? Anything I can do to help?" Jake asked.

"No, everything's good. But there is one more thing."

"What's that?" Jake asked.

"Check in on your mom every now and then. I think she's alright, but she's had a long day, and it would be nice if someone looked in on her."

"No problem, Marc," Jake replied. "Don't worry about us, we'll be fine." He glanced toward Ann Marie. "And I'll make sure to check in on Mom."

Satisfied the kids and Laura were where they should be, Marc went back down to the lobby. He noticed it was beginning to fill up as more guests straggled in from their day at the golf course. Several were missing their hats and most looked tired and bedraggled from the ordeal. He glanced at his phone. It was just after eight o'clock. With a few more hours to wait, Marc ordered a glass of white wine and took a seat at the bar. As he was contemplating what he needed to do, he felt someone slide onto the stool next to him.

"Figured I'd find you in here." It was a woman's voice. At first glance, he didn't recognize her, although the voice was familiar. Her long brown hair that had been tied up under her guard cap now hung loose on her shoulders. Her uniform had been exchanged for a dark, loose fitting blouse and a pair of designer jeans. She had traded her clunky work boots for a pair of light grey Sketchers. Instead of a purse, she was carrying a large envelope.

"Hello, Rebecca. I thought we were to meet around nine-thirty this evening?" Marc glanced at his phone that he had laid on the bar. "It's only a little after eight."

"Yeah, well, I came across something I figured you'd want to see before the lights went out, so to speak."

Marc felt his eyebrows raise. "Okay, I'll bite. Whatcha got?"

"You're probably aware that all visitors and patrons attending the Monarch Golf Tournament had to go through specific gates on entry."

"Yes. I believe that's standard procedure for most tournaments of this size," Marc said.

"And that all gates were monitored with high-definition cameras equipped with internet protocol and capable of identifying people we suspect of carrying out nefarious activities?"

"Uh, no not really. I mean, I was aware the course had surveillance capabilities, but not to the extent you're describing."

"Well, they do. Not long after you left the course today, I gained access to some of their video. I've printed out a few photos of people I suspect may have had a hand in the attack." She laid the envelope on the bar.

"Do you have any idea who these people are?" Marc nodded toward the envelope.

"Not really, they all have a list of aliases. We couldn't connect their real names to faces."

"Have you notified the authorities?"

"Didn't have to. They have everything we have and probably more."

"Is your vehicle nearby?" Marc asked.

"Just around the corner."

"I'd like to look at the photos, but not here. Let's go sit in your car." Marc finished his wine and picked up the envelope. He followed Rebecca out of the hotel's main entrance to a white Ford Explorer parked close to where he'd had the discussion with the Meerschaum pipe smoker earlier that evening.

The vehicle's lights blinked as Rebecca pressed the fob button to unlock the doors. Marc got in on the passenger side. Rebecca slid in behind the wheel.

When she switched the interior map light on, Marc opened the envelope and slid out four 8 x 10 black-and-white glossies. They were close-ups of three white males, captured at different entrance gates at the golf course. The time stamps indicated the photos were taken over a ten-minute span. There was also an aerial photo of a portion of the parking lot.

"You suspect these men had something to do with the attack at the course today?" Marc asked, "Why these three in particular?"

"As you're probably aware, the gates open at 7:00 a.m. These guys all showed up within the first hour, the busiest time, every day, entering through different gates."

"Okay," Marc said, urging her on.

"Each day that I observed them, all three would usually get together at a different spot about the same time for a short while. Then they would separate."

"And you thought this was suspicious because..."

"Because it revealed a pattern of behavior. Entering the grounds separately through different gates, then meeting up. Who does that? And once they were on the confines of the course, they didn't seem to follow any particular player, or even a group of players. Rather, they seemed to be focused on course layout and security."

"What do you mean?" Marc asked.

"The Monarch Golf Tournament requires that discreet surveillance be conducted to monitor the gallery, mostly to assist in evacuating the course in the case of impending inclement weather or any other emergency. But we also watch for more nefarious conduct, such as someone interfering with or impeding the performance of a particular player, shoplifting, or other criminal conduct. When I wasn't physically on the course, I was assisting in monitoring these hidden cameras."

"So you were looking at each other?"

"Not exactly. Without the proper equipment, the cameras are virtually impossible to detect. These guys seemed interested in determining routes of egress and ingress, especially in the area around the eighteenth green."

"Egress and ingress?" Marc asked.

"Sorry. That's security speak for leaving and entering. They seemed interested in determining how to get onto and off the property without being noticed."

Marc exhaled, "So they arrive at different times and through different gates. Once on the property, where did they usually meet up?"

"Different places, but usually near one of the food concessions. They arrived early for breakfast every day, at least on the days that I saw them."

"And how many days did you observe them?"

"I first noticed them on Tuesday, the day of the second practice round. When they showed up again on Wednesday, I alerted my supervisor. We then monitored their presence on Thursday, Saturday, and, of course, today."

"What happened on Friday?"

"Either they didn't come or we may have missed them."

Marc again studied the photos. "Okay, exactly what was it they did that got your attention?"

"Well, Tuesday, the first day that I noticed them, I didn't really suspect much. I mean, I saw them sitting in the bleachers near the fourth hole. They were talking and drinking coffee. But when I walked by them, I noticed that they stopped talking and looked straight ahead, even though there were no golfers in the area at the time."

"Alright," Marc said, encouraging her to continue.

"I still didn't think much of it, and like I said, I didn't see them on Friday, although they could have been there. But if they were, they got onto the course without going through one of the regular gates or the cameras would have picked them up. I think attendance that day was a little over fifty thousand, so they could have been there, just not seen. Then, on Saturday I saw them again, several times actually. And, just like Thursday, I still didn't give them a lot of attention.

People have tickets for all four of the regular tournament days and I often see the same people throughout the week. But Saturday, then again today, they seemed to hang around the area of the last two or three holes. They didn't have any drugs or explosives or my dog would have alerted on them. It was mainly their behavior that made me curious."

"Tell me a little more about their behavior," Marc said.

"It was right before the incident at the eighteenth hole, before the chlorine gas was released through the sprinkler system. The spectators who had been watching the progress of the tournament at different holes along the course began following the final twosome, which is usual for any tournament. But I noticed that right after the final group had teed off on the eighteenth hole, these three didn't follow along, they held back."

Marc considered what he'd heard. "What happened after that?"

"Later, when I heard the president of the Savannah River Golf Links introducing the winners, these three turned away and started toward the parking lot. To me, it was like they knew something was going to happen and didn't want to be there."

"Were you in the area when the gas was released?"

"Yes, I was near the eighteenth tee box. A large number of patrons had gathered around the green to listen to the club president make the presentations to the winners of the tournament. That's when I saw these three running back toward the pedestrian gate located near the concession stand."

"That doesn't sound unusual. Maybe they just wanted to leave early to get a jump on the crowd," Marc said.

"Yeah, I thought of that, but why would they be running. It was like they knew something was going to happen and didn't want to be caught up in it. Of course, about a minute later, the gas was released, and all hell broke loose."

Marc continued to study the photos as he thought about Rebecca's recital of the day's events at the course.

"Could you tell if these guys left together, or did they split up?"

"Not for sure, but I assume they left together. We don't have cameras set up at all of the exits, and I don't know what they would have gained by leaving through different gates."

"Then, for all you know, they could still be on the property somewhere?"

"No. We swept the property thoroughly as the police were conducting their interviews. We didn't find anyone."

"So, who the hell are these guys, and where did they go?" Marc asked, holding the photos.

"That's why I came to talk to you," she said.

"What do you mean?"

"Although we don't have cameras at the exits, we do have them in the parking lots. We use them to look for possible acts of vandalism during and after the tournament. We picked up their trail when they got to the main parking lot." Rebecca pointed to the last photo that Marc held. The photo displayed a time stamp.

"This is a wide-angle view," Rebecca said, pointing at the vehicle in the photo. "If you look closely, you can see the images of three people next to that minivan. Unfortunately, their faces are hidden from view, but, as you can tell by the similarity of their clothing, we believe these are the same three guys leaving right after the attack."

"Were you able to get the license plate number off the van?" Marc asked.

Rebecca pointed at a spot on the photo, "As you can see, one of the men standing at the back of the van partially obscured the plate number. With enhanced imaging techniques however, we were able to determine it was a Ford rental."

Marc studied the photo. "How do you know it's a rental when you couldn't read the license plate number."

"See that little sticker?" Rebecca said, pointing to a spot on the vehicle's rear window. "That's a rental car sticker."

Marc squinted at the tiny white rectangle, "Really hard to see it. Any luck tracking the partial plate number?"

"Very difficult. These things move around from dealer to dealer like pieces on a chess board."

Marc started to ask another question, but Rebecca cut him off. "With enhanced imaging however, we were able to connect the sticker to a rental agency. It's a black Ford Transit Connect XL belonging to Budget Rental located right here in Aiken."

"Interesting. Have you had a chance to contact them?"

"Yeah. They gave us a name," she said, then referred to a notepad. "It was rented to a David Ackerman. He used a Florida driver's license with an address in Miami. The Feds checked the address. It doesn't exist."

"Ackerman? I suppose it makes sense for a terrorist to use a family name that probably originated in the country he may be out to destroy. I assume the vehicle hasn't been returned?" Marc said.

"No, and I don't expect it will be," Rebecca said.

They were both silent for a moment as Marc studied the photographs.

"Look, Mr. LaRose, the reason I'm giving you this information is that, I thought maybe, with your background and what you did at the course today, you might have a lead. Something you could share regarding who may be responsible for what happened."

Marc thought how to answer. "How well do you know the course superintendant?"

"I know who he is. I've seen him around the course. He seems like a hard worker and is cooperative, but that's about all I know."

Marc glanced at his phone. "He's supposed to meet me later this evening."

"Why? You think he's connected with the attack?" she asked.

"No, I think he may be able to help us. Have you ever heard of the Apex Irrigation Company?"

"Vaguely. I think they had something to do with installing the irrigation system at the course, right?"

"Correct. Bill worked with the people at Apex. Don't know if you realize it, but Apex has recently, in the past year or so, changed hands."

"No, I hadn't heard. And this is significant because—?"

"It may be nothing. But, Goodspeed informed me that the new owner is a man named Sajak Akhtar."

"Akhtar? Rebecca repeated. "Do you know if this Akhtar is an American citizen?" Rebecca asked.

"I doubt it. I understand he's a recent immigrant to the U.S."

Rebecca pursed her lips in thought. "I have a contact at ICE, Immigration and Customs Enforcement. Maybe they could help us with that."

Suddenly the interior of the SUV was filled with the sounds of one of Marc's favorite tunes. It was his phone's ring tone set to Dave Brubeck's 'Take Five.' He glanced at the number, but didn't recognize it.

"Hello," Marc answered.

"Marc, this is Bill Goodspeed. "

"Hey Bill. I was just thinking about you. Are we still on for tonight?"

There was a pause. "That's why I'm calling. I can't. Something's come up."

Marc noticed tension in Bill's voice. "Bill, what's the matter? Everything alright?"

Marc waited for a long moment, and when Bill didn't answer, Marc asked, "Bill, what's the matter?"

"They've got my wife."

"Bill, who has your wife? What are you talking about?"

"I received a call a few minutes ago. I didn't recognize the voice. He just said, 'stay where you are, do not go home. Your wife is with us and if you try to leave the course, or say anything to anyone, you will never see her alive again.'"

"That's it? Did you happen to notice the caller's phone number?"

"No, it was blocked. It came in on my cell. I'm calling you on a pre-paid I keep as a backup. There's law enforcement all over the place. The course is still on total lockdown from the gas attack. "

"Have you told the police about your wife's kidnapping?"

"No, the caller said that if I did, I'd never see her again."

"So, you're doubly stuck. You can't leave because of the attack and you can't inform the police of your wife's kidnapping. I'm so sorry, Bill." Marc exhaled into his cell. "Have the cops talked to you about the attack?"

"You kidding? They grilled me for two hours. They haven't talked to you yet?" Bill asked.

"No, other than the State Department security that were on the scene when the helicopter landed, I haven't seen anyone."

"You got away just in time, but I'm sure they'll catch up to you eventually. They just haven't got around to you yet."

Marc glanced in Rebecca's direction. "Bill, I know you've got a lot on your plate, but if you wanted to look inside the Apex building for any evidence that someone there may be involved in this mess, where would you start?"

Again, there was a long silence on Marc's end of the line, and just as he was about to repeat his question, Goodspeed spoke. "At this point, all I want is to see my wife safe again. But if I thought Akhtar is hiding something, and no doubt I think he is, I'd access his computer."

"The computer at the plant?"

"No, not the company computer. That's in the main office. I seriously doubt that you'll find anything incriminating there. It's mostly full of billing information. Besides, he's too smart. No, I'd start in his office. There's a desk computer, plus he has a laptop. Trouble is, he always takes his laptop with him wherever he goes."

"So where does he usually go?" Marc asked.

"Besides work, he goes home. You know anything about the hamlet of Jackson?"

Marc thought a moment. "I've heard of it. Isn't it somewhere near the Savannah River Site?"

"Yeah, close. It's at the end of Atomic Road, near the entrance to the Bomb Plant. Akhtar has a large home at the end of the road. From his front porch you can see the Site's main security gate."

"You've been there?" Marc asked.

"Once. Just after he bought Apex. Said he needed help moving a few things. That was just before he put up the fence."

"Fence?" Marc asked.

"Yeah, he had a six foot cyclone fence installed shortly after he moved in. He said it was to keep his Dobermans from running off."

Marc thought a moment. "Does he live alone?"

"I guess so, just him and his dogs. But like I said, it's a large house, which I thought was peculiar. It's a two-story and has about four bedrooms and an attached three-car garage."

"Sounds like a lot of room for one person," Marc said.

"That's what I thought, but I wasn't in any position to pry. Also, he's a private kind of guy, keeps to himself. But like I said, he doesn't go anywhere without that laptop."

Marc thought a moment. "Bill, I appreciate the info. Hopefully, this mess can get straightened out and your wife returned to you unharmed."

"Thanks, Marc. You hear anything, let me know."

"Will do," Marc said and ended the call.

"Was that the Course Superintendent?" Rebecca asked.

"Yeah, he's in a jam. The Fed's won't let him leave the course until they're through with their investigation, and now he's learned that someone, probably whoever is responsible for the attack, has kidnapped his wife and is threatening to kill her if he says anything."

"I don't get it. What is it that the kidnappers think he knows?"

"Well, for starters, he's pretty sure that a friend of his, a former employee of Apex died at the irrigation plant just before the start of the tournament. His death has been ruled accidental, but Bill takes issue with that decision. He thinks his friend was murdered."

"Why would Bill suspect someone at Apex killed his friend?"

"His friend's name was Zach Saylor. He was responsible for designing the irrigation system at the Savannah River Golf Links. Saylor died of chlorine gas inhalation and, like I said, his death was ruled an accident. Bill had known Zach for years. Besides being a chemist, Saylor was an expert in the field of landscape irrigation and fertilization. Bill is convinced that Zach Saylor's death was no accident."

Rebecca was quiet as she appeared to think about Marc's statement. "I gotta say, this shit's getting deeper by the moment."

"I agree. And it all seems to be pointing toward Apex and its owner, Mr. Sajak Akhtar."

Rebecca seemed to mull over what Marc was telling her.

"I have to ask, Marc. Why do you care? I mean, your future son-in-law was the tournament's low amateur. Why not just pack up his trophy and boogey back on up to New York State?"

"Because somebody's put my daughter, my future son-in-law, and me in danger. Any one of us could have been seriously hurt, or even killed today. I'd have a hard time walking away from this without at least trying to find out who is responsible and making the fucker pay. Simple as that."

"I see your point, but don't you think it's about time we get the police involved?" Rebecca asked.

"And tell them what? That we suspect someone at Apex is responsible for the attack on the Israeli Prime Minister at the Golf Tournament? We have suspicions, but no direct evidence, certainly nothing they could use to get an arrest warrant. Plus, Goodspeed has been told that if the police get involved in his wife's disappearance, she would be killed."

"So, where do we begin?" Rebecca asked.

Marc glanced at the dashboard clock. It was almost 9:00 p.m. "The offices of Apex Irrigation. That's where this mess started. Hopefully, there's still something there we can use."

"Sounds good, but just how do you propose we get inside? I suppose we could knock on the door and pretend we're police officers and demand to look around inside?"

Marc looked over at her with a grin, "No, already tried that, didn't work out so well." Marc held up the key he had received from Zach Saylor's wife. "I have a different plan."

"Where did you get—"

Marc held up his hand. "You don't want to know."

Rebecca returned the photos to the envelope and turned the key in the vehicle's ignition. "Which way to Apex?" she asked.

Chapter Twenty

Five minutes later Marc directed Rebecca to the deserted Texaco gas station where he had parked a few nights before. He pointed her to the spot at the back of the lot and told her to cut the engine. Leaving the vehicle, Marc motioned for Rebecca to follow him around the deserted gas station. With the help of a partial moon and clear skies, he led the way through the brushy field toward the Apex building. The cyclone fencing and the outline of deserted vans were clearly visible along the back of the property. A sudden rustle in the brush nearby caused them to stop in their tracks.

Rebecca quickly withdrew a semi-automatic firearm from her belt and crouched in the standard policeman's 'ready' position.

Marc held up his hand. "It's okay, just a wild boar."

"If you say so," she whispered as she slowly re-holstered the gun.

Cautiously the pair continued toward the perimeter fencing that outlined the rear portion of the Apex property. Marc located the channel under the fence that he suspected had been created by the wild boar. Laying on his back, then grasping the bottom of the fencing, he pulled himself under the fence to the other side.

"Okay, your turn," he whispered.

In a few seconds, Rebecca was crouching next to Marc, inside the fence.

Marc could see a few lights on inside the building. Most of the external lighting filled the parking area off to the building's right-hand side. Keeping low, Marc continued toward the rear of the structure following the same path he'd used on his previous visit. He passed the large window that he'd tried to open before, and headed toward the side of the building where the perimeter fencing ended. Just inside the fence, he spotted an exterior door. Unlike the main door out front, there was no window in this door and no light over it. Through the fencing he could see that the front and side parking lots appeared empty, save for two vans with the Apex name and logo imprinted on them.

Marc retrieved the key he had obtained from Zach's widow, and slowly inserted it into the door's keyway. Alert for any alarm that unlocking the door might cause, he turned it slowly. A muffled metallic click indicated the lock was disengaged. He carefully turned the knob and pulled it open. If there was an alarm, Marc figured it would be of the silent variety that would alert someone off the premises, giving him at least a few minutes to look around. After the two entered the building, he eased the door closed behind them.

They had entered a dark hallway. For a moment, they both stood still, listening for any sounds. Dead silence. Marc retrieved his cell phone and turned on its flashlight. A quick look around revealed three interior doors leading from the hallway to other parts of the building. He carefully cracked the door open to their right. Lights glowed from computer monitors on desks. He could see a long counter and an exterior door leading to the front parking area where he and Laura had been when they visited a few nights before.

Marc closed the door, then turned the knob on the center door. A lone florescent ceiling light had been left on inside. It was a work room with several drafting cubicles along one side. In the center of the room he observed a large green polyethylene tank, probably the type that had been installed at the Savannah River Golf Links, he suspected. The tank was suspended from the ceiling by a heavy chain. He also noticed several workstations around the room. Likely the main production area, he figured.

Glancing toward the third door he saw that it was protected with a commercial keypad locking device. He suspected that messing with it could set off an alarm.

Rebecca re-opened the center door. They both slid through and entered the production room with the ominous polyethylene tank, swaying ever so slightly with the gentle currents of air that surrounded it. It hung from a chain that was attached to a track on the ceiling. The track led to an overhead door at the opposite side of the room.

Marc led Rebecca past the first cubicle. Off to their left, a small window appeared to lead to the room that was guarded by the keypad locking device.

"That must be Akhtar's office. I bet he uses that window to keep tabs on his employees," Marc whispered.

Marc went to the window and peered inside the room. There was a large metal desk and several TV monitors attached to the wall. Two more monitors sat toward the back of the desktop. A few of the monitors had been turned off; however, two were left on. One looked to show the outside of the building, at the front of the office.

"That's why they saw us coming when Laura and I visited here a few nights ago," Marc said.

The other monitor seemed to show an entrance or exit gate and a roadway to some kind of facility. Well-lit security booths monitored incoming traffic.

"Wonder where the hell that is?" Marc said pointing to its screen.

Rebecca leaned over Marc's shoulder and studied the monitor for a moment. "Marc, I know where that is," she said. The tenor of her voice tensed. "This guy's monitoring one of the main gates to the Savannah River Site, probably from where he lives, out near Jackson."

Marc was momentarily stunned. "You think Akhtar is keeping tabs on who's coming and going at the country's primary nuclear weapons production site?"

"It looks that way, but why?" she asked.

Marc hesitated, "Probably for the same reason someone would attack the golf course with chlorine gas and try to kill the Israeli Prime Minister," Marc said.

Rebecca seemed to consider Marc's statement. "Marc, you think the attack and monitoring the Site from here are somehow connected?"

"One thing that I've learned in my line of work is that you can't believe in coincidences." Marc continued to stare at the monitor. "Rebecca, do you have any contacts inside the Site?"

She was quiet for a moment. "Maybe," she said.

"What's that mean?" Marc asked.

"Remember when you saw me the other night at the billiards place?"

"Yeah, you were sitting with some people who work out at the Site."

"Right. A few of my friends work out there. They usually meet at Billiard's Restaurant once a month or so and they asked me if I would meet them there."

"Okay?" Marc said.

"Anyway, I used to date a guy who worked security at the Site. But that was almost a year ago. He worked odd shifts and we hardly saw each other, so I cut it off."

"You think he'd be interested in knowing that someone like this Akhtar guy is monitoring one of the Site's main gates?" Marc asked.

She hesitated, "Maybe. Not sure what he could do about it, I mean…" Rebecca's thought was interrupted by the muffled sound of a car door closing.

"I think we may have visitors," Marc whispered.

When he pulled Rebecca toward the back of the workroom, they heard someone rattling the outside entrance door that they had entered just minutes before. The two ducked behind the walls of a tool crib that was set along the back of the room. Marc knew it wasn't much of a hiding place, but he figured they would be out of view of anyone entering the room or through the window from Akhtar's office.

A moment later, Marc heard the faint sound of someone punching the buttons on the office door keypad. A slice of light came through the office window. Someone had switched on the overhead lights in Akhtar's office. There was the sound of a door closing, then Marc could hear muffled voices.

Either there were two of them, or someone was talking on a phone, Marc thought.

About a minute later, the office door closed. Almost simultaneously, there was the sound of the workroom door opening, then a bank of overhead florescent lights buzzed to life. Staring from beneath the tool crib shelves, all that Marc could see were two sets of shoes entering the workspace. The sounds of shuffling feet on the concrete floor echoed around the room. Peering from under the tool shelf, Marc could see that one of the men wore dress pants and a pair of black leather dress shoes. The other man wore jeans and work boots. Work Boots was carrying a tower for a desktop computer.

"I'm not going to miss this fucking place," one of them said. His voice was thick with an accent Marc couldn't place. "Are you sure you grabbed all the flash drives that were in my desk drawer?"

"Got'em right here, in my pocket, Mr. Akhtar."

Work Boots patted his jean's pocket.

"Good. According to our contact, the convoy carrying the nuclear material and the warhead Pits is scheduled to depart the Site in a little over an hour. It should be in Atlanta right around eleven o'clock tonight."

"Yes sir, your timing is perfect. They will have no idea what hit them. Most will be tucked into their comfy little beds or watching their pathetic late-night news shows as their own country's nuclear arsenal is unleashed on one of its most advanced urban centers. Absolutely genius!"

"Too early to gloat," Akhtar said. "We have already failed once today. That fucking Israeli Prime Minister is still alive. He needs to pay for the deaths of General Suleimani as well as our best nuclear scientist. To fail again could be catastrophic, not only for you and me, but for our entire movement to regain our position in the Middle East as its primary superpower."

"Yes. I'm afraid that today's episode at the golf course was most unfortunate, Mr. Akhtar. There were unforeseen circumstances and…"

"Enough excuses!" Akhtar said forcefully. "You have only one thing left to do. Our informants have done their job. We know the time and the route the convoy carrying the plutonium Pits will take when it leaves the Savannah River Site. Your job is to see that the convoy is intercepted at the precise location and time we have decided on. How that truckload of nuclear material is deployed is none of your affair. Our team is waiting for us to neutralize the shipment. They will handle the rest."

"Certainly, Mr. Akhtar. Nothing will interfere with the plan. I give you my word."

"I hope so. Your life, your family's lives, and mine depend on it."

Marc was stunned. His hand brushed the grip of his H&K that was secured to his belt, and for an instant, he even contemplated taking the two conspirators into custody and calling the local police. However, the thought quickly passed. He knew that the authorities needed more information to act on. Besides, he suspected any plan as complicated as the one he had just learned about was sure to have built-in redundancies…plans within plans.

"Let's get out of here, there's plenty more to do," Akhtar said. With a soft click, the bank of lighting was extinguished and the door to the work room closed. A few moments later, Marc heard car doors slamming shut, then an engine starting. The sound of the car's movement on the crushed stone parking area diminished and soon it was quiet again.

Marc and Rebecca remained frozen for a full two minutes after Akhtar left, making sure they were indeed alone. Finally, Marc said, "You still have your boyfriend's cell number?"

"Old boyfriend," Rebecca said. She pulled her phone from her pocket. Marc watched as she scrolled through her contacts.

"Yeah, here it is. He's probably either getting ready for work, or sleeping. He often works the midnight shift. I guess we'll find out shortly," she said and pushed the call button.

A moment later Marc listened to the one-sided conversation, "Hello? Hope I didn't wake you. Good, you're still home? Okay, look, I, uh, we have a situation here and I think you should know about it."

Rebecca glanced at Marc, then raised her eyebrows, "It's something I don't think we should discuss over the phone. Your place? Okay, that'd be great. See you in a few and thanks." She ended the call.

"He's scheduled to go in at midnight and was just watching a rerun. I think he was happier to hear from me than to hear about what we saw and heard."

"Good. Does he live very far from here?" Marc asked.

"No, he has a place just off Whiskey Road on the south side of town. We can be there in ten minutes."

"Time's running short. Let's go," Marc said. He led the way back out of the building and through the field to where they had left the SUV.

Heading to the other side of town, they passed by Rose Hill. It was still early and the parking lot was full of cars. With the glow of the streetlights, he spotted the SUV Laura had rented, still parked where it was left upon their return from Augusta.

After passing through the commercial area on Whiskey Road, Rebecca hit the turn signal lever. A restaurant offering barbecued pork sandwiches sat on the corner. A neon caricature of a blinking pink pig rubbing its belly and sporting a wide smile helped advertise its specialty. The sign reminded him of one he'd seen on a trip to

Montreal the year before. The left-hand turn took them down a two-lane county road.

"What is it about barbecue that people around here like so much?" Marc asked.

She gave Marc a funny look. "You don't?" she asked.

"Never mind," he said.

A quarter mile later, Rebecca turned onto a single lane dirt driveway.

"Phillips place is up ahead, just off the road. He likes his privacy."

The fifty-yard-long driveway took them to a double wide mobile home surrounded by a growth of trees. There was a red Ford F-150 pickup parked near the steps that led to the entrance. An outside flood light snapped on, welcoming them.

When Rebecca stopped her SUV alongside the pick-up, the door to the home opened. The silhouette of a large man filled the doorway.

Rebecca and Marc got out of her SUV and climbed the short flight of steps to the top of the landing.

"Hey, Phillip, thanks for seeing us on such short notice."

"No problem. Who's your new friend?" Phillip asked, tipping his chin toward Marc. His inquiry had an accusatory tone.

"This is Marc LaRose. He's a PI from New York, came down to watch the golf tournament in Augusta."

Marc approached Phillip and extended his hand. "Hello, Phillip. Thanks for taking time to talk with us." Although Phillip's large hand completely surrounded Marc's and his grip was firm, it was surprisingly soft.

After an awkward few moments, Phillip stood beside the door and said, "Well, come on in before the bugs carry us away."

Inside the home, Phillip motioned to a couch. "Have a seat." A five-foot flat screen television occupied the wall across from the couch and a rocker/recliner that Philip claimed for himself. A clip from the movie, "War Dogs," was frozen on the screen.

Phillip apparently noticed Marc glancing at the TV and turned it off.

Marc estimated Phillip to be about the same age as Rebecca, a bit taller than Marc and possessing a former athlete's build. *Probably a weight-lifter, or a left tackle in his younger years.*

"So Becky, what's this all about? Your call sounded kinda mysterious."

"I suppose you've heard about the incident at the golf tournament today?"

"Who hasn't. It's been on the TV practically all day. I looked for you on the newsreels. Thought you'd be working security there."

"Yeah, been there all week. That's where I met Marc, I mean Mr. LaRose. He was caddying for his daughter's boyfriend on the eighteenth green today when this whole thing went down. He may have even saved the Israeli Prime Minister's Life."

"Well, I wouldn't quite…" Marc started, but Rebecca held up her hand for him to stop talking. She continued.

"Anyway, I'd been keeping an eye on a few characters at the course for the past few days, and when I learned that Marc was a PI, I thought I'd pass my suspicions on to him. As it turned out, he was already looking into some activity that tied the golf course to the Apex Irrigation Company in Aiken."

"Okay, so how does this concern me?" Phillip asked.

"I'm getting to that. Like I said, I'd been watching a few guys at the course during the week, and when I relayed my suspicions to Marc, he told me he had been working with the golf course superintendent regarding the death of a friend of his that recently passed away due to chlorine gas inhalation at Apex."

"And you think that the Apex death is somehow connected to the incident at the golf course today?" Phillip asked.

"Yes, and I'll tell you why. Just this evening, we went to the Apex building and discovered that the manager, a man named Akhtar, was watching the Savannah River Site's entrance gate in Jackson with a TV monitor he had set up at his office in Aiken."

Phillip seemed to consider what Rebecca had said. "Although, it's kinda strange, I doubt that's illegal. So, how do you know this Akhtar guy?"

"I don't. And how we got this information is sort of confidential," Rebecca said.

"Is that code for trespassing, or worse?" Phillip asked.

Marc cleared his throat, "Look Phillip, how we obtained this is not important. I believe the information we have involves national security and is of utmost importance. Rebecca called you because she trusts you and you are in a position to act on it."

"National security? Everything we're involved with at the Site deals with national security. We make parts for nuclear bombs. I doubt you can get any more security conscious than that."

"You know what Pits are?" Marc asked.

Phillip hesitated, "Of course. It's no secret that the Site produces Pits. They're the core of any nuclear bomb, made of Tritium, a hydrogen isotope that magnifies nuclear weapon power. They're the triggering device for a nuclear bomb. It's what makes the bomb explode, sorta like a bomb within a bomb, and every Pit needs to be replaced from time to time, about every thirty years or so. Why are you asking me about Pits?"

"You seemed pretty well versed on the function of a Pit, so you're no doubt aware that there's a truckload of nuclear material including several Pits leaving the Site later this evening," Marc said.

Phillip's face seemed to lose some of its color. "How do you—?" He stopped in mid-sentence and glanced toward Rebecca. "I don't know, and even if I did, that information is classified."

"Look, Phillip," Marc glanced at his watch. "We're wasting time here. There are some very bad people who have learned about the timing of the convoy and are planning to hijack the cargo and explode it when it passes through Atlanta."

"Impossible. They're armed to the—." Again, Phillip stopped mid-sentence.

"It's not only possible, unless something is done, it's going to happen. You need to take this information and advise your supervisors. I don't know who is in charge of transporting these things, but they should know that an attack on the convoy tonight is imminent. "

Phillip was quiet as he seemed to think about what he'd just heard. He glanced at Rebecca, "I gotta make a call." He picked up his cell from the end table and punched in a number. "Hey, it's Phil. I got an emergency situation. Is there a supervisor around?"

Phillip appeared to listen, "No, shithead, I'm not calling in sick. I need to speak to a supervisor, now!" Phillip's tone had taken a serious, almost military tone.

Phillip's call appeared to have been put on hold. His foot jogged up and down in a nervous tick. A few seconds later his call was apparently transferred. "Mr. Trombly, it's Phil." He listened, then exhaled again. "No, I'm not calling in sick. I think we may have an emergency situation here." Phillip glanced at Rebecca and Marc. "I've just received some information about tonight's outbound load. Apparently the timing and the route the load is to take has been compromised."

Phillip stopped, listening to what Trombly was telling him.

"Yes sir, I know that's the responsibility of the Office of Secure Transportation, but the information I have is that there will be an attempt to hijack the load and possibly blow it up."

Again, he stopped to listen. "Atlanta. Supposedly someone, terrorists I guess, are going to try to hijack the load in the Atlanta area as it passes through later this evening."

"Who? My old girlfriend, and some guy from New York State that she's met. He's some kind of a private detective up there."

Phillip was quiet as he listened to what Trombly was telling him.

"I know. You can't make this shit up. What would you like me to do?"

There were a few moments of silence on Phillip's end, "Yes sir. Hold on."

Phillip covered his cell with his hand. "My supervisor wants me to bring you both to the Site so he can speak to you."

Rebecca looked at Marc.

"Fine with me," Marc said.

"We'll be there in twenty minutes, Mr. Trombly."

Phillip ended the call. "Okay, Trombly's expecting us. You ready to go?"

Marc glanced at Rebecca. "We're ready."

"We'll take my truck. Mr. Trombly has expedited your passes and alerted the gate that we'll be coming through."

Phillip hesitated, then looked at Marc "Uh, look, if you're armed, you should leave your weapon here. It'll be confiscated if you're caught bringing it on the Site."

Marc pulled his jacket open, revealing his H&K. "Where can I leave it?"

"Whoa, heavy metal. Yeah, you better leave that here, somewhere," Phillip said.

"I'll lock it in the trunk of my car," Rebecca said.

Fifteen minutes later Marc saw the glow of the Site's floodlights lighting up the dark sky ahead, then the security booths came into view. Phillip maneuvered the F-150 into one of the entrance lanes.

"Let me do the talking," Phillip said as he rolled up to one of the security booths.

"Hey Phil, we've been looking for you. Mr. Trombly has been in communication with us. Understand you're bringing in a couple of visitors."

"Yeah, he said you'd have their visitors badges ready," Phillip said.

"Yep, they've already been processed. Got 'em right here," the guard said. He reached around a computer screen and retrieved an envelope. Just have them clip them on, you know the drill. Trombly's waiting for you at the Main Security Building."

"Thanks, later," Phillip said. He handed Rebecca the envelope, and pulled away.

Entering the Site, Marc noticed that the entire roadway was bright with HID lighting. Within a few minutes he saw a discreet "Security" sign mounted on a pole in front of a two-story brick building. Phillip pulled the truck into a small parking area that was designated for "Visitors Only." There appeared to be a man in a business suit along with two other men wearing camouflage gear standing near the front entrance, one much taller than the other. "Looks like Trombly has arranged a welcoming committee for you," Phillip said.

The three of them walked quickly to where the man was standing.

"Mr. Trombly, this is Rebec…" Phillip started, motioning toward Rebecca, but was quickly cut off.

"We'll do introductions inside," Trombly said. The taller uniformed man opened the glassed entrance door. "Inside, everyone. Take them to the conference room, upstairs."

Inside the building, Marc noticed a receptionist's desk with a tired looking woman sitting behind it. She glanced up, and then returned her attention to the computer screen in front of her.

Trombly motioned toward Phillip, "You can return to the main security building."

"Yes sir, but…"

"No worries. You did good, but we need to discuss what these people know in private."

"Uh, yes sir." Phillip said, reluctantly.

Trombly motioned toward the camouflaged men who turned and led the way toward a set of stairs. At the top of the stairwell, a short hallway led to a room with a long table. There were at least a dozen chairs arranged around it.

Trombly directed Rebecca and Marc to seats at one end of the table, across from each other. Trombly took the chair at the end, facing them. The uniformed men took their seats next to Rebecca and Marc. The shorter uniformed man retrieved a recording device from his jacket pocket and laid it on the table. The guard pressed a button and a red light blinked on.

Trombly cleared his throat, apparently to get Marc and Rebecca's attention. "First of all, I want to thank you for your cooperation. I, we, the United States government appreciate your coming in to talk to us about what you have learned. As you can imagine, if what Phillip has informed me is true, then we have to assume that there has been a serious breach of intelligence. Although we are recording what is said tonight," Trombly said, tipping his head toward the recorder, "Please understand, this is highly confidential. You are not to repeat anything you hear or learn while you're present here at the Site or anywhere else. Is that understood?"

Both Marc and Rebecca nodded that they did.

Anywhere else? Marc thought.

"Good. For the purposes of this recording, my name is Jack Trombly, head of security at the Savannah River Site. Today's date is April the tenth. We are meeting at the Site's Security office regarding the matter of a possible security breach. There are two witnesses to this breach and they are present here at the Site to give their statements. Please state your names, one at a time starting with you, miss," Trombly said, motioning toward Rebecca.

Rebecca's voice was firm, "My name is Rebecca Tripp, with two p's."

Marc glanced down at the device. "Marc LaRose," he said in a clear voice.

"Fine. Now let's discuss just how you learned of this possible security breach. Ms. Tripp, let's begin with you. Please speak clearly, and in the interest of time, keep your remarks succinct and to the point."

"While working security at the Monarch Golf Tournament in Augusta this past week, I noticed a group of men, three men, of possible Middle Eastern descent acting in a manner that caused me to believe that they could be up to something and appeared to have little interest in the golf tournament. During my surveillance of the men earlier today, I noticed they had gathered in the vicinity of the eighteenth green, when suddenly they vacated the premises just before the gas attack. I have since conducted a trace of their vehicle. It was rented to a man by the name of Ackerman who used a Florida driver's license. I met Mr. LaRose as he was leaving the tournament grounds today and advised him of my suspicions. Then, earlier this evening, Mr. LaRose and I had the opportunity to visit an irrigation company in Aiken that does business at the golf course. While we were there, we learned that the owner of the business is monitoring the Jackson entrance to the Savannah River Site via a video camera.

"Ms. Tripp, what does the presence of these men at the course have to do with monitoring the Jackson gate?"

"While we were at the Apex plant earlier this evening, we overheard the Apex plant manager, a man named Akhtar, say that he intended to hijack the load of nuclear material that is leaving the Site this evening with the intent of detonating the load as it passes through the city of Atlanta later tonight. That's when we called Phillip, and here we are."

Trombly was silent for a moment. "Do you have anything to add, Mr. LaRose?"

"No, I think Rebecca's told you all that we know."

"Can either one of you identify this Akhtar?"

"We could hear what he was saying, but we didn't actually see him," Rebecca said.

Trombly drummed his fingers on the table as he seemed to consider what he'd heard. He motioned for the guard with the recording device to turn it off. "I'll have to alert the OST, uh, Office of Secure Transportation, of what you've told us. It will be their decision, of course, but I doubt this revelation will change the timing or the route of travel of any shipment they have planned."

Trombly glanced at the clock on the wall. "If you'll excuse me a moment, I'll be right back." He rose from his chair and left the room.

Marc and Rebecca sat facing each other as they waited for Trombly to return. The two camouflaged guards remained sitting patiently on either side.

Ten minutes passed before Trombly finally came back into the room.

"Good news and bad news," he said. "The bad news is that this shipment is time specific, it cannot wait."

"So even though there's information about a possible attack on the shipment, they're going ahead with it anyway?" Marc asked.

"Circumstances dictate it. The good news, however, is OST is sending out two identical trucks, five minutes apart."

"So they're sending a decoy truck to try and confuse any would-be terrorist? How original," Marc said.

"It's the best they can come up with on such short notice. Of course, in light of what you've told us, security will be greatly enhanced."

"That's comforting. You're risking the lives of millions of people, hoping that a terrorist who has come into possession of the exact timing and route of travel of tons of highly explosive radioactive material will be fooled by the presence of a look-alike truck."

"Sorry you don't approve, Mr. LaRose. But you have to understand, OST has been moving radioactive material over the roadways of this country for the past forty years with never so much as a close call, much less a terrorist incident."

"Whatever," Marc said, his tone ripe with sarcasm.

Trombly hesitated. "Look at the bright side," he said, his lips curling in a smirk.

"There's a bright side?" Marc asked.

"In the interest of national security, and because you both have first-hand knowledge of this threat, the OST has directed that both you and Ms. Tripp will accompany the convoy as it travels through Atlanta tonight."

Rebecca eyes widened. She looked at Marc. "I understand your reluctance. This is a first for us as well, but given the circumstances, OST had no other option. They have applied for, and received an emergency order from the district federal judge. Because the specific nature of the information you have come across could prevent an impending national disaster, you will remain in our custody until the threat has either been determined to be unfounded or has been neutralized."

"You're saying that because we came to you with this information, you're forcing us to take a midnight ride to Atlanta along with a truck load of nuclear bombs?"

"Actually, there are only four, and they're called Pits. In laymen's terms, they're the firing pin for a nuclear bomb. Practically speaking, they cannot be exploded on their own. It's a highly complicated process for a Pit to become critical. However, the psychological effect of an impending nuclear explosion in a metropolitan area could cause massive panic."

"Just four nuclear firing pins? Now that's a relief," Marc said, his sarcasm obvious.

"Look, Mr. LaRose, I understand your concern, but national security dictates that in situations such as the one we're facing tonight, it is imperative that we follow certain protocols."

Marc knew there was no use arguing. He glanced over at Rebecca, "Look, Mr. Trombly, there is no use involving Ms. Tripp in this. I know as much about this as she does, probably more."

"Maybe you do, but according to her statement she apparently observed the terrorists at the golf course earlier today. That experience could be useful in identifying suspects that are encountered on the road." Trombly glanced at the wall clock. "At any rate, time is not on our side. The load is scheduled to leave in a little over an hour. These two gentlemen," Trombly motioned to the camouflaged duo, "will accompany you to the OST hanger. There you will meet your handlers who will brief you on the mission and get you suited up. I understand why you may have reservations about your impending journey, but the OST people are professionals. They're the world's best at what they do."

Trombly arose from his chair. "Good evening Ms. Tripp, Mr. LaRose. Nice to have made your acquaintances and, like they say over at OST, "Bomb voyage!"

"Bet you just made that up?" Marc said as Trombly opened the door.

"Just for you, Mr. LaRose." Trombly replied with a wide grin, and with that, he left the room.

The two uniformed men rose from their chairs. One of them, the taller of the two motioned toward the door. "Like the man just said, we're up against the clock. Our job is to escort you to the hanger. There, you will receive further instructions."

"Doesn't sound like we have much choice," Marc said.

The big guy just grinned while the other guard opened the door.

The taillights of an unmarked SUV blinked as they walked across the parking lot from the security headquarters.

"Mr. LaRose, please sit up front with me. Ms. Tripp will ride in the back seat."

A short five minutes later, Marc observed a large Quonset hut type structure coming up ahead of them. The building's two overhead doors were wide open. Bright light spilled out onto the pavement in front, illuminating the expansive parking lot. Marc noticed four oddly shaped vehicles of differing colors parked along the side of the building. Inside, Marc could see two tractor trailer trucks parked side by side, both facing the open doors.

"There's your ride to Atlanta," the driver said. He drove through one of the openings and parked off to one side of the semis. "Let's go, I'll introduce you to your handlers."

Oh good, now we're being handled.

Exiting the SUV, Marc observed a group of men sitting around a long picnic table at the back of the room, and like the two men that had brought him and Rebecca to the building, they were also dressed in military camouflage uniforms. As Marc got closer, he noticed a box of plastic take-out bags emblazoned with the "Chick-fil-A" logo on them.

One of Marc and Rebecca's escorts approached a man sitting at the end of the table. The man appeared a bit older than the others and had just taken a bite of his sandwich. "Hey Tom, here are the people Trombly called you about." Then pointing, he said, "This is Marc, and that there is Rebecca."

Tom nodded, then casually took a draw from his drink. He wiped his mouth with a paper napkin. "Care for a sandwich? We appear to have an excess tonight."

Rebecca shook her head. "No thanks."

"Not hungry," Marc replied.

"Last chance," Tom said. "Looks like we may have a long night ahead of us, and once we start there's no stopping until we get to where we're going."

"And just where would that be?" Marc asked

Tom looked up from the remains of his sandwich. "If I told you, I'd have to kill you."

At first Marc thought Tom was kidding, but when he didn't return a smile, he wasn't so sure.

"Do we get to ride in one of those big rigs?" Rebecca asked.

Tom laid the uneaten portion of his sandwich on the wrapper in front of him and again wiped his mouth. "The short answer is no. Neither of you have the appropriate clearance or the training to sit in an SGT semi carrying nuclear material. No, you'll both be assigned to ride in separate MGT's."

"SGTs, MGTs? Can you translate?" Rebecca asked.

"Sorry, that's OST speak. SGTs are the haulers, semi tractor-trailer trucks, called Safeguard Transporters. They're specially built to carry nuclear Pits as well as any other radioactive material over the nation's roadways. MGTs, or Mobile Guardian Transporters are those odd-looking buggies parked out front." Tom motioned to the vehicles Marc had noticed before. "We use them to help guard the SGTs from attack. We'll have four MGTs on this trip, one following each semi, plus one in the lead and another trailing behind. And because you asked, young lady, you have the privilege of riding with me in the lead MGT. Your boyfriend will follow us in the tail," Tom said, nodding in Marc's direction.

"Sounds like you have this pretty well covered," Marc said.

"As you can imagine when it comes to hauling nuclear material over public highways, it's best to err on the side of caution. We'll also have a bird, a helicopter, with spotters above us at all times.

Plus, we have people covering the overpasses just in case someone gets cute and decides they'd like to drop something on, or in front of, one of the trucks."

"Impressive," Marc said.

Tom eyed Marc, then he looked at Rebecca. "You'll both need to get dressed. We can't have you standing around in your civvies. Some people could get the idea you were nuclear physicists or something. Just as well have a target on your backs. There are locker rooms over there," he said motioning toward two doors at the back end of the building. "I'll have one of the guys show you where we keep the extra suits. I believe we still have a couple female sets left."

"You mean, at one time there were more?" Rebecca asked.

"You don't want to know," he said with no change in his expression. He then eyed his watch. "Better get to it. We only have thirty minutes 'til show time."

Chapter Twenty-One

A few minutes later Rebecca and Marc emerged from their respective changing rooms. Marc stretched his arms out to his side. His shirt sleeves were a bit short, but his pants seemed fine.

"Not bad," Tom said.

Rebecca's set was obviously about two sizes too large.

Tom appeared to stifle a grin. "You'll have to roll up your pant legs and maybe button up the top of your shirt. But other than that..." he said, not finishing his thought.

A set of headlights turned in the parking area in front of the building.

"This should be our SGT drivers," Tom said.

A van pulled up in front of the open doors. Two men, one black and one white, along with two women emerged from the vehicle. They walked to where Marc, Rebecca and the OST men were gathered.

One of the women, the heavier of the two, glanced at her watch, then over to Tom.

Marc noticed a tattoo of a string of daisy flowers creeping up her neck from under the collar of her blue work shirt.

"Almost that time. You guys about ready to mount up?" she said.

"We're ready. Just a small change of plans," Tom said.

The woman looked at Rebecca, then at Marc. "Yeah, I heard we were going to have some company on this run."

"We've developed some intel that the timing of our trip may have been compromised. Mr. Smith thinks these two," motioning toward Rebecca and Marc, "may have come across some information that could be useful. He's obtained a federal court order to retain both, pending the outcome of our run this evening."

"What kind of intel?" one of the drivers asked.

"We overheard a conversation between two men that we suspect may have had something to do with the gas attack at the Monarch Golf Tournament today," Marc said.

"Okay, but how does that concern us?" the tattooed lady asked.

"We heard one of the men, an Iranian national, tell his friend that a truck carrying some nuclear material along with a load of Pits was going to be attacked when it reached the Atlanta area later this evening. He went on to say the material would then be activated."

Tom looked at the driver. "The FBI has been notified and will be working with the State Troopers. Of course, for security purposes, the police were only told about a possible hijacking attempt, not about the cargo."

"Good," Tattoo said, again glancing at her watch. "Well, let's get started. By the time we perform our pre-op's and initial communication checks, it'll be time to roll."

Tom motioned to Marc and Rebecca. "Follow me. I'll show you where you'll be riding."

Trailing behind Tom, they made for the four vehicles lined up just outside of the building. Tom motioned to Rebecca. "You'll be sitting right behind me in the front MGT, code named, G-1." He then pointed toward the last vehicle in line. "Mr. LaRose, you'll be sitting behind the driver in that one, G-4." You'll each have a side window seat and you'll be equipped with helmets and headphones. We'll instruct you how to use them. Remember the number one rule, if you see something, say something. Do not hesitate. Communicate your suspicions to the team leader immediately. The team leader will pass the information onto the mission coordinator who will decide what action, if any, will be taken. Do you understand?"

Rebecca and Marc nodded.

The truck drivers climbed into their respective cabs, then the security personnel got into their assigned transporters. Along with the driver, there were three security people assigned to each MGT. Like Marc and Rebecca, everyone was outfitted with helmets, a set of headphones and mikes. All the security officers carried a nine-millimeter Glock sidearm neatly secured in its holster, and except for the driver, the remaining officers also carried sub-machine guns that, to Marc, looked surprisingly like Glock pistols on steroids. He recognized the guns as the new APC-9Ks, Austrian-made automatic weapons capable of firing over a thousand rounds per minute with a single pull of the trigger. Marc figured from the size of their magazines, they each carried thirty rounds. Each member of the detail also carried extra magazines on their belts.

Thirty rounds fired at full automatic could be mistaken for a man zipping his fly, Marc mused. He sat behind the driver and Tom sat in the front passenger seat. He saw Tom glance at his watch.

After calling for radio checks to make sure communications between the vehicles were operating properly, Marc heard someone, apparently the mission coordinator, call for the lead MGT, code named G-1, carrying Rebecca, and the first tractor-trailer truck, code named T-1, to start out. G-2 fell in behind the lead semi.

A long five minutes later, the same voice came over the radio with the command for the second semi, T-2, and its accompanying security vehicles, G-3 and G-4 to move out.

By the time the second semi with Marc's MGT had cleared the Site, he noted that the lead truck with its accompanying security vehicles had been swallowed up in the darkness of the unlit country highway. From the limited radio chatter advising of each semi's progress, Marc knew Rebecca was somewhere up ahead.

Fifteen minutes passed and Marc's section of the convoy was rolling through the town of Beech Island with its family-owned food markets, laundromats and gas stations displaying the now familiar metal security grids over their windows. A short while later, the procession turned onto the four-lane ring road that took them around the city of Augusta. Despite the melee that had occurred at the Savannah River Golf Links earlier in the day, the city looked to have returned to somewhere near normal. Few cars were on the road and the streetlights cast their usual yellow glow. Most of the houses were darkened, their inhabitants having turned in for the night. Marc watched his unit's semi, T-2, lumbering ahead as it drifted onto I-20, the interstate that would take them to the Atlanta Metro area, two and half hours to the west.

Marc found riding in the Mobile Guardian Transporter fairly comfortable, but he knew the vehicle was not built for its accommodations. It was built to protect a lethal cargo, probably the world's deadliest, from falling into the wrong hands. Although the MGT's exterior appeared somewhat odd at first glance, given its wide axles and low roofline, riding in it gave Marc the impression that it was heavy and sturdy. The rhythmic thumping of the vehicle's thick, oversized tires on the concrete pavement was muted and hardly perceptible. When the driver needed to accelerate, the MGT's engine responded effortlessly with minimum engine noise.

Inside the vehicle were three rows of seats. The front passenger seat was for Tom, his submachine gun lying across his lap. Marc sat in the second row of seats behind Charlie, the driver. Another agent named Glen rode on the seat beside him. Tyrone, the lone African American in the group, rode on a single seat behind Marc. Tyrone appeared to be in charge of a stack of gear stashed in the corner next to his seat, probably more armament or firefighting equipment, Marc figured. Although the vehicle's windows were tinted, their configuration allowed for a mostly unobstructed 360° view around the vehicle.

On the road, everyone spoke into their microphones. Whatever was said was heard by everyone, including those in the other MGT's, plus the occupants of the semis. So chatter amongst the crews was discouraged and held to a minimum.

The night was clear and with a full moon, visibility was excellent. The traffic conditions were perfect to transport a truckload of nuclear weapons over interstate highways.

Although the speed limit on the open road was seventy, the convoy moved along at a steady sixty-five miles per hour, the standard limit for Department of Energy transporters. Traffic was moderate, allowing for a relatively steady stream of cars, vans and tractor-trailer trucks to move past the convoy. Marc kept an eye on the line of traffic as it passed by him, alert to anything suspicious. The trouble was, he wasn't completely sure what something suspicious might look like.

An hour into the trip, Marc saw a road sign indicating the exit for Lake Oconee. As the convoy passed by, he noticed the convergence of the on and off ramps was lit-up from the lights of various eateries and gas stations that dotted the area.

A perfect location for anyone watching and waiting for a particular vehicle to pass by.

As the convoy re-entered the darkness of the open road, Marc's mind drifted back to the events of the day and what had brought him to where he was, traveling to Atlanta in the middle of the night in a Department of Energy security vehicle. Despite the long day at the golf course and the ensuing terrorist attack, then his trip to the irrigation plant with Rebecca, Marc had to force his senses to stay sharp. Following a truck carrying a load of triggering devices for the world's most powerful nuclear bombs had really put a cap on his day. He suspected however that this day was far from over.

Outside of the occasional "Radio Check," initiated by the mission control officer wherein the commander of each vehicle in the convoy replied with the standard "10-4," the ride to Atlanta seemed to proceed smoothly. That was, until they were about a half hour east of the city when a semi, hauling an unmarked trailer passed Marc's MGT, then changed lanes and slid in between his vehicle and their assigned semi, T-2.

Before Tom could communicate the issue to G-1 and the lead MGT, another semi passed them at a high rate of speed. Charlie calmly steered their vehicle into the passing lane and slowly worked his way past the intruding semi, reclaiming the position directly behind the tractor trailer they were guarding, T-2.

"Fucking truckers. Some of them think they rule the road," Charlie blurted into his microphone.

"Hey, watch what you say about us truckers," a female voice came back over the radio. Marc recognized the voice as the driver of T-1, the one with the daisy tattoos.

A minute later, the voice of the mission control officer came on the air. "All units, the city of Atlanta's coming up in just a few. You're familiar with the drill. Stay sharp. Stay alert."

Marc felt his MGT decrease its speed as the convoy entered the outer band of Atlanta's city limits. Despite the hour, the night sky burned with yellow light that reflected off the low hanging clouds. Years of experience sitting surveillances, first as a state police investigator looking for criminal suspects, then to the garden variety marital complaints in his role as a PI, Marc was a veteran, always looking for that something, that one thing that seemed out of place. Despite this, Marc was keenly aware he was operating in a completely different environment compared to the sparsely populated Adirondacks of upstate New York.

One thing remained the same, however. Small time burglars and cheating husbands as well as professional thieves and gangsters all eventually made the same mistake. As hard as some may try, something made them stand out from their surroundings. A lit cigarette in a dark corner, exhaust rising from the tailpipe of a parked car on a cold night, a clear windshield on a vehicle parked in a light rain, even fresh tire tracks in the snow. Except for the tracks in the snow, these were the kind of signs that Marc was looking for tonight in Atlanta, Georgia in mid-April.

The convoy continued deep toward the heart of the Atlanta Metropolis. Despite the hour, there seemed to be an unending stream of lights from cars, trucks and buses crisscrossing the bridges above and below the interstate highway.

The crackle of Marc's headset brought him back to the moment. It was the pilot of the DOE helicopter flying somewhere above.

"Mission control, you have a disabled fourteen-wheeled tanker partially blocking the right lane at the I-20, route 401 interchange causing a backup. Someone's put out a line of flares. Looks like you'll be down to one lane, westbound, for a few hundred yards."

Over the report, Marc recognized the sound of the accompanying helicopter's blades slapping the air as it followed the path of the convoy from overhead.

A moment later, Marc heard the voice of mission control, "Roger that, H-1. G-1, did you copy that?"

"Roger that, brake lights up ahead."

From G-1's reported location, Marc estimated his half of the convoy was about a quarter mile behind the lead semi that was slowly closing in on the reported disabled tanker truck. Although disabled trucks were a common sight along any interstate, Marc also understood the role that bad actors could employ using such a tactic to their advantage.

Ahead of his MGT, Marc noticed there was a red cast in the night air made by the reflection of brake lights from the line of vehicles ahead. The ripple effect of the slowing vehicles was making its way through the line of traffic to Marc's location.

As Charlie slowed their MGT to a crawl, Marc's attention was suddenly diverted outside the vehicle, off to his right. Looking past Officer Glen, he noticed the darkened shape of a sedan parked in an empty lot behind a warehouse that was adjacent to the interstate. A security light at the far end of the lot revealed the silhouette of the seemingly innocent vehicle. But it was the flash of light coming from the back seat of the sedan, its side window partially open, that grabbed Marc's attention. As his MGT slowly worked its way adjacent to the lot, a lone puff of smoke drifted from the sedan's partially opened rear window. Instantly, Marc recognized the car. It was the vehicle the man with the Meerschaum pipe had left in after speaking with Marc earlier in the day. But what could he be doing here in Atlanta at this hour? His thoughts immediately raced to the lead semi and Rebecca.

"Stop the convoy!" Marc tersely announced into his mike.

"What's up G-4?" The voice of mission control instantly responded.

"Possible bogey in the parking lot off to our right-hand side. A lone black sedan. Male in the back seat made threatening remarks earlier today. Believe he could be coordinating an attack."

Again, mission control acted immediately. "Mission Control to T-1 and T-2. Cease progress. Pull off the highway and stop. G-2, wait with T-1. G-4, wait with T-2. G-1, continue on and check on reported disabled vehicle ahead. Mr. LaRose, are you still in sight of that bogey?"

"That's affirmative. We just passed him. He's approximately fifty yards to our rear," Marc replied.

"The local police have been advised and will engage the subject."

"10-4," replied Marc.

Mission control was on the air. "H-1, did you copy? Do you have eyes on subject sedan?"

Marc again heard H-1's rotors fighting the wind as the helicopter pilot keyed his mike. "Affirmative, but be advised, bogey appears to be on the move."

Marc craned his neck and scanned the parking lot from his vehicle's rear window. Although the sedan's headlights had not been activated, Marc could see through the chain link fencing that separated the parking lot from the interstate highway. Its dark silhouette was indeed moving slowly along the rear of the warehouse.

Mission control came back on the air, "G-4, Mr. LaRose, the Georgia State Patrol has been made aware of the situation. They are dispatching a unit. They advised they will arrive in your area in approximately five minutes.

"10-4," Marc responded. Trouble was, Marc knew the sedan could be long gone in five minutes. "Charlie, stop this thing or we're going to lose him."

Charlie's head turned toward Tom in the passenger seat, apparently looking for some direction from the officer in charge of their MGT.

Marc opened his side door. "Charlie, stop this thing. Now!" Marc yelled again, removing his helmet and laying it on his seat.

Tom gave Charlie a nod of approval. As the vehicle slowed to a crawl, Marc jumped out and onto the pavement. He quickly caught his balance, then ran around the rear of the still-moving MGT. Keeping low, Marc made his way off the side of the roadway toward the chain link fence. Just then, the driver of a vehicle traveling behind Marc's MGT blinked his headlights in an apparent expression of confusion about someone running across the lane of traffic in front of him.

At least he didn't lay on his horn. That would've definitely attracted the attention of the Meerschaum man, Marc thought, as he continued toward the fence. Through the links of the fence, Marc could see the outline of the sedan as it slowly continued in his direction.

Marc crouched down along the fence line, which appeared to be about six feet high. He knew he could easily scale the fence, but that could expose him to anyone in the sedan.

Suddenly there was a screeching of tires, then the sickening sound of crunching metal a few car-lengths behind Marc's MGT. Apparently, someone had rear-ended another vehicle in the line. Noticing the outline of the sedan had come to a halt, Marc took advantage of the distraction and quickly scaled the fence, then dropped to the other side.

Marc lowered himself in the cover of thick weeds growing along the fence line. Scanning the mostly deserted lot, he estimated the sedan was about thirty yards away. It remained still, the driver apparently distracted by the accident. Adding to the confusion was the sound of multiple car horns. Because the accident had blocked the only open lane, the already slow traffic had come to a dead stop. The chorus of horns increased as the ripple of traffic behind the accident began to take the shape of a single lane parking lot. A few people got out of their vehicles, some to help with the accident, some anxiously searching for a way to get around it.

As Marc lay among the weeds surveying his dilemma, he heard, "Marc, what's your situation?" It was the voice of mission control coming through his earpiece. Although he had removed his helmet, he'd left his headphone attached.

"Still have bogey in sight. Will keep you advised."

"Georgia State Patrol advises their unit has been delayed due to their involvement in an automobile accident. They are in the process of dispatching another unit."

"10-4," Marc quietly acknowledged.

Fuck's sake, tell me this can't get any worse.

Marc carefully raised his head above the level of the weeds to get a view of the sedan. It had again begun its slow procession in his direction. When Marc repositioned his arms in anticipation of moving toward the sedan, his hand brushed against a metal object in the grass. It was a length of pipe. He grasped it and pulled it toward him. It felt cold, like a piece of steel, and about three feet in length. There was one thing he couldn't figure out, why the sedan was moving at all? A quick glance toward the interstate gave him a clue. The reflection of brakes lights from the cars on the interstate was partially obstructed by a large billboard that Marc had not noticed before.

When he looked back, the sedan was now about fifty feet away. With the ambient light cast by the line of stopped traffic, he had a partial view of the face of the man in the back seat. It was indeed the Meerschaum pipe man. As another plume of white smoke escaped the partially opened rear window, Marc noticed the driver, sitting directly in front of the Meerschaum man. He appeared to have one hand on the steering wheel while his other hand held something close to his face. Whatever the driver was holding seemed to emit a green glow that gave the chauffeur's face an eerie expression.

"What the hell is he holding, a cell phone, maybe?" Marc muttered to himself as the driver continued to inch his vehicle closer to where Marc was lying.

Through the din of blaring car horns, Marc could hear the sedan's tires interacting with loose impediments that had been strewn around the parking lot. Through the vehicle's side window, he saw that the driver's face was locked in a sinister expression. When the vehicle came to a point where it appeared to have cleared the billboard, it came to a stop. It was then that Marc saw a hand reach up from the back seat and hover over the driver's left shoulder. It was the hand of the Meerschaum man. He about to signal the driver to do something, possibly with the device the driver was holding in his hand. But what?

Not waiting to find out, Marc scrambled to his feet. Clenching the pipe in one hand, he sprinted toward the sedan. When he was just a few feet from the vehicle, Marc saw the driver's surprised expression, his face still backlit by the device's green light. Wasting no time for introductions, Marc, grasped the iron pipe with both hands in a classic baseball grip and swung with everything he had. The driver's side window immediately shattered as the pipe passed through and made hard contact with the side of the driver's face.

The sound of a steel pipe colliding with facial bones was one that Marc, and certainly the driver, had probably never heard before, and not one either would soon forget. The green glow from the object the driver had been holding slipped from his hand and now lay on the vehicle's front passenger seat.

Although the initial shattering of the car's window seemed to take the backseat passenger by surprise, he recovered quickly. The man grasped his Meerschaum with his right hand and leaned forward, extending his free arm through the split between the front two seats, frantically patting the passenger seat, feeling for the device. Marc again reared back and, with the precision and power of a Major Leaguer, swung the steel pipe through the vehicle's rear door window. Another dinger. The length of steel glanced off the back of the Meerschaum man's head as his hand was about to grasp the device.

Marc opened the driver's door and retrieved the glowing cell phone from the front passenger seat and slid it into his pants pocket. He pulled the unconscious driver from the car and laid him on the pavement. It was then that he noticed the boots the driver was wearing. They were the boots that the man who accompanied Akhtar had been wearing at the Aiken Irrigation plant earlier that evening. Then, he pulled the dazed Meerschaum man from the back seat and laid him next to the driver.

Marc pressed his intercom button and advised mission control of his situation. As he was doing this, he saw two sets of flashing blue lights rounding the corner of the building that separated the parking lot from the street on the other side. Two Georgia State Patrol cars screeched to a halt in front of the black sedan. A single trooper emerged from each vehicle, guns drawn.

"Received that, and thanks. We'll advise the state of your position," the voice of mission control responded.

As the troopers approached, Marc dropped the pipe, then raised his hands.

He identified himself, "Officers, my name is Marc LaRose. I'm working with the U.S. Office of Secure Transportation. We believe these gentlemen were intent on blowing up a shipment of nuclear materials." Marc motioned toward the line of flashing lights along the interstate.

"What the fuck are you talking about?" one of the troopers asked as he looked from the bleeding men sprawled on the pavement to the pipe lying nearby. "We got a call to check out a suspicious vehicle parked behind that building," he said, motioning to the warehouse behind them. "We get here and find you and them," he said, glancing toward the bodies sprawled on the ground. "Right now, mister, you need to get down on the pavement, arms out to your side."

Marc knew the drill and complied.

Over his intercom, Marc heard, "Marc LaRose, are you still there? I see blue lights coming from your position."

"Boys, if you don't mind, I think the convoy carrying the nuclear material is trying to communicate with me," Marc said.

He watched as the troopers exchanged a glance. This was obviously something they had not expected and were apparently unsure about how to proceed.

"Better call Troop HQ and tell them what we got. Also advise them we'll need an ambulance," one of them said to the other.

"Mister Marc LaRose, mission control speaking, what is your situation?" Marc heard on his personal intercom. He lay still, watching, and waiting for the troopers to react.

Then, the older of the troopers went to where Marc was lying. He knelt down and frisked his backside and asked him to roll over. "He's clean."

The trooper motioned toward Marc, "Mr. LaRose, you're free to respond to your mission control."

"Mission control, this is Marc LaRose. The state police are here. We have two subjects in custody that I suspect were about to initiate an explosion on the interstate."

"Roger that, Mister LaRose. Great work."

The voice of mission control continued, "G-1 and 2, break off from the convoy, take the next U-turn and proceed to Mister LaRose's location. You'll see the state trooper's blue lights in the parking lot. G-3 advises the situation with the tank truck has been remedied. A hazardous materials unit has been called to that location. T-1, follow your GPS coordinates around the disabled vehicle and proceed as planned. G-2 and G-3 will accompany you. I am contacting the Georgia State Police and will apprise them of our situation."

A few minutes later, an ambulance arrived along with two Atlanta city police vehicles. The driver of the sedan was tended to as he lay on the pavement. It was obvious he had lost some blood due to the blow that Marc had inflicted with the iron pipe, but appeared to be regaining consciousness. As both men were loaded into the ambulance, the Meerschaum man looked over at Marc who was standing off to one side. "See you around, Mister LaRose," he said with a twisted grin.

Marc reached inside the sedan and recovered the meerschaum pipe where it lay on the floor of the vehicle. He reared back and flung it to the other end of the deserted parking lot. Even through the dim lighting, Marc saw fragments of meerschaum scatter as the pipe hit the pavement. "Don't think you'll need that where you're going," he said.

The man's grin slowly disappeared as the rear doors of the ambulance slammed shut. The ambulance turned and, with its siren emitting a loud wail, left the lot with one of the police vehicles following behind.

"We'll need a statement from you about what happened here," the remaining police officer said. Marc was still distracted with the ambulance as it left the area. "Sorry officer, were you saying something?"

"He said he wanted you to give him a statement."

A man approached Marc from where he had been standing in the shadows of the parking lot.

"Oh yeah, sure," Marc said, somewhat confused by the appearance of this third man, although his voice sounded familiar. He was dressed in fatigues similar to Charlie and the rest of the men in the MGT. He approached the police officer and flashed his ID. "We'll be taking care of any statements, officer. You good with that?"

The officer glanced at the man's ID. "Uh, yeah, I guess. Anything we can do, just let us know, sir." With that, the police officer retreated to his vehicle.

The man turned toward Marc and held out his hand.

"You must be Mission Control," Marc said, taking the man's hand in a firm handshake.

"Before we leave the area and wrap this up, I just wanted to meet the man who saved us - and the city of Atlanta - a lot of trouble. Great job, Mister LaRose."

"Yeah, well, uh, thank you, I guess. But, you know, I had a lot of help."

"If you're referring to Rebecca Tripp and the rest of the team, you're right. I just wanted to personally thank you for your service. And just so you know, we have plans for Ms. Tripp as well. I think she'd be a big asset to our team."

"I'd have to agree," Marc said.

The man turned, then hesitated. "Of course, you understand, what happened here tonight didn't really happen, if you know what I mean."

"I guess. As long as you have all the details," Marc said.

The man hesitated, his expression serious. "If you're referring to Mr. Akhtar and his surveillance capabilities, yes, I believe we have. He'd actually been on our radar since he located to Jackson a little over a year ago. Unfortunately, we underestimated his reach. I have it on good authority that the issue is being dealt with as we speak."

Marc thought about what he'd heard. "Well then, if my services are no longer required, any chance of getting a lift back to Aiken?"

"Of course. One of our MGT's should be here shortly."

Marc saw another set of headlights turning toward them from the street.

"As a matter of fact, looks like your ride is approaching as we speak."

Chapter Twenty-Two

The MGT with Charlie at the wheel, the same one that had brought Marc to Atlanta, came to a stop just short of where the two men were standing. Marc saw Rebecca smiling at him through the vehicle's side window.

Marc looked back at the man he knew only as Mission Control. "You're sure the police won't need my statement regarding what happened this evening?"

The man had already turned to leave. "It's all taken care of. Have a pleasant ride back to Aiken, Mr. LaRose."

With that, Mission Control climbed into a waiting MGT and left the area.

"Never figured you to be a big swinger - with an iron pipe that is," Rebecca said as their MGT turned onto the I-20 on-ramp headed back to Aiken.

"Bad news travels fast. He was lucky I only had the pipe."

"Word is he has a nice concussion that should keep him in the hospital a few days. So, how's that lucky for him?"

"If I had had my H&K 40 caliber, he'd be spending the night in the morgue."

They rode in silence for a few miles as the bright lights of Atlanta slowly dimmed in the rearview mirror.

Marc glanced at his watch. It was 12:30 in the morning, and he knew Laura wanted to leave for Columbia shortly after breakfast. With the two-hour drive to Aiken in front of him, he knew he wouldn't get much sleep tonight.

"I understand you were offered a job with the federal government," Marc said.

Rebecca glanced over at Marc. "Talk about news travelling fast."

"Yeah, so what do you think?"

"I haven't actually accepted the offer. But given what I saw tonight, the work looks challenging, so I guess, yeah, I'm considering it. What's next for you?"

"Barring another national security incident, I'm heading back to the relative peace and quiet of the Adirondack Mountains in upstate New York, first thing tomorrow morning."

"I've never been there," she said.

"You should try it sometime. The change might do you good."

"I don't know," she said. "Been living here in the South since I was born. It's the only life I know. Besides, I looked Plattsburgh up on the map. Seems like it's smack dab in the middle of nowhere."

They both rode in silence for a few miles.

"So, how did you find out I lived in Plattsburgh?" Marc asked.

With the dim green light from the vehicle's dashboard that seeped over the front seatbacks, Marc thought he noticed a smile on Rebecca's face.

"Ever heard of the internet?" she asked. "I was curious after we met at the Savannah River Golf Links, so I Googled your name. Amazing what you can find out about someone with just a few keystrokes."

"Okay. What else did you learn besides the fact the City of Plattsburgh is located at the top of New York State, a long, long way from New York City."

"Well, outside the fact that Plattsburgh played a pivotal role in the War of 1812, not much. But I did learn that you're apparently no stranger to excitement."

"Oh, really?"

"Well, first off there was something about a wild train ride you were involved in that left Montreal for New York City and ended up in Lake Champlain."

"Yeah, well, you see..." Marc started, but was cut off as Rebecca continued.

"Then there was this thing about a foiled terrorist plot to take the Village of Lake Placid out of future Olympic contention."

"Well, it really wasn't..." Marc started.

"Those were just the articles I had time to read before we met up last evening. But there were a few more, and from those and what I've seen so far this evening, it appears, Mr. LaRose, you don't have to look for trouble. Trouble seems to have you on speed dial."

"Actually, my number's unlisted, but these days even the telemarketers have no trouble finding me."

Marc noticed the exit sign for the city of Thompson, Georgia reflecting in their vehicle's headlights coming up. He figured they were about forty minutes from Aiken.

"So, what time you think you'll be leaving?" Rebecca asked.

"We fly out of Columbia. I believe our plane departs around two-thirty in the afternoon, so I figure we'll have to be on the road by ten or so."

"I see. So, uh, how would you like to spend the rest of the night at my place?" Rebecca asked.

She said this while looking straight ahead, appearing to watch the white lines on the road sweeping by the vehicle.

Marc glanced at the dashboard clock, then back over at Rebecca. "Sure, I'll just need a lift back to Rose Hill in the morning."

"That can be arranged," she replied. "I just have to retrieve my SUV. It's still parked in Phillip's driveway," Rebecca said.

"Yeah, along with my gun. Is that going to be a problem, I mean, with Phil and all?"

It was her turn to glance at the time. "It shouldn't. He'll be at work, won't be home for another few hours, maybe a little longer with all that's occurred this evening."

Rebecca gave the MGT driver Phillip's address.

It was after 3 a.m. when Rebecca turned the SUV into her condo's parking lot on the outskirts of Aiken. Her unit was nestled in the center of about ten others, and, like many condominiums, the only difference between one unit and another was the unit number attached to the door. Marc followed as she led the way to the entrance. Upon entering, he noticed that the interior, although a bit small for Marc's taste, appeared quite neat.

"I know it's getting late, but you think we have time for a drink?" Rebecca asked.

"After what we've been through tonight, I think that should be a requirement. Whatever you're having will do."

She disappeared around the corner to where Marc suspected was the kitchen area, "I have vodka and bourbon."

"Bourbon, with ice, please."

As he listened to the sounds of Rebecca preparing the drinks, he glanced around the living room. Like Phillip's trailer, there was a wall mounted flat screen TV hanging opposite a reclining chair, about half the size of Phillip's. There was also a coffee table and an end table with a lamp, and a couch.

"So, where's your dog?" Marc asked.

"My dog?" she answered. There was the sound of ice cubes being dropped into glasses.

"Yeah. At the golf tournament, I saw you with a Belgian Malinois."

"Oh, you mean Buster. Yeah, when I'm not working, I board him at a kennel. I don't have a lot of room here, and besides, the security company pays the kennel fees. He's a great companion and a super drug sniffer."

Marc took a seat at one the end of the couch. Rebecca reappeared, holding two glasses of brown liquid.

"Looks like I found another bourbon fan," Marc said.

Rebecca handed Marc a glass and took a seat next to him.

"How many other bourbon fans have had the pleasure of your company, Mr. LaRose?" she asked, peering over her glass.

Ignoring her query, Marc brought the glass up to his nose and inhaled. He took a sip and savored the aroma of his drink. "Um, Wild Turkey," he said.

"You're as bad as Buster. He knows drugs, you obviously know your bourbons. Is there anything else you can tell from a single sip?" she asked.

Marc held his glass up to the light, examining its contents. "I believe it's Wild Turkey's Long Branch brand," he said, then hesitated, giving his drink another swirl. "The notes of aged Texas mesquite charcoal are a dead giveaway. It appears you appreciate good whiskey," Marc said. He then took another slow sip and held it in his mouth for a long moment before swallowing. "Yep, sweet heat, definitely Long Branch. Haven't had this lately, but it's good to be back," Marc said.

"Glad you like it. You know, Marc, quality bourbon isn't the only thing I appreciate."

The sexual inference was not lost on him. "So, you're really going to accept that offer to work for the Office of Secure Transportation?"

Rebecca hesitated. "Probably. The security job I had at the golf tournament is done, although I'm sure I could work for them somewhere else. But OST is close by, right there at the Site. Federal benefits are good, looks like there'll always be work to do and they like the fact that I have a trained police dog."

As Marc was thinking how to respond, he noticed the flash of car headlights through the picture window facing the parking lot. Probably someone coming home from a late shift, he figured. He took another slow drink and set his glass on the coffee table.

"So, what time do you think you'll be leaving?" she asked.

"Whenever you want me out of here, or 7:00 a.m., whichever comes first." As he spoke, he noticed a shadow flit across the panels of sheer curtain covering the window. Then the shadow stopped. Someone was standing outside the window. Marc put a forefinger to his lips, leaned over and grabbed the half empty bottle of Wild Turkey by its neck. With his free hand, he switched off the lamp sitting next to him on the end table.

"Marc, what's the…" Rebecca started, but stopped when she felt Marc's hand grab her arm and pull her down to the carpet. "Oh, so you want to do this in the dark, huh?"

"You still have your car keys on you?" Marc asked, his voice tense.

"Yeah, but…"

"Hit the panic button."

"But Marc, why…"

"Someone's lurking outside your front door. Do it…"

Rebecca had her car keys in her hand, and as she pressed the emergency button, a volley of gunfire came through the door's window glass, striking the wall and the back of the couch where Marc had been sitting seconds before.

As Rebecca's SUV horn blared, Marc pulled her along the condo's floor toward the curtain-covered window. When they reached the wall just below the window, another volley of gunfire came through the glass, punching holes in the curtain. A moment later, Marc heard the condo's front door rattle. Someone was trying the doorknob, but it was locked. Marc slid across the floor toward the door, keeping close to the wall.

Suddenly the door burst open, followed by a large work boot. Then the silhouette of a man holding what appeared to be a gun filled the now-open door.

Marc rose from his crouch and, wielding the half-gallon bottle of Wild Turkey in his right hand, smashed the bottle across the man's face. The man, caught by surprise, let out a yelp, then fell back over the railing and off the landing. Marc flipped on the outside light switch. The attacker was down on all fours in the parking lot. Blood was spewing from his mouth and nose. Another burst of gunfire from someplace in the parking lot caused Marc to duck back inside the condo.

There was the sound of a car's engine starting, then revving up. Keeping low, Marc drew his sidearm and poked his head around the open door. The attacker that Marc had struck with the bottle was gone. Then, several flashes of light, followed by the sound of gunfire, came from a vehicle at the end of the parking lot. The outside light next to Marc's head shattered, sending splinters of glass in all directions. He quickly recovered and saw a small dark-colored van exiting the parking lot. Marc watched as the van, its tires squealing, speed away in the direction of the city of Aiken.

"Are you hit?" Rebecca asked, still crouching on the condo floor.

"No, come on, we're going after those bastards," Marc yelled, shaking bits of glass off his shirt.

Fifteen seconds later, with Marc in the passenger seat, Rebecca was backing her SUV out of the parking space. A few porch lights had switched on. The gunfire had apparently awoken the neighborhood.

"Turn left!" Marc yelled when they got to the end of the parking lot. By the time Rebecca turned onto Whiskey Road, there were no vehicle taillights to be seen.

"Floor it! It was a small van. They can't be far ahead!" Marc yelled over the noise of SUV's powerful engine. Thirty seconds later, brake lights appeared in the darkness ahead. Marc figured, whoever it was, was driving by the light of the full moon with the headlights extinguished, but they couldn't hide the brake lights. The brake lights came on again, this time making a right-hand turn.

A long fifteen seconds later, Rebecca turned right on the same road. Again, there was nothing but darkness ahead of them, but Marc knew the van was somewhere up ahead and Rebecca was a better than average driver.

"Marc, do you think they're heading back to the Apex Irrigation plant?"

"Possibly, we'll soon find out. Just keep doing what you're doing. We're gaining on them."

Then, as if on cue, brake lights appeared again, this time turning left. They were indeed closing in.

"You're doing great, but whoever it is, looks to be heading downtown," Marc said.

Marc could see there were lights on in a few of the houses as they sped by. People were just getting out of bed to start their day.

Marc's concentration on the vehicle's tail lights was interrupted as a newspaper delivery person pulled out from a side street in front of their SUV, the carrier tossing folded editions of the daily newspaper out the window onto subscriber's driveways. He noticed a street sign that read, "South Boundary."

Rebecca braked, then swerved around the delivery vehicle in time to see the brake lights of the van up ahead. She pushed down hard on the accelerator. Giant live oak trees lining both sides of the road formed a thick canopy overhead, giving Marc the feeling they were speeding down a living tunnel. Ahead of them, in the darkness at the far end of the tunnel, a traffic light turned red, then the van's brake lights illuminated again.

"Doesn't look like they're headed for the Apex building. Maybe, they've simply lost their way," Marc said.

Marc caught the reflection of the van as it passed under the traffic light. A few seconds later, Rebecca slowed their vehicle as they approached the same intersection, the traffic light still red.

"Good on your right," Marc said.

Rebecca made it through the intersection in time to see more brake lights, she had managed to gain valuable distance on the van as it made a right-hand turn two blocks in front of them.

"They've turned onto Laurens Street, that will take them right into downtown Aiken," Rebecca said, her voice strained.

When she turned onto Laurens Street, Marc could see several cars up ahead of them. Although the street was well lit, there was no sign of the van.

Rebecca slowed as she concentrated on the road and the intersection up ahead. Just then, Marc heard a chorus of car horns that seemed to come from the intersection. It appeared that a vehicle had run a red light.

Looking beyond the intersection, Marc saw a set of brake lights veering to the left before disappearing behind a building.

When their SUV arrived at the intersection, the traffic light had turned green and the stopped vehicles had moved on, some turning left, some continuing straight. Rebecca slowed their vehicle. Marc looked for any movement. As they slowly passed through the intersection, he noticed a stately building that sat at the corner,

"That's the Old Post Office building," Rebecca said, motioning toward the structure.

Marc continued to concentrate on the street in front of them; however, other than a city refuse collection truck, the street was void of traffic. Then, off to his left, in the shadows behind the Post Office building, Marc caught a movement and the spark of a vehicle's interior light just before its doors closed.

"Kill the headlights, take this next turn and park on the other side of the street," Marc said.

Rebecca did as Marc instructed. "I think our visitors have parked their car behind the old post office," Marc said.

"Curious," Rebecca whispered.

"How so?" Marc asked.

"Just that I believe the building's tenants may have a connection to the Site."

"So why would they be trying to kill us?" Marc asked.

Before Rebecca could answer, a flash of light came from a window at the back of the building.

"Come on, let's find out," Marc said.

He opened his side door and slid out. Quietly, he clicked his door shut, then headed across the street, Rebecca following close behind. A black Ford Transit was parked at the back of the building.

Rebecca pointed to a white sticker on its rear window, "that's the sticker that connects this vehicle to the photograph of the one we saw at the golf course and to the rental agency here in Aiken."

They peered inside the van. With the first light of the early morning sun just breaking through the trees, Marc could see a dark stain on the passenger seat. He opened the door and felt the area of the stain. He knew what fresh blood felt like and what it smelled like. "There has to be at least two of them, and one is injured."

"Marc, I think we should call the police."

"Yeah, go ahead and make the call. Tell them what we got. I'm going to take a peek inside the building," Marc said.

"Marc, be careful. They're cornered and they probably know it. Desperate people are the most dangerous."

Marc crossed the street. There was a railing along the side of the building that guarded a short flight of steps leading down below street level. A metallic sign, "Atomic City Tours and Travel," was attached to the railing. The sign swung ever so slightly in the early morning breeze.

As he slowly descended the four steps, the light he had noticed coming from the travel agency's window was suddenly extinguished. Thinking that possibly someone inside had seen him approaching; Marc stayed off to one side of the window.

As he waited, trying to decide what to do next, he heard a noise from somewhere inside. It was the sound of a door opening, or closing, he couldn't tell. Someone was leaving the office space through another door. Ducking under the window, he tried the door. It was unlocked. Pushing it open, Marc called out, "Put down your gun! The police are on the way!" There was no response. He waited, then called out again, but still no response. Keeping low and with his handgun in front of him, he eased inside. With early morning light seeping through the window, he could see two chairs and a desk. There were several posters hanging on a wall, but in the near darkness, it was impossible to see what they displayed, probably the Eiffel Tower, Big Ben, or St. Mark's Square, he figured. Behind the desk, he saw two doors. One was partially open.

Probably the one used by the terrorist attempting to escape.

Slowly, he approached the door. Using the tip of his handgun, Marc pushed the door open a little more, just enough to peer around it. There was nothing but darkness. Then, he heard the sound of another door closing somewhere at the far end of the hallway.

As he was about to enter the hallway, he heard a thumping sound, but it didn't come from the hallway. He hesitated, trying to determine its source. The thumping continued. It seemed to come from behind him. He reversed course and backed into the tourist office. He stopped in front of the second door he had noticed before. There was more thumping, this time accompanied by a muffled groan. Marc, his handgun at the ready, carefully pulled the door open just a crack. Immediately, the groaning became louder, but in the darkness, he still couldn't determine its source. Just inside the door,

Marc felt a light switch along the wall. He flipped it on to see a woman bound to a chair with plastic zip ties, her mouth covered with packing tape. He immediately suspected the woman was the wife of the Savannah River Golf Links superintendent, Bill Goodspeed. She had been kidnapped the day before.

Chapter Twenty-Three

Marc secured the handgun in his waistband. When he went to remove the gag covering her face, however she became hysterical, apparently thinking Marc was part of the terrorist gang that had kidnapped her.

"Shhh," he whispered, and put a finger to his lips in an attempt to calm her. "I'm a friend of your husband. I talked to him last evening; he told me you had been abducted. He couldn't call the police because the people who kidnapped you warned him not to."

This seemed to quiet her a bit, but by the frightened look in her eyes, Marc could see that she wasn't convinced.

Marc went back to the window that faced the street. He could see Rebecca was on her cell phone. He tapped on the window to get her attention. Rebecca looked up. Marc heard a bit of the one-sided conversation. She was apparently giving the police her location. She ended the call and came to where Marc was standing.

Rebecca looked past the open closet door and saw the woman in the chair.

"She's Bill Goodspeed's wife," Marc said. "The terrorists were holding her hostage so her husband wouldn't contact the police. Help her with her bonds. The terrorists are here, somewhere in the building."

"Marc, I've taken a tour of this place once. It's a freaking maze of rooms. Maybe it would be better to wait and let the police look for them. The officer I spoke to said they'd be here in a few minutes."

"The terrorists are probably more familiar with the place than the police are. Stay with her. She'll need an ambulance," Marc said.

Before Rebecca could protest any further, Marc turned and left through the open door that led back to the hallway. Feeling his way along the corridor, his hand touched another light switch on the wall. When he flipped it on, he saw that he was alone in the hallway. Up ahead he spotted an open door. Inside he could see a sink and a toilet.

Continuing past the toilet, he saw another door at the far end. It was closed. As he approached, he heard the shuffling of footsteps on the concrete floor. Standing off to one side of the doorway, he slowly pulled the door open. Inside however, there was only darkness. There were no windows. He stepped through the doorway. The sound of his footsteps echoed through the room. It seemed to be fairly large, but with no light, it was impossible to tell. As he advanced through the room, he saw a line of illumination leaking under another door on the opposite side of the room. Keeping along the wall, he found another light switch. He snapped it on. Several rows of florescent lights instantly buzzed to life. The room was large, filled with folding chairs and an oversized wooden desk along the wall next to yet another door. The ceiling was domed, a large concave rotunda in its center.

He hesitated. "What the fuck?" he whispered, awed by the room's size and the dome in its center. Marc slowly made his way toward the desk. As he passed a metal folding chair, he noticed the back of the chair seemed to shine in the florescent lights. When he got closer, he saw what caused it to shine. Fresh blood. Marc stopped, then crouched down. With his gun aimed in the direction of the desk, he said, "Okay, show's over. Put your hands in the air. Cops are all over the place. There's no escape."

Nothing. No sound. No movement. Marc repeated the command.

"Look, you're hurt. You need a doctor. Give yourself up and I'll make sure you get one."

Slowly, a man's bloody hand rose up from behind the desk, "Don't shoot, please."

The voice seemed rattled, like he was having a hard time speaking, like he had a mouthful of something.

"Stand up," Marc ordered.

A few moments passed, then the other hand appeared and grasped the top of the desk. Whoever it was seemed to need the desktop for leverage to help him stand. Slowly, the man's head appeared, his face bloodied. Finally, he was on his feet, but he still leaned on the desk for balance. He was a big guy, dark-complected and over six feet tall.

"Keep your hands flat on the desk."

Marc quickly approached and went around the back of the desk. Using his foot, he kicked the man's legs back, forcing him to lean over and put his weight on his hands. Marc secured his gun in his waistband then spotted a semi-automatic pistol in a holster on the man's right-hand side. With his free hand, Marc pulled the gun from the man's holster. The gun was a nine-millimeter Glock, the most popular handgun made. Marc shoved the Glock in the back of his waistband. Then from somewhere outside, he heard the faint sound of a police siren.

"There were two of you. Where's your partner?" Marc asked. His voice had the strong tenor of a cop with over twenty years of experience locking up bad guys.

The man mumbled something unintelligible.

"What? What'd you say? Speak up!" Marc yelled.

"Don't know where he's at," the man mumbled with a thick accent. Blood dripped from his mouth and formed a small puddle on the desktop. Blood also ran from the man's nose and lips. He looked to have recently lost one of his front teeth.

"I bet you're the fucker that tried to break into the condo. How'd you like that little taste of Wild Turkey Bourbon I gave you?"

The terrorist gave Marc a dazed look, "Fuck you," he said, spitting out a mouthful of blood.

Grabbing a handful of the man's hair, Marc pulled his head back, "Tell me, where's that fuck-head that was with you in the car? Tell me or I'll slam your face right into this desktop." Marc pulled the man's head back further.

"Kay, I tell," the man managed. His words were impeded by his accent, blood filling his mouth, and the apparent loosening of a few teeth.

"Well?" Marc yelled.

With his injured hand, the man motioned toward the door next to the desk.

"What? He went that way, through the door?" Marc yelled.

The man gave a quick nod in the affirmative.

Marc had to go after the mastermind of this affair, but he couldn't leave this guy free to warn whoever had been with him, whether he was handcuffed to the table or not. "Sorry, buddy," Marc said, and with that he slammed the man's face back onto the desktop. There was the sound of another tooth snapping, sending a bit of enamel skidding across the desk. The man's legs collapsed. Marc let him slide to the floor where he immediately began snoring.

"Sweet dreams, asshole. I doubt you'll need that tooth where you're going anyway," Marc whispered. He turned toward the door the man had nodded to, and carefully pulled it open. Poking his head around the corner, he saw another dark hallway that appeared to lead further back into the interior of the building.

"Rebecca was right. This place is a fucking maze."

Marc listened for a long moment, then, above his hostage's snoring, he heard the shuffling sound of someone climbing stairs somewhere in the distance. Heading toward the sound, he located a short stairway. It was narrow and dark. Then he heard another door closing somewhere above. With his handgun at the ready, Marc slowly ascended the stairs and came to another door. He carefully pushed it open. Using the faint streaks of the early morning light coming through a set of tall, arched windows, he could see into a large open room with a row of desks and a counter. The twenty-foot-high ceiling had been formed into another rotunda. A carved sign above a door off to his left read "Postmaster." When he silently closed the door behind him, there was the sound of footsteps climbing yet another flight of stairs.

This fucker's got to be a mountain goat!

Following the shuffling footsteps, Marc located the staircase and, as quietly as he could, while taking two at a time, ascended the steps. Before reaching the top, he stopped and listened. From somewhere outside, he could hear the sound of police sirens. As he was about to continue the climb, he heard a muffled "thump." It didn't sound like a door closing, but whatever it was, it came from somewhere near the top of the stairway.

With the increasing morning's sunlight trickling through the windows, he ascended another flight of steps. He reached the top and quickly scanned the area. There were more desks, two rows of them, and a huge bookcase that completely covered one wall. Marc scanned the area under the desks looking for the second terrorist, but there was no-one here, and there was not another door to be seen. He knew he wasn't hearing things. Someone was up here, but where?

Thinking his quarry could be hiding beneath one of the desks, he started toward the first row then stopped. He noticed a section of the book shelves was uneven and appeared to have been swung outwards. When he pushed on the wall of books, the shelves rotated.

Pushing further, he stepped past the opening made by the open wall of books, and stared. It appeared to be some kind of secret passage. Using his cell phone light, he could see he was in the building's attic. Bare wooden ceiling joists were filled with a sea of blown-in insulation, and not far from where he was standing was yet another set of steps. Like he did while hunting deer in the Adirondack forest, he stood stock-still, and listened. Then, just overhead, he heard a creaking sound. Footsteps. Someone was on the roof.

Quietly, Marc climbed the short flight of steps. At the top of the steps was a metal hatch with a hasp that would lock it shut. Only now, the hasp was in the open position. Marc slowly pushed the hatch upward a few inches. Through the opening, he was hit with the orange and yellow of the early morning sky. The sun was just breaking over downtown Aiken.

Slowly, Marc pushed up on the hatch and cautiously ascended another step. From around the hatch's door, he saw a short railing that he assumed ran along the edge of the roof, but no sign of an assailant. Cautiously, he continued pushing on the hatch until it locked open. With the early morning light he could see the tops of a few buildings that ran on either side of Laurens Street, the business hub of the City of Aiken. Standing on the last step, Marc peered around the hatch. Crouched along the railing, was the dark shape of a man about fifteen feet away. Marc could see the man was using the railing to steady his aim as he pointed his pistol downwards, toward the street, and Rebecca's car.

Using the hatch as a shield, Marc slowly brought his firearm up, covering the man with the sights of his gun.

"Drop the gun!" Marc commanded. His voice was clear and authoritative.

The man flinched, surprised by the sound of Marc's voice. A few seconds passed and he slowly got to his feet. He raised his arms over his head, still clutching the firearm in his right hand and turned, bringing himself into a standing position to face Marc. The rising sun shone down on the man's face.

The terrorist wasn't a large man, maybe 5'10" or so, but he was holding a big gun. Marc recognized it as a Sig Sauer 40 caliber, which he knew was powerful enough to penetrate the steel hatch he was using as cover. Marc also recognized the shoes he was wearing.

A pair of black leather dress shoes, just like the ones he had seen while he and Rebecca were hiding in the Apex Irrigation building the evening before.

"Who the fuck are you, anyway?" the man asked.

Marc noticed the accent, Middle Eastern, Marc suspected. "You have a short memory, asshole. I'm the guy you tried to kill twenty minutes ago."

The man's facial expression turned from indignation to a sneer. "You have no idea what you've done, what you've cost us."

The voice of a policeman using his vehicle's public address system called up from the street below. "You, up on the roof, this is the police. The building is surrounded. Put down your gun! Give yourself up!"

Upon hearing the policeman, the man turned and glanced over his shoulder in the direction of the policeman's voice.

"From where I'm standing, it appears you're in kind of a tight spot. The cops have the place surrounded, and I'm here with a gun pointed at your head. What's it going to be, Mister Akhtar?"

The terrorist's facial expression remained unchanged. "It appears that we have underestimated you, Mister Marc LaRose."

The policeman's voice called again, "You, up on the roof, this is the Aiken Police Department. The entire area is surrounded. Put down your weapon and give yourself up."

Akhtar again glanced at the gathering of police on the street below.

"It seems your police friends are getting anxious for this to end. But first tell me, what are you doing here? We know you're just a small-town private detective from upstate New York. You came here to caddy for your daughter's boyfriend at the golf tournament in Augusta. So why do you choose to interfere? Our plans had nothing to do with you."

Marc held his pistol steady. He suspected the terrorist was attempting a last-ditch effort to divert his attention and create a moment's hesitation so he could strike.

"Give it up, Akhtar. There's an old saying in the U.S. that you're probably not aware of."

"Oh? And just what is that?"

"Blood is thicker than water," Marc said.

Akhtar hesitated. "So how does that concern me?" The sneer on the terrorist's face held steady.

"You and your crew have caused more than your share of mayhem, leaving a bloody trail of sick, dead and traumatized people from Aiken to Augusta to Atlanta. But the biggest mistake you made was when you needlessly frightened my daughter."

"All this is about one of my men pushing your daughter around? Surely we can work something out."

"Yes, you can. You can either give yourself up, which we both know you are not prone to do, or you can do the right thing," Marc said, remembering an article he had read concerning the 'Old Post Office' that he found in his room back at Rose Hill.

Akhtar seemed to consider Marc's words. "'The right thing? What do you mean? What is this 'right thing' you speak of?'"

"About a hundred years ago, when this building was a working U.S. Post Office, there was a flagpole mounted in the middle of that rotunda over there," Marc said, motioning with his pistol toward the mound of cement that formed the interior rotunda just a few feet away.

The terrorist's eyes flickered toward the mound.

"It rained that day. This man, no one seems to remember his name, carried out his duty and came up through this very hatch, the same one we both used to get here. Because of the storm, it was his duty to lower the flag."

"So?" Akhtar spat, his lips curled downward.

"The rain caused the mound to be slippery, and while he was attempting to bring my flag, the flag of the United States of America, inside, he slipped on the wet surface of the rotunda and fell off this roof to his death. He was trying to do the right thing, and he died for it. We both know your situation. You're surrounded. Your accomplices have been captured or are on the run. It's the end of the line. It's time for you to do the right thing."

Akhtar's face was expressionless. He inhaled deeply. "Suicide is not an option, Mr. LaRose." With that, he lowered his weapon and fired, the bullet penetrating the hatch's steel lid, but missing Marc.

Marc ducked below the level of the roof and prepared to return fire. But, before he could react, there was an explosion of gunfire from the street below. For whatever reason, Akhtar had decided to take on the Aiken Police Department. Raising his handgun, Marc peered around the side of the hatch's lid. Akhtar stood motionless next to the railing at the roof's edge. Bullet holes had ripped through the back of Akhtar's shirt. The gun fell from the terrorist's hand, and he teetered. Just before tumbling over the railing, his face turned slightly back toward Marc. The evil sneer that Akhtar had worn before was gone, replaced with the placid look of surrender.

A moment later, Marc heard a sickening "ka-thump" as Akhtar's body hit the cement sidewalk thirty-feet below. Without looking over the railing, Marc turned and quickly went down the three sets of stairs to the building's basement. Rather than heading out through the tourist office however, he exited the building through the rear service entrance.

When Marc rounded the corner of the building, several police officers were gathered around Akhtar's remains now in a bloody heap on the sidewalk. Rebecca and Mrs. Goodspeed were standing on the opposite side of the street.

A detective noticed Marc exit the building. He came across the street to where Marc and the two women were standing.

"Sir, I need some identification."

Marc had noticed the detective eyeing him as he joined Rebecca and Mrs. Goodspeed. He removed his New York State Police retirement ID and shield from his back pocket and handed it to the detective.

The detective looked at the photo on the ID, then back to Marc. "Are you familiar with that man?" the detective asked, motioning toward Akhtar's body lying on the sidewalk.

Marc hesitated. "Yes, I believe he's the terrorist responsible for the attack at the Savannah River Golf Links yesterday as well as an attack on me and Ms. Tripp earlier this morning. He also kidnapped this woman, Mrs. Bill Goodspeed." Marc motioned toward the woman, her face still red from the packing tape that had been wrapped around her face. "In addition, I believe he's responsible for the death of a former employee at the Apex Irrigation Company, Mr. Zach Saylor. Moreover, he masterminded an attack on an Office of Secure Transportation convoy carrying nuclear material in Atlanta last night."

"You seem to know quite a bit. Do you know his identity?" the investigator asked.

Marc hesitated, then exhaled. "His name is Sajak Akhtar. He owns, or owned, the Apex Irrigation Company. He and one of his sidekicks, who you'll find on the floor of one of the rooms in the basement of this building, attacked me and Ms. Rebecca Tripp earlier this morning."

"There's someone else here, inside the building? Show me," the detective said.

The detective motioned for another police officer to join him. Leaving Rebecca and Mrs. Goodspeed on the sidewalk, he followed Marc through the building to the second terrorist, who they found still passed-out under the table.

When the detective started to search him, Marc retrieved the pistol from his waistband that he had taken from the man earlier. "This belongs to him. I suspect it's the gun he used when he and his friend out on the sidewalk attacked us earlier this morning at Ms. Tripp's condo."

The detective retrieved a pair of disposable gloves and a plastic evidence bag from his pocket. He put on the gloves, then dropped the handgun inside the bag.

He turned toward the uniformed officer and motioned toward the terrorist, "Give me a hand. Let's get him up off the floor."

The two men lifted the terrorist into one of the chairs around the table. The man was groggy, but appeared to be coming-to. When his eyes focused on Marc, he flinched and put his hands in front of his bloody face." Don't hith me, pleath," he cried through a mouth full of busted teeth as more blood trickled from his chin.

"What the hell happened to his face?" the detective asked.

Marc looked down at the cowering man. "Don't know, probably fell, or something."

The detective gave Marc a knowing glance, then looked at the fresh smear of blood on the tabletop. He ran his hand across the table and felt a fresh indentation. He picked out a broken piece of incisor made when the terrorist's face came in contact with the table and shook his head. A corner of his mouth turned up. "Guess he's going to have to learn to watch his step."

The detective then retrieved a radio from his belt and signaled that an EMT was needed. He told the terrorist to put his hands flat on the desk, searched him and retrieved a wallet from the man's pants pocket. Other than a few hundred dollars however, there was nothing that would help identify him.

"What's your name?" the detective asked.

The terrorist gave the detective a confused look, then pulled his bloody lips back in a ghoulish smile. "Fuck you," he mumbled, but with blood dripping from his swollen lips and around a mouthful of broken teeth it sounded like "fuff ooh."

The detective stood the man up, pulled his arms around his back and secured handcuffs to his wrists.

A moment later, two EMT's arrived with another uniformed police officer. "He's under arrest for felonious assault. There'll be a few more charges, but that will hold him for now. Take him to the emergency room and get him patched up. When the doctor is through with him, bring him to the police station," the detective said.

"Fuff ooh," the terrorist blurted again as the EMTs helped him out of the room. The detective and Marc followed the EMTs and watched as they loaded the terrorist into a waiting ambulance. A police car with two uniformed patrolmen left, following the ambulance to the hospital.

The detective turned toward Marc. "What'd you say your name is?"

"Like my ID says, my name is Marc LaRose. I'm in town with my family. We attended the golf tournament in Augusta." He looked around and saw Rebecca. Pointing toward the two women on the sidewalk, he said, "I'd suggest you talk to those ladies over there. The younger of the two is Ms. Rebecca Tripp. It was her condo that the deceased and the guy with the busted face tried to break into. The older lady, Ms. Goodspeed was kidnapped by the terrorists last evening. We found her here, earlier this morning in the bathroom next to the tourist office. She was bound and gagged."

The investigator caught the ladies' attention and walked over to them. "Ms. Tripp, I understand you had a run-in with the deceased earlier this morning."

"Run-in? Yeah, if you call having someone break into your home, then fill your living room with bullet holes, yeah, I guess we had a little run-in."

The detective shifted his attention to the woman next to Rebecca, "Aren't you Bill Goodspeed's wife?" the detective asked, apparently recognizing her from a previous meeting.

She nodded, "Yes, I'm Gloria Goodspeed," She said, still shaking from her experience with her kidnappers.

"I thought you looked familiar. Are you injured?"

Rebecca, knowing Gloria was unwell, jumped in. "Officer, Ms. Goodspeed was kidnapped by those men last evening. She's been tied to a chair and wrapped in tape all night. She should be examined by a doctor."

The detective again pulled out his radio and directed that another ambulance respond to the scene. Then, returning his attention to Marc and the women, he said, "Why don't we all take a seat in my car while we wait for the ambulance?"

While they waited, Rebecca described the attack at her condo and the pursuit that led her and Marc to the Old Post Office. As she was talking, several more detectives arrived, as well as a black SUV with the word, "CORONER" emblazoned on its license plate.

When Rebecca finished, the detective motioned toward Rebecca and Marc, "As soon as the ambulance gets here, I'm going to ask you to follow me in your car to the police station. I'll need written statements from both of you. Mrs. Goodspeed's can wait until she's discharged."

Marc, aware that taking witness statements can be time consuming said, "Detective, I have a situation."

"What's that?" he asked.

"Before our encounter with the terrorists this morning, Ms. Tripp and I had just returned from Atlanta. We had been directed by the Office of Secure Transportation to accompany them as we had information regarding a possible terrorist attack on a convoy that was leaving the Site and traveling through Atlanta. We had just returned from that, when these guys tried breaking into Ms. Tripp's condo in an effort to take us out. We haven't slept for over twenty four hours, plus, I have to catch a flight out of Columbia at 2:30 this afternoon."

"The detective glanced at his watch, "Sounds like you folks have had a busy evening. Don't worry, Mr. LaRose. I'll personally see that you're on the road in plenty of time to catch your flight.

After the ambulance left with Gloria, Marc turned his phone on and dialed Ann Marie's cell number.

"Daddy, where have you been? We didn't see you last evening and this morning, when you hadn't returned, we were getting worried. I tried calling, but couldn't get through."

"Sorry. It's a long story. I'm just calling to give you a heads-up. Right now, I'm enroute to the police station."

"The police station! Daddy, what'd you do? What happened?"

"Nothing that you should worry about. I'll fill you in when I see you at Rose Hill. I should be there shortly, probably in an hour, maybe two."

Two hours later, Marc and Rebecca left the police station.

"If you have time, I know a nice place for breakfast, my treat," Rebecca said.

"I'd love to but it's running late," Marc replied, glancing at the time on his phone. Any chance on getting a rain check?"

"I guess," Rebecca said with a disappointed look.

"With all that's happened, I'm sure either the city or the Fed's, probably both, will need me to return here to testify. I'm sure we'll have time then for some breakfast, or dinner, or whatever else you'd like to do," Marc said.

With a sad look she peered up at Marc, "Okay, I'll hold you to that."

In an effort to console Rebecca, Marc wrapped his arms around her. "We've only known each other for a few hours but, you know something, Ms. Tripp?"

"What's that, Mr. LaRose?" Her eyes filled with tears.

"I think you're someone I'd like to spend a lot more time with."

She smiled and blinked the tears away, then raised herself up on her toes and kissed him.

Marc returned the kiss. Then, with his arms still around her, he said, "but now that you're going to be a federal agent, when will you find the time?"

"You underestimate a woman's power of persuasion. Leave that little detail to me," she said.

They held each other in a long embrace.

Two cops, who were leaving the police station to begin their day on patrol, observed the two in the parking lot, whistled and clapped.

"Better save some of that for later," one of them shouted.

Marc smiled, waved at the officers, then returned his attention to Rebecca. "Got time to give me a lift to Rose Hill?"

"I have time to take you anywhere you want to go, Mr. LaRose."

Chapter Twenty-Four

Six weeks later, Marc was sitting at his kitchen table drinking a cup of decaf coffee while reading his hometown newspaper, The Plattsburgh Standard. At his feet, his cats, Brandy and Rye, made kitty noises, reminding Marc it was time for their breakfast.

"Just a moment, fellas," Marc said. An article at the bottom of the second page had caught his attention; "Keeseville man accused of burning his house down, then filing an insurance claim for damages, pleads guilty to arson and insurance fraud charges." Details of the article continued on the fourth page. "The accused, Mr. Cecil Robare of Keeseville, on advice of assigned counsel, pled guilty to the reduced charges and was sentenced from three to five years at the Bare Hill State Penitentiary near Malone, New York."

Marc smiled, remembering Robare's smugness when he had talked to him about the cause of the fire two months prior.

Couldn't happen to a nicer guy.

Just then, Rebecca emerged from around a corner from the living room. Freshly showered, her hair wasn't quite dry. She was wearing a housecoat she had left from her stay there three weeks prior.

Marc looked at her over the top of the newspaper, "Hey beautiful, you hungry?"

"Sure, as long as you have something beside the kibbles you feed those poor cats."

"Poor cats, my eye! They probably eat better that we do."

Rebecca smiled. "Wouldn't know, I've never tried eating kibbles."

Marc grinned, "When do you start your training with the Office of Secure Transportation?"

"Next Monday. I report to the OST training center in Fort Chaffee, Arkansas."

"Arkansas, huh. Never been there."

"Neither have I. It's just for twenty weeks."

"Twenty weeks? That's a stretch," Marc said.

"Yeah, I know, but I'll be free on weekends. You could come out and see me once in a while."

"Suppose I could, but I doubt there's a direct flight out of Plattsburgh, although there may be a connecting flight through Columbia," Marc said.

"Columbia? You're flying from Plattsburgh to Columbia to see me, Marc? That would work."

"Yeah, especially since Columbia is where I'm actually headed."

"Okay? I'm confused," she said.

"The United States Attorney's Office called. Their office is in Columbia."

"Oh?"

"According to the federal attorney who called, the terrorist who accompanied Akhtar to the Aiken Post Office after our wild chase has changed his mind and has decided to open up."

"Wonder why?" Rebecca asked.

"Not sure, but according to the attorney, when my name came up as someone he was calling on as an eye-witness, the terrorist suddenly had a change of heart. He said he would only talk on two conditions."

"Oh, really. So what were his conditions?" she asked.

"The first one was he didn't want to be alone in the room with me. That his lawyer and the Federal Attorney had to be present."

"Guess I can understand that," she said with a smirk. "So, what was his second condition?"

"That after pleading guilty, he wanted to serve his time at the Super Max federal prison in Florence, Colorado."

"Any idea what he wanted to talk about?"

"The Federal Attorney said the terrorist - he still hasn't given his name - revealed that on the morning before the attack, he, along with four others, swam across the Savannah River and covered the water intake pipes leading from the river to a formerly mothballed reactor at the Site. The reactor was slated to be fired-up while the Israeli Prime Minister was visiting there. Luckily, however, due to the Prime Minister's incapacitation from the gas attack, starting up the reactor had to be called off."

"Any idea what happened to the other terrorists?" Rebecca asked.

"That's what the FBI and the federal attorney's office are trying to determine. They've recovered a few things from Akhtar's residence and a camp on the Georgia side of the river where they think the terrorists had been holed up, but so far, nothing."

"Do you really think this guy will open up on just who the other terrorists were, or where they were going after the attack?"

"I seriously doubt that. They could be anywhere by now."

Rebecca was quiet as she took in this new revelation.

"So, we were talking about you travelling to Fort Chaffee. Classes start next Monday," she said.

"I don't know. Guess it depends on how long I'll be needed in Columbia, and I doubt the feds will want to pay for my flight to Arkansas," Marc said with a grin.

"'Like the saying goes, 'Life's not about the journey, it's what can be accomplished upon your arrival,'" Rebecca said. She went to Marc and wrapped her arms around him.

Marc looked deep into her eyes, "Leave it to a woman's power of persuasion to reconstruct an age-old maxim to suit her mood."

Just then Brandy, the larger of Marc's cats began circling his feet.

"Speaking of desire, Mr. LaRose, you should fill your cat's bowl, while you can. I have an immediate assignment for you that can't wait."

"Meow," Brandy and Rye cried in unison.

I sincerely hope you enjoyed reading *Masters of Terror*, my fourth book in the Marc LaRose Mystery Series. My previous works include, **Borderline Terror, Southbound Terror** and **Placid Terror.**"

As an independent author, I depend on you, the reader, to spread the word about my stories, which can be done through social media and word of mouth. I publish my books through 'Kindle Direct Publishing.' (KDP)

Amazon.com offers the reader the opportunity to 'Review' my stories. Reviews are important for readers and authors alike, whether the author is an indie, like me, or an established published author using one of the big publishing houses.

I invite you to review this book as well as other stories in my series by going to Amazon.com and typing **"Masters of Terror."** Click on the book title, then the "Reviews" tab. This will bring you to the page where you can "Write a Review."

Thanks again,
R. George Clark

ACKNOWLEDGEMENTS

First, I thank God for bestowing me with a full life, one that has allowed me to meet so many wonderful people, endowed me with a loving family and has provided me with a multitude of diverse experiences that have helped formulate the stories for the "Marc LaRose Mystery Series."

Early on in my writing career, I was fortunate to associate myself with Aiken Writer's Block, a special group of talented, patient and knowledgeable people who freely shared their time and expertise to help others with their writing aspirations.

I owe a special debt of gratitude to my editors: Ms. Carolee Smith and Mr. Walter Church, my readers: Ms. Carol Morenc and Ms. Rita Malloy, Ms. Betsy Hart, and to Mr. Arthur Osborne for his technical expertise. I also received words of encouragement from a list of friends, much too long to mention on this page. You know who you are. Thank you.

Lastly, I am most grateful to have been assisted by my best friend and soul-mate for the past fifty-five years, my lovely Delena, who, without her unrelenting encouragement and reassurance, this story would have truly been impossible for me to write.